CIRCULATE

AUTHOR	CLASS
MORROW, J.	AFG

TITLE   Slainte

SLÁINTE

SLÁINTE

James Morrow

The Book Guild Ltd
Sussex, England

First published in Great Britain in 2002 by
The Book Guild Ltd
25 High Street
Lewes, East Sussex
BN7 2LU

Typesetting in Baskerville by
SetSystems Ltd, Saffron Walden, Essex

Printed in Great Britain by
Antony Rowe Ltd, Chippenham, Wiltshire

A catalogue record for this book is
available from the British Library

ISBN 1 85776 682 2

sláinte: (Irish) *nf* health;
(toast) good health, cheers.

In memory
of
A.H.W.D.

It takes a great deal of history to produce a little literature.

Henry James

Later on in my life I may well look back and regret some of the things that I have done. I do not, however, want to look back and regret some of the things that I have not done.

PROLOGUE

There are a small number of life events that are generally recognised to cause disproportionate stress and unease to the human condition. These traumas (in alphabetical order) are usually held to be:

1. Bereavement
2. Divorce
3. Moving house
4. Serious illness

Any of the above can or could happen or may have already have happened to any of us at any time. Indeed it's likely that most of them will happen to most of us, given time.

If these trials are then out there, lying in wait, as it were, for most of us, most of the time, what are we to do if we are not to become terminally depressed at the prospect?

It's true that eventually we do tend to overcome the fall-out from these major life events, usually through an elaborate array of coping strategies, aided and abetted by the fact that it is rare to suffer more than one affliction at any one time.

But just imagine what would happen if they started hunting in packs.

Now that really would ruin your day.

1

September 1999

'Your first patient is here, Dr Wallace.' The voice came from behind the partition that divided waiting area from reception desk.

Harry barely had time to shoulder his way through the glass double door, which slammed closed behind him. The suddenness of the announcement and the heaviness of the door nearly made him drop the large and awkward bundle of notes that he was clutching tightly to his chest. As he passed the large semi-enclosed reception area, he saw that it was Mary, the practice manager, who had noted his somewhat belated arrival and spoken. She lifted her head from the computer screen and nodded knowingly in his direction. In her late fifties and with greying and stubbornly untinted hair, Mary had been at the Albert Street health centre for as long as anyone could remember, certainly well before Harry's partnership had been confirmed.

She regarded Harry critically; his close-cropped sandy hair, his green Helly Henson, beige chinos and Timberland shoes were what she had reluctantly come to accept in these more informal days of general practice. Mary was less forgiving, however, of Harry's stubborn refusal to wear a tie to work. She was of the old school and, whilst Harry's partners had made some concessions to modern times and were now less inclined to wear the suits that they had in the

1

past, she was of the opinion that they at least had the good grace to still dress as if they were professionals.

Harry scanned the waiting area. It was early and there was only one patient waiting; sitting hunched up in the corner, engrossed in his newspaper was Jimmy Rodgers.

It was going to be one of those days.

Jimmy Rodgers was a regular with the practice, and well known to Harry, though he tended to switch allegiance between physicians. Clearly, Harry was in favour this month. Jimmy's problems usually entailed an ongoing battle with the social services, for whom he held a total contempt as they regularly refused him a range of benefits. Perusal of Jimmy's medical notes would reveal that some fifteen years ago he had been working on a short-term contract as a labourer on a building site when he had the misfortune to trip over a piece of discarded piping. Falling awkwardly to the ground, he had twisted and injured his lower back. Due to continuing discomfort and pain, Jimmy Rodgers had never worked again. A clever solicitor had sued his employers and obtained some form of compensation for the original injury, but that had long since been spent and now Jimmy eked out a living by pursuing benefits through the DSS. His major hurdle was now, and always had been, the clinical opinions of the constellation of doctors, including some of the most respected orthopaedic surgeons in the land, most of whom the DSS had paid for him to see, often at great expense to the national purse. However, despite some of the most modern investigations, including a number of CT and MRI scans of the lumbar and thoracic spine, abdomen, pelvis and hips, no one, as yet, had been able to come up with a diagnosis or indeed to formulate a logical or clinical reason for Jimmy Rodgers' continuing problems. Without a firm diagnosis the DSS tended not to view Jimmy's applications for incapacity benefit and DLA with the compassion and understanding that Jimmy, at least, felt he deserved, especially after all his years of suffering and misery and his faithful dedication to the cause.

'I'll just dump this stuff in the room and then give him a call.' From the corner of his eye Harry noted Jimmy's head rise to look over the top of his paper. He nodded in Harry's direction and gave him a wry smile.

Returning from the inner sanctum that was his office clutching Jimmy's not inconsiderable folder of notes, Harry summoned him from the waiting room.

'Well, Jimmy what can I do for you, today?'

'Ah, it's the pain, Doctor.' He moaned, grimacing and indicating his lower back in a single movement. 'Bad as ever. It's the weather, always worse in the winter time, plays havoc the damp does.'

'What about the new tablets I gave you last week?'

'No good, Doc. Went for my stomach something shocking. I tried them, though. I took them for a few days but in the end I had to stop them.'

'This back pain of yours goes back a long way, Jimmy,' said Harry, flicking absentmindedly through the file. 'I fear we're dealing with a chronic problem – probably one that's not going to go away. To be brutally honest, Jimmy, I'm really not sure what more I can suggest.'

'I know, Doc, you've done your best. I appreciate that but there must be some painkillers somewhere that would give me some ease.'

'What about physiotherapy?' Harry suggested, more in hope than expectation.

'Useless, worse than useless, tried it lots of times. Usually sent by one of the hospital docs. Wouldn't listen to me. I told them that it never helped – in fact it usually ended up making me worse.'

'A chiropractor?'

'Can't afford one. Unless you can get me to see one on the National Health.'

'I don't think I can, to be honest.'

'Look, I'm happy to try some other pills, if you can prescribe something.'

Harry knew that tablets were not the answer and would only prove, as the saying went, a victory for optimism over experience, but as in so many cases before Jimmy and cases since Jimmy, writing a script for a supply of medication was likely to be the path of least resistance. He reached for the prescription pad.

'By the way, Doc . . .'

There was always a 'by the way' or 'just one other thing I thought I should mention'. This codicil always arose just as the interview was about to terminate and was by no means unique to Jimmy Rodgers. This 'other thing' invariably would turn out to be the real reason for the appointment and the earlier proceedings merely a subterfuge.

'Yes, Jimmy?'

'I need you to fill in these DLA claim forms for me, I hope you don't mind.' He reached down below his seat for a plastic bag. From this emerged what appeared to be the complete works of Shakespeare. He thrust the bundle of papers across the desk. Harry's heart sank. There goes my coffee break, he thought.

'Okay, I haven't time right now, but if you leave them with me, I'll sort them out and send them on.'

'No problem, Doc. Cheers.'

With that, he got up effortlessly and left.

There followed the usual procession of headaches, minor lacerations, sprains, colds and wheezy chests that constitute the bulk of any GP's practice. One of the major roles of any doctor in a community setting is to act as a gatekeeper to the more specialised and expensive hospital sector. The key to being a good GP, apart from the obvious clichés of being caring and a good communicator, Harry had always felt was in the ability to recognise just when you were out of your depth and hence when to call in the cavalry.

As Julie McCormick made her way across the waiting area towards Harry's office she flicked her long dark hair back from where it had strayed over her face, to reveal the broadest of smiles, but Harry already could hear a bugle sounding somewhere in the distance.

Harry had known Julie for many years. Her parents and his father had been friends in the past, and on the many visits to their house during his childhood Harry had got to know her quite well. He had patchy recollections of first seeing Julie as a screaming pink bundle lying in her Moses basket when his parents had taken him round to visit their friends and celebrate the birth of their only daughter. He thought that he had been about four at the time. Over the succeeding years Harry had recognised Julie only as a hindrance and as a nuisance. Her persistence in tagging onto her elder brother Michael and himself as they endeavoured to have serious boyhood fun only served to annoy them intensely. Everybody knew that girls in general, and baby sisters in particular, were incapable of keeping up with boys or playing an active role in their games. Michael, being exposed to her entrapment more often, got more resentful than Harry, the infrequent visitor.

The years passed and, as an independent observer, Harry had watched Julie blossom and mature. She grew through her obligatory rebellious teenage years to reach maturity and adulthood almost imperceptibly. After leaving school she had spent some years in nursing. In fact they had both once worked in the same hospital for a short while and Harry recalled that they had shared childhood reminiscences over soup and sandwiches in the canteen. When his father had learned of this, Harry, could see that he was delighted. Harry thought that his father had secretly hoped that he, the bachelor son, and the daughter of his best friends might somehow hit it off and hence go on to unite the two families further in a matrimonial bond. However, nothing could have been further from the truth. Whilst Julie and Harry did harbour some affection for each other, the fact that they had spent long periods of their childhood together meant that this affection could never be more than that which is felt between brother and sister.

Julie had in fact married C.J. Despite the differences in their backgrounds, Harry had warmed to C.J. from the first time Julie had introduced him as her fiancé. He had never heard anybody call him anything other than by his initials, except perhaps somebody making the occasional reference to his alleged parentage, but certainly never by a proper name. C.J. was a journalist on one of the local newspapers. His appearance always gave the impression of being slightly unkempt and disorganised, in need of a good woman, but then, Harry thought, he had a good woman, he had Julie. Others, less well informed, had thought them an odd couple, C.J. and Julie. Some had even postulated that their relationship wouldn't last. Julie the vibrant, athletic and attractive nurse and he the somewhat shambolic, chain smoking journalist. Later, when their relationship blossomed, some suggested that Julie would change him and his ways. But now, years later, C.J. was still exactly as Harry had always remembered him. Despite, or perhaps because of this, their relationship had gone from strength to strength, being finally cemented by the arrival of two children. Harry, in the intervening years, had often reflected on Julie and C.J.'s marriage, only to contrast their successes with his own failures.

For some years Harry had lost contact with Julie and C.J. when he had worked abroad, but on his return he had been pleased to find them living in the locality and they had signed on with his practice on the strength of his presence. Harry had come to know their children, Becky, who was three, and Tom, who had only been born just over six months ago. Julie was clutching onto Tom's pushchair as she made her way towards Harry's consulting room. Harry could clearly see that there was something wrong. There was a look of brave determination etched across her face as she approached, but her gait was stiff and clumsy, no longer the light skipping motion that he associated with their earlier meetings.

'Hello, Harry how are you?' she said.

'Hello, stranger, it's not often we see you here,' he replied.

'No, it's usually one of the kids that brings me down here. I try to avoid you guys – no offence.'

She made her way unsteadily past Harry as he held the office door open for her. She reached the waiting chair and thumped down into it, blowing hard.

Harry took his seat at the desk and, ever the professional, opened the conversation with some innocuous remarks about her husband and family. He moved quickly on, though, given the constraints on health service time, to ascertain the purpose behind her visit.

'So what brings you down to see me today, Julie?'

'I don't know really where to start. It was C.J. who finally forced me to make the appointment. It all seemed to start just after Tom was born. While I was in the maternity unit, a day or two after Tom's birth, I noticed that my feet were tingling. To be honest it was quite mild and I just thought that it was something that happened after labour or I'd lain in an awkward position and trapped a nerve or something.'

'Seems a reasonable thought. What changed your mind?'

'Well, it didn't get any better. In fact, the pins and needles feeling seemed to be slowly spreading. It went up my legs and then up to my waist. I was going to come and see you, but then it stopped just about the level of my lower ribs.'

'How long did it take to go from your feet to its worst point?'

'About two weeks.'

'Then what happened?'

'It seemed to stay stable for a while and I even thought that it was getting a little better on its own. In fact, the feeling has definitely got better. I've still a sensation like a band round my middle but my feet and legs feel fine.'

'But . . .?'

'But, although the feelings got better, the next thing was that my right leg wouldn't work properly and it seems to be getting slowly worse.'

'What do you mean, it won't work properly?'

'I seem to drag it and I can't run. If I try to walk quickly I'll trip and fall. C.J. used to laugh at me at first. He kept on accusing me of being on the gin. I think that originally he suspected I'd some kind of postnatal depression and become a secret drinker. But as time has gone on it's just got worse and worse. Now other people are starting to notice. When I go out I always bring Tom's buggy, it gives me the support and the confidence to get around. I don't know what I'll do when he's too big for it, I'll not go out at all.'

'Why do you think you fall? Is it because of the leg being weak or is your balance affected?'

'I think it's a bit of both. I know my leg feels weak but there's more to it than that. I feel generally quite . . . what's the word?'

'Clumsy?' he added.

'Yes, clumsy, I trip and I bump into things.'

'If I asked you to go on a long walk, what would happen?'

'At the moment, I just couldn't'.

'If I forced you?'

'If you forced me to walk, I'd probably start off okay, but very quickly I'd start to drag my right leg. I would seem to throw it, and my foot would slap as if I couldn't control it properly. Eventually it just wouldn't work at all and I'd have to stop.'

'How far can you go before all this seems to start?'

'That's the worrying part. It's getting less and less. To be honest, I can only get a few hundred yards now before I'm in trouble.'

Harry detected the despair in her voice and could see the moisture gathering in the corner of both her bright blue eyes. Julie was a brave and courageous girl with a great strength of character, but he knew that she was afraid, very afraid.

'What about the left leg?' Harry wanted to keep her focused.

'I think it's all right.'

'And the arms?'

'No. Sometimes I think there's a little tingling in my fingers but it's not really a problem.'

'Any difficulties with bladder or bowel function?' he asked.

'I have to run to get there sometimes and, with my leg the way it is, I have had the odd accident. But I think that the bladder problem just relates to childbirth, don't you think?'

Harry noted that the moisture had now gathered to a glistening tear which was attempting to break free from the confines of the sclera and escape down Julie's cheek.

'Well, it could be. Anything else you've noticed wrong?'

'I do feel tired all the time, but anyone with two kids and a husband to look after does, don't they?'

'Quite so. Look, can you pop up on the couch and let me have look at your legs, so we can decide what to do?'

Harry beckoned towards the examination couch against the back wall of the office.

Julie struggled to her feet and made her way, now without the support of Tom's pushchair, with some difficulty across the short distance between desk and couch. She slipped her shoes off and climbed awkwardly up onto the couch itself.

Harry stood beside her and looked intently at her legs. They looked perfectly normal. In fact, they appeared well toned from years of aerobics at the local gym; whatever the recent problem was, it had not yet induced any obvious wasting, he thought. He rolled each leg in turn and lifted it gently upwards. There was an abnormal resistance to the movement, as if Julie was actively impeding him.

'Just try and relax and let the legs go loose,' he requested.

'I am trying, but that's part of the problem, they just won't seem to relax for me.'

Although Julie felt that the right leg was the abnormal one, there was little doubt when Harry examined her that both legs were stiff and, worse still, both legs felt weak. He could easily overcome her hip flexors and her hamstrings. These Harry knew to be very powerful muscles that he should not be able to overpower. Certainly the right leg was the stiffer and the weaker, but to Harry's mind both legs were affected by whatever was going on.

He reached for the patella hammer to test the reflexes. He hardly needed it. The slightest of taps on the tendon sent the leg into paroxysms of jerking.

'I forgot to tell you, that's another thing,' said Julie once the jerking had ceased. 'My legs are always jumping like that and I get terrible cramps at night.'

'Just one final test,' said Harry, an idea beginning to form. 'This is everybody's favourite. I'm just going to tickle your feet. It's a bit uncomfortable, I'm afraid.'

Harry stroked an orange stick along the outer aspect of

the sole of each foot in turn, slowly drawing it forward and gently turning it inwards to run along the pad at the base of the toes.

This was the clincher. As he performed this manoeuvre on each of Julie's feet, the big toe on that foot rose upwards into extension. As every medical student knows this is abnormal, the toe should flex not extend. The abnormal response immediately indicates to the observer a problem within the central nervous system.

Harry helped Julie down from the examination couch and steadied her as she put her shoes back on. He sat her down again beside his desk and then sat down himself. He placed his hand on Julie's.

'That bad, Doc?' she said, looking down.

'I don't know, Julie, I really don't know. There is something wrong, you don't need me to tell you that.'

'I know.' The teardrop finally broke free and ran down her cheek.

'I don't actually think that the problem's in your leg.'

'Well where is my problem then? Don't tell me I'm imagining it. I'm not, you know.'

Why do so many patients these days, when the doctor can't immediately ascribe a diagnosis, assume that he thinks that they are imagining it or, worse still, manufacturing it, thought Harry.

'No. No. You're definitely not imagining it. I just think that the signs suggest that the leg itself isn't the problem; the problem is that you are not getting the messages down to the legs properly. And I do think, what's more, that both legs are affected, though the right is worse than the left, so that you notice it.'

'That's exactly what it feels like. that they won't do what I tell them to do. So what's wrong and what can I do about it?'

11

'That's what I don't know, at the moment. I want to try to arrange for you to see a colleague of mine in the hospital. A neurologist.'

'A neurologist?'

'A specialist in conditions affecting the nervous system.'

'Is that what you think is wrong with me, something is wrong with my nerves?'

'The nervous system, that's my professional opinion.'

'And what can be done about that?'

'That I don't know either. It really depends on exactly where the problem is and on what exactly is causing it. That's why I want to send you to the hospital. You're going to need special tests, tests that I can't do, but tests that will help us to answer those questions.'

'Okay.' More tears followed in the track left by the first escapee.

'I'm going to arrange some blood tests right now, and while you are having them done I'll try to ring the hospital and get you an appointment.'

Harry quickly scribbled some details onto a number of blood request forms and led Julie, once more clutching her pushchair, over to the nurse's office.

Returning to his own room, Harry reached for the telephone and dialled.

The number that he dialled was that of the Royal Victoria hospital, the biggest and, in most eyes, the best hospital in the area. It also housed the Neurological Centre for Northern Ireland. Neurology is and always was one of the Cinderella specialities, chronically understaffed and underfunded and, with growing patient expectation, beginning to strain at the seams. Waiting lists for outpatient referrals could be anything up to nine or even twelve months, such was the demand to see one of the very few neurologists in

Northern Ireland. Hence the telephone call. Harry knew if he could get through to the consultant that he had in mind, he could try to persuade him to see Julie much more quickly.

The first problem . . . he hung on . . . and on . . . was the Royal never seemed to answer the telephone. A recent poll in one of the local newspapers had confirmed what many GPs already knew, that the Royal group of hospitals were the worst in the Province at answering incoming calls. Finally . . .

'Royal hospital. Caroline speaking.'

'Hello, It's Dr Wallace here. I'd like to speak to Dr Anderson from Neurology.'

'I'll put you through to his secretary.'

There followed the obligatory taped music before John Anderson's secretary answered and reluctantly agreed to put him through even though he was in clinic and didn't usually like to be disturbed there. Harry knew John Anderson from his training years. He had often given lectures on a variety of neurological subjects. Harry thought him to be, as most hospital consultants, a bit self-opinionated but, in contrast to so many others, generally quite approachable.

The traditional caricature of a neurologist, in Harry's mind, was of an older, bespectacled and dark-suited physician interested in the academic side of medicine rather than the day-to-day job of patient care. There was little doubt that the last decade had seen a radical change in this regard. With new investigative techniques, the newer drugs and better, safer and more directed neurosurgery, the practice of neurology had undergone a seismic shift. Dr John Anderson represented to Harry one of this new breed of neurologists. He had committed to memory something that he had once heard Dr Anderson say in a lecture, though in truth he had forgotten most of the rest of what

13

he had tried to impart. He had said that a good doctor should model himself on the archangel Gabriel. Not because he should radiate goodness and light, nor indeed because he was next to God, but because the archangel Gabriel was an example of a good communicator. He must have been; after all, it, was he who persuaded an unmarried fourteen-year-old girl in a strict Jewish society to allow herself to become pregnant by some invisible and unseen entity.

'Dr Anderson here, what can I do for you?'

Harry recognised the voice immediately. He explained Julie's case as best he could, detailing all the physical signs that he had found.

Being a specialist, John Anderson, of course, had to ask about a few things that Harry had forgotten to elicit. But finally and after some consideration, he said, 'Harry, you've done the right thing to ring me. I can fully understand your concern. I think we should get her up here fairly soon. My next clinic here is on Wednesday next week in the morning. I'll just ask the secretary here if I can add her on then . . . She's shaking her head at me . . . Hold on . . . Two extra new patients already . . . No, that's all right, one more we can manage . . . Harry, send her up at about twelve thirty p.m. at the end of the clinic. I'll see her then myself when the juniors have gone off for lunch.'

'Thanks, Dr Anderson. I'll send a covering letter up with her.'

Julie was still in the nurse's treatment room. She was pressing a cotton wool ball onto the exposed pit of her elbow where she had just been punctured when he passed on the appointment details to her.

Returning to his clinic, Harry was aware of the growing crowd of disgruntled faces accumulating outside his door.

14

As always, there was a restriction on the time with which to deal with each patient. If, as frequently happens, a complicated case presents, or more than the allocated time is required, it results in a backlog that will carry on throughout the entire length of the day. For whilst some cases may take longer than expected, none ever takes less time than expected. So it was that Harry struggled on, constantly trying to catch up and yet deal with each and every case on merit. And he still had Jimmy Rodgers' benefit forms to fill out.

At the end of the day, when his final patient had left and he had appended the notes appropriately, Harry leant back in his chair and breathed a sigh of relief. It had been a busy one, a snatched sandwich and a cup of black coffee was all that he had managed to consume during its course. It was now 6 p.m. and it was already pitch dark outside. He was still concerned about Julie McCormick. Harry knew deep down that there was something very wrong. He ran through her symptoms and signs in his mind, trying to come up with the answer, the diagnosis, that he knew had to be there. He wished that he had paid more attention in those neurology lectures and ward rounds. But Harry, like most generalists, had always found the subject to be complicated and was prepared, like most others, to defer to the specialists in that field. Finally he decided that what he needed was just to switch off and relax. He lifted the phone to ring home and tell Olivia that he was going to call in at the leisure centre and he'd be late home. Then he remembered that he didn't live there any more. Harry just couldn't get used to his new circumstances. He replaced the receiver, feeling more than a little embarrassed at his own stupidity.

Having ploughed up and down the length of the pool thirty times, fifteen lengths breaststroke, fifteen lengths front crawl, the aching in his muscles now sufficiently distracted his mind from the day's toils and tribulations. Harry retired briefly to the jacuzzi at the far end of the pool complex. As he relaxed in the warm water and allowed the jets to massage his muscles back to health below the surface, life started to feel bearable again.

At the far end of the pool, Harry spied C.J. pushing his way in through the heavy door leading from the changing rooms. Wearing faded multicoloured swimming trunks and with an even more faded and somewhat ragged towel draped over his bare shoulders, he made his way along the side of the pool towards the jacuzzi. C.J. in a state of undress was not an inspiring sight. His greasy, lank, unkempt hair and his pale spotted skin, flabby musculature and incipient beer belly hanging over the elasticated top of his swim wear did little for the image that The Body Building, as the gym was euphemistically called, would probably wish to portray. Watching him navigate the unfamiliar terrain of the gym and pool area, Harry was reminded of a story that somebody had once told him about C.J. Somewhat bemused by the idea of C.J. joining a fitness centre, they had asked him what sort of machines the gym had. In all innocence C.J. had replied that 'they have a state-of-the-art expresso maker'.

C.J. discarded his towel and hung it on one of the pegs on the wall beside the jacuzzi. He was about to step in beside Harry when he was interrupted by a series of loud blasts from the lifeguard's whistle. Startled, C.J. and Harry looked over in his direction. The lifeguard, who was stationed at the far side of the pool from them and was perched on an elevated seat, was gesticulating wildly in C.J.'s direction.

'What's up with him?' C.J. asked innocently.

The lifeguard's whistle sounded again.

'I think he's got a problem with your cigarette,' replied Harry.

'What cigarette . . .? Oh shit.'

C.J. smoked so much that he had been unconscious of the presence of the half-smoked butt hanging from the corner of his mouth. He removed the butt from his lips, threw it to the floor and immediately stamped on it grinding its flattened remains into the tile.

'Shit . . . Shit . . . SHITE . . . FUCK!'

He hopped furiously around on one leg, gripping the other foot with both hands. C.J. had made the simple mistake of forgetting that when hanging up his towel he had simultaneously discarded his flip-flops.

'Thanks for seeing Julie, she told me all about it.'

That was all he said. Harry knew that he was worried.

2

C.J. sat at his cluttered desk in the *Belfast Spectator* offices. His mind, however, was elsewhere. He had never been a person who coped with illness stoically and the fact that the illness wasn't his but Julie's only served to heighten his sense of hopelessness. C.J. loved Julie. He felt that he had always loved her. He recognised, now more than ever, that he had not been the ideal husband; he drank too much, he was away from home too often, late nights, working weekends, he spent too many hours working, hours, days, weeks and months that he should have been devoting to his wife and family. All his perceived inadequacies seemed to have suddenly been brought sharply into focus by recent events. But despite his shortcomings, he knew that he and Julie had a bond. He felt that he was a part of Julie and she a part of him.

Last night, after Julie's visit to the doctor, the two of them had sat in silence hand in hand, staring blankly at the television screen. Neither one knew quite what to say to comfort the other. There was something wrong, that they both had known, but now their suspicions had become a reality and yet, still, they didn't know what they were facing and, as the cliché goes and C.J. was starting to realise, there is no greater fear than the fear of the unknown.

The loud ringing of the telephone on the desk summoned C.J. sharply back from his gloomy deliberations.

The call being put through from the switchboard was from Patsy Harte, a Sinn Fein councillor based in West Belfast with whom C.J. had had a number of dealings over the years. Usually it was Patsy who would contact C.J. about a potential storyline, rather than vice versa. C.J. was acutely aware that he would usually be fed the party line on some aspect of political, paramilitary or social life and that he was unlikely to be able to ascertain any more information from Patsy than he had been instructed to divulge by his political masters. Nevertheless, despite being fully aware that he was being presented with a slanted view (and sometimes in his final copy not entirely reflecting that view), he and Patsy maintained their contact over the years.

'Hello . . .?'

'Hello, C.J., how's about ye?'

C.J. had never entirely warmed to this traditional Ulster form of greeting.

'Hello, Patsy, how are you?'

'Well as can be expected this weather . . . Listen, I have some information for you. Can you meet me later today?'

'What time?'

'How about half twelve, then you can buy me lunch . . . the Crown bar, okay?'

'Okay, I'll see you there . . . twelve thirty.'

The *Belfast Spectator* employed C.J. as a political journalist. He frequently wrote on other issues as well, as did most of his colleagues, but political affairs were his main area of interest. He'd been in the job now for sufficient years to make a number of valuable and useful contacts, which in turn had increased his standing with the newspaper. Having an interest in politics in Northern Ireland was a fruitful speciality given the constantly shifting state of affairs, or indeed shifting affairs of State. C.J. had returned to the Province not long after his graduation from Manchester. He had spent a short while hawking his journalistic talents

19

around various English cities but had finally realised that being a small fish in a large pond was paradoxically nowhere near as satisfying as being a small fish in a goldfish bowl. And that was what Northern Ireland was in the seventies and eighties; a goldfish bowl into which the rest of the world would occasionally focus its attention, especially if one of the goldfish had become particularly anti-social and disruptive towards the rest of the shoal. Thus the role of a resident political journalist had its rewards for C.J., life was occasionally hectic and even at times frankly dangerous, but dull and boring it was not, and this was the atmosphere in which he thrived. C.J. wouldn't swap it for the world . . . most of the time, anyway. At the moment, he reflected, the political difficulties of the Province would at least offer some respite from his own troubles.

The Crown bar is the oldest bar in Belfast. It is situated directly across the road from the Europa hotel in the centre of the city. Whilst the Crown bar revels in its reputation due to its antiquity, the Europa hotel languishes under another form of notoriety, as it is, allegedly, the most bombed hotel in Europe. Despite its proximity and its age the Crown has come through the years of conflict essentially unscathed. It boasts an original tiled facade and internal decor and by reputation serves one of the best pints of the 'black stuff' anywhere in the island of Ireland. It was not, however, for the antiquity, nor for the decor, nor the Guinness, that Patsy had chosen the Crown as the venue. The Crown as part of its homage to earlier times retained a collection of 'snugs', small-benched areas around a table, partitioned off and with a door which could be closed to seal in the occupants, thus allowing a variety of secret deals or private assignations to be concluded well away from prying eyes. Situated around the outer wall of the central chamber, these snugs survive our more eclectic times. Even to this day they still contain a push bell to summon a waiter in order that drinks may be replenished without the occupants leaving the privacy of their surroundings. However, in modern times most of the push bells have been disabled and even those that have not are steadfastly ignored by bar staff, who remain more intent on simply pulling pints for those who conventionally present themselves at the bar counter.

It was in one of these snugs that C.J., arriving late and breathless from hurrying, found Patsy. Pint in hand, Patsy glanced up as C.J. peered over each of the barred doors in turn, attempting to locate his contact. Patsy slipped the bolt. He was alone in the cubicle.

'You're late.'

'I know, I see you had to buy your own pint then . . . Do you want another?'

C.J. proffered a packet of twenty Marlboro Lights in Patsy's direction. The 'Light' was C.J.'s only real concession to the nineties health epidemic.

'Don't mind if I do.' Patsy took one of the offered cigarettes. '. . . And mine's a Guinness, thanks.'

C.J. elbowed his way through the lunchtime crowd to buy the drinks. As he returned, Patsy swung the door closed and bolted it shut.

'Well, why did you drag me down here?' C.J. asked.

'I've got some information that you might want.'

'What sort of information?'

'Information about an IRA arms dump. I can tell you where it is and what it contains.'

C.J. looked a little surprised. With Patsy's political connections, he didn't expect him to make any revelations that might upset the IRA.

'Am I hearing you right? You want to tell me where the IRA are storing some weapons? . . . Why?'

'Let's talk money first.'

Patsy, no matter what the mission, whether on his own behalf or on the bidding of others, never let an opportunity to raise a little cash slip by.

'It depends on the information and how I can use it. But Patsy, I don't understand, why do you want me to uncover an arms dump?'

'I feel it's my duty as a concerned citizen to have this particular stash discovered.'

What ever else it was due to, C.J. thought, it was hardly Patsy's social conscience that had promoted this meeting.

'Look,' Patsy continued, taking a large gulp of Guinness, 'I know where there are some Armalites and handguns hidden away in a derelict house in West Belfast. I'm a local councillor and I'm concerned that some of the local kids, who you and I know are in and out of those old houses all the time, will discover the guns and injure themselves or worse.'

'And that's the only reason?'

'Of course.'

'Come off it. This dump has probably been there for years. Why only tell me about it now?'

'Okay, smart arse. If I tell you something, it goes no further, agreed?'

'Agreed,' replied C.J., intrigued.

'Do you believe that Sinn Fein are committed to the peace process?'

'Mmm . . . Yes?'

'The IRA army council are split right down the middle on the issue as to whether to continue the armed conflict or to pursue the political agenda. As you know, the peace process is starting to fall apart due to the Brits demanding decommissioning. The IRA can't give up their arms to the Brits just because they say so. Yet if something doesn't happen soon, the whole process will fall apart because the Unionists will pull out of Stormont. If that happens, Sinn

Fein will get the blame and the hardliners in the IRA will restart the war. If that were to happen, you and me, and anyone else who supports the peace process would have no place once again.'

'You and *I*,' corrected C.J.

'What's wrong with you and me?' asked Patsy.

'Well for a start I don't fancy you, that's what's wrong with it.'

'Oh very funny. Ha bloody ha.'

'Okay Patsy, so what are you saying? That this information that you're giving me is some form of covert decommissioning?'

'To a degree that's right, but you can't print it. We'd just deny it. As far as the public is concerned, it is a tip-off from a concerned citizen. But you have to let the Brits know exactly where the information came from.'

'Why don't you just report to the RUC directly?'

'You are joking, aren't you? A Shinner give information to the RUC? No chance! And anyway, if that got out it would blow the army council clean apart. This way we can deny everything.'

C.J. finished his drink. He wrote down the address and location of the arms then slipped Patsy a couple of twenty-pound notes, got up, let himself out of the snug and made his way to the outer door and out into the busy street beyond. He walked around for a while, trying to formulate how he could present the information that he'd just received into some form of story – one that he could print and one that he could stand over. It had the potential of a huge story: the IRA finally agreeing to give up its arms. Something that had been striven for by prime ministers, politicians, and ordinary people from all sides of the divide over many decades. It had not been thought achievable despite the progress of the current talks. But here it was, the actual moment, no matter how small the handover, no matter how covert or secretive, it was the immense symbolism that it portrayed that was the important issue. And here he was, right in the thick of it. C.J. felt that it was his own personal opportunity to contribute to the peace process, in which he, as so many others, believed. But then there was the rub: no one was to know, it was all to be so covert, so behind the scenes. All that C.J. and his newspaper would and could achieve in the short term, at least, would be a small column entitled '*Arms Find*'. Not hugely newsworthy. Not likely to increase circulation figures. Perhaps, though, having an inside track, even if at present he couldn't make full use of it, might, just might, in the longer term lead to more fruitful copy.

Returning to the *Belfast Spectator* building, and having resolved at least some of these issues in his mind, C.J. knocked on the door of his editor's office.

'Come' echoed from behind the glass panelled door.

C.J. pushed his way in to find George Thompson, the paper's editor in chief, sitting with his feet resting high up on the desktop while he read his way through some of the next day's proofs.

'Hi, George, can I discuss a potential storyline with you?'

'No problem, C.J., but you'll have to be quick – these proofs need to be down in the print room pronto.'

C.J. proceeded to relate the details of his lunchtime meeting with Patsy, though Patsy's name was not offered, or asked for. C.J. then went on to explain how he intended to publish the material.

'Yeah, yeah, but what's in it for us?' said George Thompson. 'The big story's the IRA willingly giving up its arms, but we can't cover that. By your own admission there's no proof and everyone will just deny it anyway.'

'Surely we can at least speculate on the possibility? What

harm can it do? And if anybody believes it, it can only help the peace process move along.'

'I don't know. As I see it, we only have about a column inch on the fact that we know the whereabouts of some guns. We can accompany the police or army in picking them up, which, I suppose might provide a picture. But really that's it ... Look, I tell you what I'll do, I'll have a think about it. Perhaps I'll talk it over with some friends in Special Branch and see if we can squeeze anything more out of this. Is that okay? Is your informant going to be happy enough with us passing your info over to the police?'

'Apparently that's exactly what he wants us to do.'

'It just occurs to me, though, this couldn't be some sort of elaborate trap for the RUC, could it? How much do you trust your guy?'

'No, no. He's genuine, I'm sure of it. Anyway, the IRA are on cease-fire.'

'I know, but others aren't. Okay, if you're sure, give me the address and I'll get on the case.'

To be honest, C.J. hadn't even thought about the possibility of some sort of ambush. But he had dealt with Patsy before and although he had his connections, C.J. didn't believe him capable of the sort of terrorist subterfuge that George was suggesting.

C.J. passed over the piece of paper onto which he had written the details that Patsy had divulged. Having done so, he exited George's office and made his way down between the rows of desks to find his own, near the back of the large open plan office. There he sat and mulled over in his mind how to reveal the truth behind what Patsy had told him, and how best to publicise the IRA's willingness to finally give up its weapons.

Eventually having come to an impasse, C.J. turned his attention to some of the many papers scattered over his desk-top. Work that he had been meaning to do last week, earlier this week, this morning and again this afternoon. He decided to make a start.

Later that afternoon, face focused on his computer screen, he applied the finishing touches to a story about a local politician's attempts to reverse the beef ban in the European Parliament, on the basis of Northern Ireland's advanced cattle tracking system. From the corner of his eye, he glimpsed the pair. They entered the communal office and made their way, guided by one of the girls from reception chirping away as she indicated the route between the desks to the editor's office. Two large men, sports jackets, plain flannels, shirt and tie, both had moustaches.

Why, C.J. asked himself, do all policemen have moustaches? It was a bigger give-away than the bulge in their jacket. These must be George's Special Branch contacts, thought C.J. Presumably they'll want to talk to me. C.J. watched the two men enter the office. Through the glass panels he saw them sit down on the opposite side of the desk from George. Some intense talking appeared to be going on. Initially George shook his head violently and seemed to be gesticulating but later the conversation appeared more amicable, until both men rose, shook George's hand in turn and left. C.J. had not been asked in, he had played no part in the conversation or deal that had been struck.

During the discussions C.J. had hovered around just outside the office, trying to catch even snippets of the conversation. He caught none. As the office door opened, he turned to make it appear as if he was fetching a drink from the water cooler in the corner of the office. As he turned back he accidentally caught the shoulder of one of the policemen. C.J. apologised, the policeman merely grunted and continued on his way.

When the two officers had left the building, C.J. made his way to George's office. He didn't bother to knock. He just walked in. George was on the phone. As C.J. entered, the editor saw him coming and put the phone down.

'What's going on?' demanded C.J.

'What do you mean?' responded George.

'You're not going to deny that that was Special Branch.'

'No. Of course not.'

George knew that C.J.'s undoubted investigative skills would have sussed his visitors out within seconds of their arrival.

'Well, would you mind telling me what's going on? Why was I not involved? And what have you agreed with them?'

'Look, C.J., there's more to this than meets the eye. That's all I can say at the moment. But they were very grateful for the information and I think at the end of the day we, no you, will get a good story out of this.'

'What do you mean more to this than meets the eye? I already told you that.'

'Look, C.J., just drop it. At the moment I don't want you to do anything. I don't want you to write anything about this arms dump. And especially I don't want you to go anywhere near the area. Just let it lie. Do you understand? I really mean this, okay?'

'But I don't understand why.'

'Cool down, and I'll explain,' George rose from his desk, came round from behind it and gestured for C.J. to sit down in the empty seat on the other side. When C.J. had sat down and calmed a little, George perched himself on the corner of his desk and tried to explain the meeting he'd just had.

'As you quite rightly guessed, that was Special Branch. I invited them here in the light of your information. Their view on things, it has to be said, however, differs somewhat from your informant's.'

'Mandy Rice Davies.'

27

'What?'

'They would say that, wouldn't they.'

'Okay. But their view also has some credence.'

'So what are they saying?'

'Your informant says that he's telling us where these arms are hidden for those within the IRA who believe in the peace process to kick-start the talks by initiating a decommissioning process.'

'Basically, yes.'

'But no one can know about it.'

'Well, not at the moment, certainly.'

'Okay, well Special Branch have an alternative viewpoint.'

'Which is?'

'Which is that, yes, the IRA army council is deeply divided on the peace process. Some certainly support it, but others, the more hard-line Republicans, don't – and some even have a desire to resume the armed conflict right away. Special Branch believe that the hardliners, those with links to the breakaway Real IRA or Continuity IRA, are planning to rearm.'

'So?'

'So, who has all the arms?'

'The IRA.'

'Exactly, and they're on cease-fire. So all the guns are lying idle in dumps around the country. Special Branch believes that the Real IRA, or whoever, are being tipped off where the dumps are.'

'What, and they are raiding the dumps and stockpiling the guns for their own use?'

'Yes. The police believe that your tip-off is simply an attempt by the more peace-minded among Sinn Fein/IRA to stem this flow.'

C.J. considered the alternative thesis. There was no doubt that it was certainly plausible, though clearly it was not, to a confirmed pacifist such as C.J., anywhere near as appealing as the original explanation for the revelation of the whereabouts of the arms dump.

'Also, the police believe that the Real IRA and other dissident groups are planning a series of attacks in order to scupper the peace process entirely and hence gain the upper hand over the moderates for the support of the rank and file Republicans. They believe that these guns would have been used for that purpose. The moderates must have got wind of what was happening and decided to do something about it.'

'So, what happens now?'

'Nothing. Special Branch have asked us not to print anything just yet. They say they'll deal with the guns and have promised to give us an inside track on future developments.'

'But, surely . . .'

'But, surely nothing. I've given them my word and that's an end to it. What does it matter anyway what the correct explanation is? The outcome's the same, guns in police hands, potential for violence averted. Either way there's no real story for us. Drop it.'

C.J. still felt unhappy. There had been a big opportunity both for a splash in the newspaper and also, perhaps more importantly, a chance to help the failing peace process. But if the police now collected the guns and gave no credence to the explanation that he had promoted, there was little he could do.

He decided to go home and exchange the frustrations he felt at work for the concerns he felt for his family.

3

Head buried in his hands, Harry crouched over the small table. The light from the 40-watt bulb in the desk lamp barely illuminated the pile of paperwork in front of him. It never failed to amaze and irritate him just how much bureaucracy the modern NHS encompassed. But partly it was his own fault; Harry liked people and he enjoyed being able to meet them, to listen to their problems and to help in whatever way he could. Harry, however, did not enjoy the resulting paperwork and would inevitably put it off until, like tonight, he could defer it no longer – but by that time it had grown into an unwieldy mountain. Organised was not a word that sat easily on Harry's shoulders. He continued to plough through the pile of forms and notes, slowly moving them from the large pile on his left – those waiting to be dealt with – to the smaller pile on his right – those already completed. Totally absorbed, if not totally enthused, by his labours, he nearly missed the doorbell when it rang for the first time. Partially alerted, though, he heard it clearly on its second ring and rose quickly from the table, knocking over the chair on which, up till that moment, he had been seated. As the chair toppled backwards it landed, back first, on the floor with a dull thud. Harry stumbled over it in his haste to get to the door.

Leaving the flat door ajar, he stepped out into the cold of the dimly lit communal corridor beyond and bounded down the flight of stairs, taking two at a time. Finally, and not a little out of breath, he reached the heavy outer wooden door. Through the frosted glass inserts, he could see the blurred outline of his unexpected caller silhouetted against the streetlights beyond. Harry was not an accustomed host. He had received very few visitors since he and Olivia had split up and he had moved out of the house they had once shared. Even before the break-up it was Olivia who had been the more sociable, the more outgoing. Harry was happier to sit at home, catching up with work, watching television or just enjoying the quiet pleasure of their own company.

'Hello, Harry.'

He recognised the voice, even before he had prised the door open wide enough to see who it was.

'Oh . . . Hello, Olivia . . . Umm, what are you doing here?'

Harry was certainly surprised to see the woman to whom he was still officially married but from whom he was most definitely separated. Olivia had not previously made any attempt to contact him – not since she had, in forthright terms, told him exactly how little she thought of him and of their three years of what she had referred to at the time as their 'so-called' marriage. The last he'd seen of her was as she had driven off, allowing him only the time to remove his belongings from the house, under her ultimatum to be gone by the time she returned.

He had left, initially to lodge with some friends. He was grateful for their hospitality but felt distinctly uncomfortable from the outset. Harry had never been one to impose on others and, more than this, he had detected an unwelcome air of pity that he had proved incapable of sustaining a relationship, unable to prevent his marital breakdown. So, as quickly as he could, Harry had found himself a small bedsit and moved out. That the flat was small was no understatement. In the last few years property prices in

31

Belfast had risen as the peace process started to show signs of success. In earlier years, house prices in the North of Ireland had been well below other areas of the United Kingdom or, indeed, other areas of Ireland. Now they were playing catch-up. Many properties were being bought up by outside entrepreneurs, fuelling the housing market further. In parallel to the climbing house sales prices, rented accommodation was also at a premium and rent prices had also risen sharply. General practitioners' pay scales had not, however, followed a similar trend. Thus it was, just at the time that Harry had found himself homeless, that the differential between his income and the outlay required for a rental property was at its least attractive. His choices of potential domiciles had, therefore, been severely curtailed.

'Can I come in?' Olivia asked, already pushing past. She paused, and regarded the bleak hallway in which Harry stood dumbly holding the door ajar. She glimpsed the peeling paint, illuminated by a single bare light bulb, itself hanging limply by a frayed wire from an equally distressed ceiling rose. The noise of the footsteps generated by her expensive leather soles reverberated around the empty interior, echoing off the linoleum-covered floor.

Harry still marvelled at Olivia's beauty. She had an angular face which came to a point at her chin, and fine-boned features, in the middle of which was delicately placed that which others better informed in these matters than he would refer to as a retroussé nose. A thin neck swept down to a slim but perfectly rounded size ten figure. Her hair was blonde but her eyebrows, being of darker hue, belied its naturalness.

Harry had met Olivia shortly after qualifying. She was working as a researcher for a national television company and he was immediately attracted to her not just for her looks but also because of her worldliness, her knowledge and her boundless abundance of ambition. Her drive was what he had liked most, and least, about her. She had seemed equally enthused by Harry, then a promising junior hospital doctor. At that time the world had seemed to have been his oyster with many possible options leading to personal and professional success opening up ahead of him. Olivia, Harry knew, had harboured high hopes of him becoming a wealthy and respected orthopaedic surgeon. Harry, on the other hand, had realised that his talents lay elsewhere, and when he settled for a career in general practice the seeds of Olivia's discontent had been sown. When he finally accepted a partnership in an unfashionable and socially deprived area of the city, those seeds had germinated. After three years of marriage, an attempt to renovate an old farmhouse (in an area that he had hoped would become sought after – but was probably never likely to be), two dogs, one cat and six chickens (now dead – throttled after failing to provide the level of self sufficiency of eggs that they had expected), but no children, Olivia had finally thrown in the towel and they had parted company. She, he had heard, had returned to work for a local production company. Her temporary departure as a house-wife, builder's apprentice and smallholder was simply put down to experience and presented in as favourable terms as possible in her updated *curriculum vitae.*

'I'm up on the second floor,' Harry offered as he turned to lead the way. As he clambered awkwardly back up the stairs, he tried to figure out just why Olivia had come to see him now, having previously shown no interest in doing so. He was also concerned about the present state of the flat, he hadn't yet washed his dinner plates or cooking utensils, which, he remembered, were scattered around the kitchen area. Olivia had long berated his tendency to untidiness and Harry was not really in the mood for one of her ticking offs. He heard Olivia stop on the stairs. He turned around; she was attempting to scrape something off the heel of one of her shoes. Her face contorted as she did so into a look of grave displeasure.

'Sorry,' he said. 'It's the students in the other flats. They are always dropping things . . . Oh dear, it looks like chewing gum.'

Olivia scraped her foot back and forth on one of the steps until, satisfied that the offending item had been dislodged, she carried on up the stairs in his wake to the second floor.

Harry paused outside the open door.

'Um . . . It's a bit of a mess, I'm afraid. You should have told me you were coming.'

'I don't care what it's like, Harry. Can we just go on in, please? I don't want to stand in this grotty hallway any longer.'

He ushered Olivia in. To call it a flat was something of an exaggeration for it really just consisted of a single room which doubled as a sitting room and bedroom. Off this main living quarter on one side was an archway leading to a small kitchenette and on the other side there was an even smaller en suite bathroom. Olivia regarded it all with an air of critical disdain.

Immediately sensing her disapproval, he offered, 'It's just temporary, till I get properly sorted.'

'No, no, don't get me wrong, Harry,' Olivia replied. 'I was just thinking how much this place suits you – small, cheap and unfashionable.'

'I'm sure you haven't dropped by just to insult me.'

'No, you're quite right. In any case, I don't have to try to belittle you, you are quite capable of doing that for yourself.'

'Oh, ha ha. Look just what do you want, Olivia?'

Olivia walked around the small apartment, demonstrating particular distaste for the furnishings. Finally, after firstly picking up and tossing aside a newspaper that was lying on the seat of the one cushioned armchair, she sat herself down. Still stiff backed, she crossed her legs.

Harry picked up the fallen chair and sat down opposite his formerly dearly beloved.

'It's nice to see you again,' he said. 'To what do I owe the pleasure?'

'I want a divorce,' came the frosty reply.

Harry froze. Although he and Olivia had been living separate lives for the last few months, Harry, at least, had not given up all hope of a reconciliation. When Olivia had appeared at the front door and as she had sat down in this grim little flat, he had harboured the inkling of a hope, somewhere deep within his brain, however unlikely the reality, that she had come to ask him to come home.

He still found her attractive, and no matter how unpleasant she could be at times, he would have no difficulty in forgiving her and rekindling their relationship. Harry respected her drive and her ambition. He recognised that it was his fault that he did not live up to her hopes and aspirations; his fault that they had always seemed to be in debt; his fault that he had been unable to provide her with the level of financial security for which she yearned. Olivia had mocked his failed attempts to try to lift them out of the abyss into which they had sunk. Still, Harry could forgive her anything. He recalled the good things their relationship had brought, much preferring them to the bad times.

As a child, Harry had longed for love and affection. His mother had died when he was very young, too young in fact for him to have any true memories of her. What recollections he did have were formulated from things that his father had told him about her, intermingled with his own, probably fantastical, imaginations of her. Harry thought of his mother as the cleverest, most beautiful and loving woman in the world. She possessed only good qualities, never any negative ones. His negative thoughts were reserved, quite unfairly he recognised now, for his father. Deep down, he could not deny that he had been a good and caring man, it was just that he was never there for him. Harry understood it better now with the knowledge of years behind him, but then as a small lonely child Harry could not understand his absences. A widower with a young child to look after, Harry now supposed, he had had little alternative, he had had to work to provide for his family, and so young Harry's care was abdicated to a variety of aunts and housekeepers, some of whom he had liked, some of whom he hadn't, but none of whom he had loved and none of whom had loved him. When in later years he had met Olivia, she seemed to offer him everything that had been missing in his life and he had fallen head over heels in love with her. Their marriage had been a roller-coaster ride from the outset. Olivia had always been able to put him through the full range of emotions, she twisted him in knots, but whatever the problems in the past, at least they had always been able to kiss and make up.

It was the word 'divorce' that had rocked him. It was the finality of the word allied with the iciness of its delivery that had struck home. Even though, as he had to admit, their relationship had been in trouble for months, if not years, even though they had been apart for some months, even though Olivia had made no previous attempt to see him, Harry still clung to the hope that things might yet work out for the best. A divorce was not really what he had in mind, nor indeed wished for. Harry knew Olivia well, though, and he knew that once she had decided on a course of action she could not generally be deflected. Harry realised that he was in big trouble.

'Umm ... okay,' he blurted out, unable to think of anything better to say.

'I've been to see my solicitor ...'

Another word that stabbed deep into his consciousness, 'solicitor'. It struck home because of its impersonality, its formality; it implied third-party interference in his affairs. Olivia had prefixed it with the word 'my'; Harry had been unaware that Olivia had a solicitor, other than the one they had used when they jointly purchased the house. Clearly she had engaged one now. His discomfiture was increased by Olivia's next sentence.

'You've probably heard of her,' Olivia continued, 'it's Sharon Rutherford.'

Harry had heard of her. Her reputation was well known by most men in the Province. It had been built on her notoriety as a feminist and by her success in upholding the woman's position in divorce proceedings – to such an extent that, to most of the male species, she was known in less than friendly terms as 'the Rottweiler'. It was rumoured that if she was acting for your wife in a custody case, it would be easier to get your kids back from a Rottweiler than it would be to prise them from Sharon Rutherford's legal grasp. Olivia had deliberately thrown in her name for the effect that she knew it would have on him.

He shifted uncomfortably in his seat. Olivia observed it, with some satisfaction. He knew that he was beaten before it had even begun.

'If we remain separated for six months, we can apply for a quickie divorce on the grounds of irreconcilable differences.'

'Is that what you believe? That there are irreconcilable differences?' Harry asked sadly. He knew the answer before the question had left his lips.

'Yes,' came the icy confirmation. 'We need to sort out the material and financial side of things,' Olivia continued matter-of-factly.

Harry detected the solicitor's tones in this statement. This was professional advice coming through.

'You didn't need to hire a solicitor. I'm sure we could have sorted things out amicably between ourselves.'

'Possibly, but I wanted to make sure I got all that's due to me.'

'Due to you? Like what?'

'I want you to sign the house over to me.'

'The house? But that's in both our names and I've been paying the mortgage. In fact, I believe that I'm still paying the mortgage, even though it's only you living in it. I thought that before I moved out we'd agreed that you would live on in it, I'd continue paying, but that you would put it up for sale and then we would split the proceeds.'

'Yes, I did say that. But that was then. This is now. Things have changed.'

The only thing that's changed, Harry thought, was that you have employed a fancy divorce lawyer and now, fired up by her advice, you are determined to push home your advantage.

'When we bought the house,' she continued, 'I sank all my savings into the deposit for it. You on the other hand had no money, so you didn't contribute.'

Harry could again hear Sharon Rutherford's voice speaking though it was Olivia who sat opposite him, apparently emotionless, like the ice queen as she delivered her demands.

'But, but . . . you gave up work, I paid the mortgage.'

'True, but I then worked around the house. That enabled you to continue at work and, by releasing you from the household tasks, even increased your opportunities. So it could be said that I contributed equally to the mortgage and, in fact, contributed to your wage-earning capacity. The fact that you were incapable of exploiting your enhanced occupational opportunity was not my fault.'

'So what are you saying?'

Olivia reached into her handbag and produced a number of A4 printed sheets. Each sheet bore a series of calculations. Clearly these had been prepared by Sharon Rutherford. Olivia shuffled through the sheets, finally selecting the one she wanted. She rose, came over to where Harry sat and placed the sheet on the desk in front of him. She stood over his left shoulder as he scrutinised the figures contained therein.

'I contributed the £8,000 deposit on the house,' said Olivia, pointing to the relevant figure near the top of the sheet. 'The house cost us £120,000. The mortgage was approximately £550 per month. Which is £6,600 per year. Over the three years we lived there we paid £19,800. Most of which were interest payments, though.'

'Okay, I'm with you so far.'

'Given that we both contributed in our own way to the mortgage, you contributed £9,900, whilst I contributed £9,900 plus the £8,000 deposit, i.e. a total of £17,900. If we sell the house, say we got £150,000 for it now, we would still have to pay off the mortgage – about £110,000, give or take a bit, as we've only paid off three years and that's when most of the payment goes towards the interest, not the actual loan. So we would each get about £20,000.'

'Uh huh, . . . but we might get a lot more for the house. House prices have fairly rocketed in the last two years.'

'Yes, we might, but we might also get a lot less. Especially as I'm still there, a sitting tenant in fact with nowhere else to go. That might put a lot of buyers off.'

Harry could imagine Olivia making it difficult to sell the house if she didn't want it sold. Perhaps, he thought, he should cut his losses.

'So we might each get £20,000, but you owe me £8,000, and that doesn't include the interest that I could have accumulated . . . Then there's the car.'

'The car?'

'Look here, about half-way down.' Olivia pointed to the sheet, and he looked to where she was indicating.

'My car still has two years' hire purchase to pay off plus

the final payment – £250 per month, plus £7,500. A total of £13,500. I need transport if I'm going to get back to work full-time.'

'What about me?' moaned Harry.

'Your car's already paid off. Which, as I've already explained, the courts would hold that I have contributed to. It would be unreasonable to leave me stranded without transport.'

Harry distinguished the Rottweiler's voice most clearly now. There was no mention of the fact that his car was a seven-year-old clapped-out Ford Fiesta. Olivia's car, on the other hand, was a brand-new BMW 318, which he had known that they could not afford, but she had persuaded him that it was just the family car they needed.

'You could use public transport,' he retorted.

'That's easy for you to say – you live here near the centre of town. You well know that there are no reliable bus routes near to our house.'

'So move. That's what we'd originally decided.'

'If we sell and I move, then I'll need somewhere else to live. I have just got the job with the production company, but you know as well as I do that it's only temporary. If I move I might not be able to get somewhere in the locality. I'll lose my job, and as I'm not working, because I gave up my career for you, you will have to fork out for the rent of the new place.'

'All right, all right, you've convinced me. What exactly do you want?'

'Going back to the figures . . .' Olivia had him on the ropes and she knew it, she wasn't going to let him wriggle free now. 'Given the profit that we might make from the sale of the house, but given that you are going to have to pay me off from your share, you will actually end up still owing me money. So by just signing it over to me now, as a sort of goodwill gesture, it will actually save you money in the long term.'

'So despite all the money, all the time and all the effort that I have sunk into the place, I just hand the house over to you and I'm actually better off.'

'That is a bit simplistic, but the figures are there in front of you in black and white.'

Ms Rutherford had trained her disciple well. Harry knew, instinctively, that the figures contained gross and even inaccurate assumptions, but he also knew that if he were to protest and to fight, then he too would have to employ a solicitor. In the end he might save a little cash, but what little he would be likely to claw back would be severely diminished by the ensuing legal fees.

'Okay, I'll let you have your divorce and you can have the house.'

Olivia let a small smile cross her frosty visage.

'Then there's just the small matter of maintenance.'

Harry sank his head into his hands, as Olivia continued unabated.

'Although we have no dependants, I am reliably informed, that because I gave up my career to support you in yours, you are obliged to provide me with an income on which to live, at least until I can re-establish my own financial independence.'

'How much?' Harry murmured.

'I don't want to be unreasonable.'

'Of course you don't.'

'You earn, what? About £35,000 per year?'

'Before tax.'

'That's about £3,000 per month,' continued Olivia, ignoring his interjection. 'If I take over the house you are going to save the cost of the mortgage. So we reckon you can afford to give me at least £600 per month. That's only a fifth of your income. Sharon said that I would be entitled to a lot more and that the courts would probably agree, but I don't want to put you through all that. I told Sharon that I would come over this evening for a chat and try to sort things out amicably, like two adults.'

All of a sudden Harry didn't feel much like an adult. Olivia was talking to him as if he was a difficult child who needed putting straight. But he didn't want to fight about it and Olivia knew that he didn't want to fight about it. Furthermore, Harry knew that Olivia knew that Harry wouldn't fight.

'Look, whatever,' he finally agreed. 'Draw up the documents, send them round and I'll sign them.'

'Sharon will get them to you within the week.'

Before I have time to change my mind, he thought. Really, though, he didn't care, money was not important to Harry, he just wanted a quiet life. He would have preferred a quiet life with Olivia, but that, he rationalised, was not now going to happen.

Olivia rose and with only the briefest of farewells, took her leave. Harry shut the door of the flat behind her, surveyed his dominion and then returned to his paperwork.

4

Julie was glad that C.J. had taken the day off work to accompany her to the outpatient consultation. They had arrived in good time but the clinic was running about thirty minutes behind schedule, so they had an extended wait in the small but busy waiting area – one of a number of outpatient suites in the tower block that was the outpatient building of the Royal Victoria hospital.

The outpatient department, as with so many other departments within the health service, had seen better times. Many of the padded seats provided had been worn thin by frequent use and many even sported rips in their imitation leather covers. The carpet in the small waiting area was also showing its age, at least in those areas where the original carpet was still visible between the stains left by the earlier drips and spills from innumerable cups of tea and coffee.

The area in which Julie and C.J. sat, hand in hand, was cramped and clearly, Julie felt, inadequate in size, given the through-put of patients, relatives and concerned friends. Julie sat in silence simply observing the comings and goings of the people who attended one of the three consecutively running clinics. They encompassed a wide spectrum of age and disability. Looking towards, but trying not to stare at, others less fortunate than her, many of whom were wheelchair-bound, Julie tried not to think of her own problems and how she had become acutely aware of her own failing abilities over the last few months. She prayed that C.J. was not thinking along similar lines. It seemed only yesterday that she was playing with Becky in the back garden of their home, running, chasing, falling, rolling on the ground and laughing out loud. She thought that she hadn't laughed much recently, everything had become such a chore, even the everyday household tasks exhausted her and drained her spirits. She remembered her joy after the birth of Tom, her pleasure in providing C.J. with the son that she had felt he had always wanted. Her life had seemed so complete. She had loved C.J. from the moment she had met him. She had never stopped loving him. Of course, they had had arguments; they had had times when they wouldn't even talk to one another. But she had never regretted a single moment of their relationship and now all she wanted, all she prayed for, as she sat with him in this faded outpatient department, was for it all to be a fuss about nothing.

But there was something wrong. At first it was hardly noticeable, just a bit of clumsiness. C.J. had mocked her and they'd both attributed it to hormonal changes following Tom's birth. When it didn't go away C.J. got worried that maybe she had become depressed, the baby blues, he thought they called it, and that she had been secretly drinking to offset her problems. She had caught him searching the house for secret supplies of gin. They'd laughed about it later. Then she found that she couldn't keep up with C.J. when they went for a walk. That had been particularly worrying. She smiled, though, as she thought of it, given C.J.'s chronic level of inactivity. But then it seemed to her that one of her legs would just give up from under her if she did too much. Most recently, she had taken to walking holding onto C.J.'s arm, or if he wasn't there she would use Tom's buggy for support. Finally C.J. had persuaded her to visit her GP, and so here they waited patiently to see the specialist that Harry had recommended. The waiting area was thinning out rapidly.

'Mrs Julie McCormick,' came the call from behind them. Julie and C.J. rose and turned in unison.

Dr John Anderson was not quite what Julie had imagined a consultant neurologist would look like. But then, Julie had had very few dealings with neurologists previously.

Her nursing days were behind her, and even then she had spent most of her working life in the geriatric wards of a small district general hospital, unaccustomed territory for a neurologist. Dr Anderson appeared to be in his early fifties, bearded but balding, and his beard betrayed his age as it was greying at the edges. His angular features culminated in a rather too prominent nose. Julie summed up her first impression as vaguely intellectual looking, in a mad professor sort of way, yet none the less a welcoming and friendly appearance. Dr Anderson didn't wear a white coat, partly because he preferred the informality and partly because since the NHS reforms and economy drives clean white coats had become increasingly difficult to obtain. He wore dark trousers, a plain white shirt and a tie that was of such vividness that it would have dazzled even the partially sighted.

He smiled towards Julie as she made her way resolutely on C.J.'s arm towards the consulting room.

Having satisfied himself of the chronological chain of events that had led to this consultation, Dr Anderson set about examining Julie. She recalled that she had gone through much the same process at the medical centre.

Dr Anderson helped her off the couch. He then asked her to walk, stiffly and unsteadily as it was, a few feet across the consulting room floor. Then he guided her on his arm back to her seat beside C.J., who had sat silently throughout, watching, trying to make sense of it all.

'What has your GP said to you about your problem?' the consultant asked.

'Very little, so far,' she replied. 'He said that he was worried, though, and he thought the problem was maybe in my spinal cord. So he sent me to see you.'

'I have to say that I share his concern and I think that he is absolutely correct. Your GP has done exactly the right thing to get you along to see us.'

'What do you think the problem is, Dr Anderson?'

'That is more difficult to say. I agree with your GP in that the problem is within the spinal cord. But whilst I can say with some degree of certainty where the problem is, what is causing that problem will require some specialised investigations.'

'What sort of investigations?'

'Well, I need to visualise the spinal cord to exclude something pressing on or growing in it.'

'You mean, like a tumour?'

'Possibly, but there are many other possibilities.'

'Such as?'

'Well, a disc, for example, but I think we are getting into specifics here too quickly. I think that we need to find out exactly what we are dealing with before we end up discussing just about every possible cause in the abstract. We should get the tests done as quickly as possible. Then I'll be better placed to discuss things in much more detail.'

'So what do you propose?'

'In order to get everything done that needs to be done in the shortest possible time, I want you to come into hospital for a few days.'

'You want to admit her?' asked C.J. somewhat taken aback.

Julie could see the distress in his face. C.J. had never been one to feel particularly comfortable around illness in general and hospitals in particular.

'What about the kids?' he asked. 'Who'll look after them? I'm out working all day.'

Typical, thought Julie, more concerned about having to look after the kids himself than worried about me.

'Don't worry about that. We'll sort something out. I'm sure my mother will help out. It will only be for a few days anyway, won't it, Doctor?'

'Obviously it will depend on what we turn up, but I would hope to have you in for not much longer than a week.'

'A week?' Julie felt the tears welling up in her eyes.

'The very specialised tests that you need do take some time to be set up, carried out and then interpreted.'

'I'll come in, Doctor. I know it's for the best. Don't worry, I'll organise everything at home. When do you want me to come in?'

'I'll try to get things moving as quickly as possible. I'd like to think that you'll be in with us within the next day or two.'

'So soon?'

'There's no time like the present.'

Dr Anderson was as good as his word. Two days later C.J. was bringing Julie back up to the hospital. This time, however, in the arm that was not linked in Julie's, he clutched her small suitcase, which contained all the things that she felt she would need for her in-patient stay. Indeed, she had spent the last two days packing and unpacking its contents, as she tried to decide what to take. She fussed about her toiletries and her make-up and then, frustrated, she would busy herself around the house, cleaning and clearing things.

The neurology unit was situated in one of the older wings of the hospital. A major hospital refurbishment was under way, but the neurological unit did not appear, at first glance at least, to feature largely in this exercise.

It was with a heavy heart that Julie kissed C.J. goodbye and then as she sat on the edge of the starched linen sheet covering the bed she watched him make his lonely way back to the car. She felt that this was going to be the longest week in her life. She had not been parted from C.J. and the kids for so long in all the years that they had been married.

The medical merry-go-round started right away. A worryingly young-looking junior doctor came and transcribed Julie's particulars into a file. He then went through the story of her illness again, detail by painful detail. Julie found it all quite trying as this was the third time she had recounted her story and by now she was becoming weary of the telling. The youthful doctor examined her, then disappeared, but only to return a few minutes later with a tray of plastic bottles, a bundle of forms, a tourniquet and a frighteningly large syringe. Julie watched in wonder as he drained dark red blood from her forearm and transferred it to each of the bottles in turn.

After the child had departed for the second time, the woman in the next bed to Julie's leant over and spoke to her.

'He's a bit of all right, isn't he?'

Julie looked over. The woman was in her late sixties, with grey, wiry hair bundled on top of her head and fixed there with a large pink ribbon. Her face had a peaches-and-cream complexion and she smiled at Julie through loose-fitting dentures.

'Who?'

'Dr McKay. He was just with you.'

'He's a child.'

'I like 'em young, more stamina.'

'Well, he's not my type, I'm afraid.'

'Glad to hear it, I don't need the competition. What are you in for then?'

'Tests.'

'That's what they always say when they haven't a clue what's wrong with you. Mark my words, they'll have you x-rayed, CT scanned, MRI scanned, ECG'd, EEG'd, they'll throw the kitchen sink at you if they can get away with it, and still won't know what's the matter with you. I've been through them all I have. Nothing showed up – they still haven't a clue what's causing them.'

'Causing them . . .?'

'My headaches. Have them all the time, day in, day out. They never shift, always there, I'm in absolute agony every minute of every day. My life's a complete misery with them and this lot here can't sort them out for me. What tests you gonna have?'

'The doctor mentioned a . . . lumbar puncture is it? Tomorrow.'

'Oh my God, a lumbar puncture, that's the worst of the lot, that is – and I should know, I've had three of them I have.'

'Why is it so bad?'

'They stick a needle in your back to drain the fluid off. They're supposed to freeze the skin first but the anaesthetic never works so it's pure agony. Then they poke about for hours 'cause they can't get the right spot, but when they do, boy! do you know about it.'

'What do you mean?' asked Julie, now even more concerned.

'This pain like a red-hot needle shoots down your leg. Pure agony it is and if you flinch at all they shout at you and tell you to keep still. I'd like to do it to one of them and see how they like it and see if they could keep still. That's not the worst of it either.'

'It's not?' asked Julie, not really wishing for any more details.

'Absolutely not. After it's all over, you get left with this massive headache 'cause they've drained all the fluid off and the brain's not got anything left to float around in, so when you try and get up the brain falls down and pulls on all its ligaments and whatever and it's pure agony. You'll be flat on your back for days. Still, if young Dr McKay's around it won't be so bad, will it?'

Julie lay down and pretended to doze. She really wasn't in the mood for any more of her neighbour's prophecies.

In fact the lumbar puncture and all of the other investigations went off without a hitch and by the fourth day it seemed from what Dr McKay had said that all the investigations Dr Anderson had ordered had now been carried out. Later that day Dr Anderson confirmed that, and said that he thought he now knew what the problem was, but he wanted to discuss it with her and C.J. together, preferably at 3.30 p.m. the next day after his ward round.

Julie didn't sleep very well that night. She had not slept particularly well since being in hospital, with the strange bed and the extraneous ward noises, which included her neighbour's loud snoring. Her neighbour seemed to sleep soundly despite her agonies, thought Julie as she tossed and turned, trying to block out the noise. But tonight the noise wasn't the problem. She missed the kids and she missed C.J., but that wasn't the problem either. Thoughts were racing around in her head. If the consultant wanted to see C.J. as well, she rationalised, then the news must be bad. She went over and over again in her head all the investigations that she'd been through in the last few days, trying to glean clues that she might have missed at the time.

She recalled the MRI scan in particular, being strapped

tightly onto a trolley top and then slid mechanically into the mouth of the scanner itself, on and on, deep into the actual bowels of the machine. The aperture was so small that her nose nearly touched the top of the all-engulfing tunnel, whilst her shoulders gently rubbed along its sides. She had to lie perfectly still for nearly as long as she could bear, while the crescendo of noise, like a pneumatic drill, pounded from inside the machine itself. She was not, nor ever had been claustrophobic, but this was as close as she had ever come. She tried to imagine how others less tolerant of confined spaces could cope. After what seemed like an eternity, but in reality was only about twenty minutes, the drilling noise ceased abruptly and the trolley to which she was bound started to make its way back whence it had come. Slowly, Julie emerged out into the subdued lighting of the scanner room itself. She blinked as the lights came on full and the radiographer entered the room and started to unfasten Julie's bindings. As the last of the straps was freed, Julie sat up and gave an involuntary shiver. Noticing it, the radiographer had praised Julie for her tolerance through the test and confirmed Julie's earlier suspicions by telling her that many patients were unable to hack the claustrophobic conditions and demanded to be released, never completing the investigation.

Now Julie tried to analyse the radiographer's reaction. Had she been overly kind and sympathetic because the scan revealed something terrible? Was there something in her tone of voice that might have given it away? No matter how many times she went over it there was nothing more – and no other emphasis she could place on it.

Then she recalled what Dr Anderson had said at their first interview: that he needed to visualise the spinal cord in order to delineate the nature of the problem. Presumably this was the reason for the MRI scan. As he had requested a meeting with both of them again, that must surely mean the news was bad – a tumour on the spine, or worse. Maybe not, maybe it was good news. But then, she thought, why did he want both of us to hear the results together? Maybe that was just routine, just the way Dr Anderson ran his practice. And there were the other tests as well – what were they for? The 'electrical tests'. She'd been asked to sit and look at a television screen on which a checkerboard pattern came and went and changed in front of her. While this was happening a technician was recording a read-out from the machine to which Julie was connected by two small wires whose ends were attached to the back of her head. What was that all about?

C.J. arrived at 3 p.m. Julie saw him briefly just before he was unceremoniously bundled out again by the ward sister, who told him to come back when the consultant had finished his ward round. When he reappeared thirty minutes later, Julie noted that he had not slept well. There were bags under his eyes and his face reflected a dull sallowness. C.J. sat down on the edge of the bed and together they waited for Dr Anderson to return. Not a word did either speak. They shared and understood each other's concerns without the need for words.

A few minutes late, Dr Anderson appeared. Apologising for keeping them waiting, he drew the curtain around the bed, as if to provide a semblance of privacy from the rest of the ward.

'Thank you, for coming in.' He addressed C.J. 'I think that it's best to go through things with us all together, rather than see you separately. This way we will all know the situation and avoid misunderstandings. Then we will be able to plan together for what is best to do and the way forward.'

Julie's nervousness increased, she could feel her heart

pounding as if it would jump out of her chest, but she suppressed it as best she could for C.J.'s sake.

Dr Anderson continued. 'I have almost all the test results through and I thought that we would discuss them together. Firstly, we carried out the MRI scan of your spinal cord. You recall that I felt clinically that was where the problem was.'

'Yes.'

'The principal reason for carrying out that test was to exclude something pressing on, or growing in, the spinal cord.'

'Like a tumour or a disc, I remember you saying at Outpatients.'

'That's right. Well, the scan did not reveal any such problem.'

'That's good.'

'Well, yes, but although the spinal cord looked normal on that scan, it still doesn't get over the fact that there is a problem within it.'

'So, what does that mean?'

'In this situation, where the cord looks normal on the scan but clinically there is no doubt that there is a problem, it usually means that there's some disease within the cord itself.'

'Wouldn't that show up on the scan?'

'Not necessarily. Even an MRI scan has its limitations. One of these is detecting disease within the spinal cord. It is often due to such a small patch of abnormality the scanner can't detect it. Because the spinal cord itself is also quite a small piece of tissue and yet because it is so compact, a tiny abnormality can result in serious consequences.'

'So you think, but you can't prove, that there is some form of disease within Julie's spinal cord?'

'In essence, yes.'

'What sort of disease?' Julie asked.

'This is why we carried out a range of other tests. When

we did the MRI of the spinal cord, I requested that they also performed an MRI scan of your head.'

'But there's nothing wrong with my head.'

'No, but some diseases that affect the central nervous system can affect the brain as well as the spinal cord. Although there may be no symptoms in the brain, the disease can be visualised more easily on the brain scan.'

'And did you see anything on the brain scan?'

'Yes we did. On the brain scan we could see a number of little patches of what looks like inflammation, or what we call demyelination, scattered around the brain. None of these little patches, however, is causing you any difficulty clinically.'

'So what does that mean?'

'It implies that there is a similar patch of inflammation, or demyelination, in the spinal cord – one so small that we can't see it but it is the one that's causing the difficulty with your walking. You recall we also carried out some electrical tests?'

'Yes.'

'These too confirm problems in the central nervous system. The visual tests showed a delay in the optic nerves, suggesting that they are involved in this process, though at present you have no problems with your vision.'

'I did lose my eyesight in my left eye once, for about three weeks, a few years back. The doctor told me that there was some inflammation in the nerve then.'

'I think, in retrospect, that was probably part of the same process.'

'So this is something that's been going on for a while then?'

'Yes, I think so. It's just that now it has affected an area which is causing you considerable difficulty. The other part of the electrical test, the "sensory evoked potentials"—'

'That was where they gave me small electric shocks?'

'Yes. They measure the speed of conduction through the spinal cord and they confirmed our clinical suspicion of a problem within the cord itself, as your conduction speeds were delayed.'

'I also had the lumbar puncture.'

'The reason for that was to have the CSF, the cerebrospinal fluid, the fluid that bathes the brain and spinal cord, examined.'

'What for?'

'One reason is to carry out a count of the white cells. White cells fight infection and inflammation. So a raised white cell count would go along with our synopsis of an inflammatory condition.'

'And was it raised?'

'Yes, slightly. We also looked for evidence of infection, but there was none and we have sent the sample off to look for what are called oligoclonal bands. They are a sort of antibody that we find in conjunction with certain disease processes. We haven't got these back yet – it can take a couple of weeks to get that result through.'

'But you have some idea of what's causing Julie's problem anyway?'

'Yes, I do.'

'I think we would rather know, wouldn't we, C.J? no matter what it is.'

C.J. nodded apprehensively.

'To be frank, there is really only one disease that can present in this way – a disease that can affect the nervous system, both within the brain and the spinal cord, that can come and go, affecting different places at different times, like when it affected your left eye, or can come and stay, as it has in your spinal cord. All the tests results are also consistent with this diagnosis.'

'Which is?'

'Which is multiple sclerosis.'

Julie reached for C.J's hand. C.J. gripped it tightly. Nobody said anything for a minute or two, while the impact of the diagnosis sank in. Neither Julie nor C.J. had previously had any direct knowledge of or contact with anybody suffering from MS, but they were fully aware of the potentially devastating consequences of the disease.

After the few minutes' silence, Dr Anderson started to talk again. Julie thought that he had been trying to emphasise that the disease may affect different people in different ways, and that it was not always the disabling condition that she and C.J. imagined. Although she and C.J. seemed to be listening and nodded at what appeared to be the correct times, neither could really recall much of the succeeding conversation. After a while Dr Anderson stopped talking. He asked if they had any questions.

No response. Only a stunned silence.

Dr Anderson said that he would see them again when things had sunk in properly and go through things in more detail. In the meantime, he wanted to keep Julie in hospital for a few more days to give her a trial of steroid treatment, to let the physiotherapists work on her walking and to get the MS liaison nurse to see her to talk things through. With that he took his leave. When he departed he deliberately left the curtains still pulled round the bed, to allow them some privacy.

Julie looked into C.J.'s eyes, which were moist with tears, and then they simultaneously fell, both with tears freely streaming down their cheeks, into each other's arms.

They were still clinging one to the other a few minutes later when the nurse put her head round the curtain, offering the steaming, milky tea that Dr Anderson had requested for them.

5

Harry was clearing up at the end of a morning surgery, writing up the notes of the last few patients that he had seen and putting them back into their individual folders in a belated attempt to keep abreast of the paperwork. He was somewhat bored but at least engrossed in this activity when the call came through. It was Mary at reception, informing him that C.J. had turned up. He was asking if he could see Dr Wallace. He didn't have an appointment, Mary added, clearly more for C.J.'s benefit than Harry's.

'Send him round, Mary. I'm just finishing off here anyway.'

C.J. came round from the reception area, as dishevelled as ever but today, Harry noted, his demeanour was a little less outgoing and he appeared more introspective. He looked a little more hunched, his features more obviously lined.

'Hello, Harry. Look, I'm sorry for just barging in on you. But this was the only time I could get round to see you. You don't mind, do you? I just wanted to ask you about Julie.'

'It's fine, C.J., honestly. Come on into the office. Do you fancy a coffee?'

'I don't mind if I do.'

Harry sat C.J. down in his office and then slipped down the corridor to the staff rest room. There was still some coffee left in the percolator which sat on the corner of the shelf near the sink and bubbled contentedly away to itself all day. By this time, the coffee was just about as concentrated as it could be. Certainly concentrated enough to revive C.J., and even Harry himself, from the trials and tribulations of their individual days.

Harry carried the two steaming mugs back into the consulting room.

'Milk? Sugar?'

'No milk, two sugars, please, Harry. Thanks very much. Just what the doctor ordered, if you'll excuse the pun.'

'What can I do for you, C.J?' Harry asked.

'It's about Julie. Have you heard anything from the hospital?'

'Not a thing. But it usually does take a little while for things to filter back to us in general practice.'

'Did you know she was admitted for tests?'

'To be honest, I thought that she would be. But I haven't heard anything since I talked to Dr Anderson, the neurologist, last week.'

'Can I fill you in then on what's been happening since and then pick your brains about it?'

'Of course you can.'

'She's been diagnosed as having MS, Harry.'

The diagnosis rocked him, but for C.J.'s sake he didn't allow any visible sign. C.J. shivered slightly as he mouthed the words. Then unable to surpress his own emotion he slumped in the chair and buried his head in his hands.

'I don't know how to deal with this, I just don't know what to do.'

'Tell me exactly what happened in the hospital, C.J.'

Having listened to C.J.'s story and chastised himself for being slow in not determining the diagnosis for himself Harry decided, once the day's surgery was finished, to call

Julie to see how she was and see how she had accepted the diagnosis. This was never, in Harry's experience an easy thing to do. It was all right if there was something to offer after bad news, some hope of a cure. In Julie's case this was not to be; multiple sclerosis remains a disease for which physicians have no cure and for many sufferers it means years of progressive disability and suffering. C.J. had told Harry that Julie had been given a short course of steroids whilst in hospital. Steroids have been for years the mainstay of medical therapy. However, steroids never cure, all that they offer is, at best, a temporary respite from the disease, and even then they don't always work. Harry hadn't yet received the discharge summary from the hospital, but he knew that despite the recent government reforms, charters and guidelines, things had not really improved much. Whilst successive governments continued to massage the statistics to match their own particular spin, the sad truth was that the NHS remained grossly inefficient and chronically underfunded. He didn't expect the official pronouncement for some weeks to come.

Harry rang the doorbell and at first he thought that nobody was home, as there was no response. Then he thought that perhaps the bell simply didn't work, so he knocked hard on the door with his fist. Again there was no reply. He was about to turn and leave, when through the leaded glass inserts of the door he detected a movement in the house. He waited and finally the door opened, Julie stood behind it, breaking into a welcoming smile.

'Hello, Harry. I'm sorry I took so long to get to the door. I'm just so damn slow.'

'Not a problem, Julie. I'm in no hurry. I just thought I'd call and see how you were doing. Can I come in?'

'Of course you can. It's nice of you to come. I haven't seen you since before I was admitted to the hospital.'

Harry went in and Julie shut the door behind him. She

motioned for him to go into the lounge. As he did so, he was acutely aware of Julie, painstakingly making her way along the corridor behind him. She was using the walls for support: when she ran out of wall she used the door pillar and then she used the furniture. It was as if without these aids she would be stranded where she was or, worse, reduced to crawling along the floor on all fours. It pained Harry to see the change in her. Even on the most cursory of observations, her walking was no better despite the hospital admission.

'Where are C.J. and the kids?' he asked, trying to keep the emotion out of his voice.

'Oh, C.J.'s out. To be honest, Harry, he was driving me round the bend. Since I got out of hospital he's been fussing around me trying to do everything for me, as if I'm some kind of invalid. I know that I married him for better and for worse, but I definitely did not marry him for lunch.'

Harry laughed.

'My mother's got the kids, she thinks I need the rest.'

'And do you?'

'I suppose she's right. I do tire very easily, but they're my children and I miss them when they're not here.'

'How did you get on at the hospital?' Harry asked, changing the subject. He didn't think C.J. would have told her about coming to see him and anyway he wanted to get a grasp of Julie's perspective of the diagnosis that she'd been given.

'Dr Anderson was very nice, thank you for recommending him. You know that I've got MS?'

She said it so matter-of-factly, it took Harry aback at first.

'Yes, I heard as much,' He managed to stumble out.

Julie went on to describe in detail the days of her hospital confinement and finished by mentioning the treatment options that had been discussed with her.

'I've been given a course of steroids through a drip, that

was last week. Dr Anderson wants to see the effect of it first of all. He also has me on a low animal fat diet.'

'And what do you think of the treatment so far' – Harry had already made his own unconscious assessment of its efficacy.

'Well, to be honest,' she replied, 'I was already eating all the right things that go with this diet anyway, even before I got ill.'

'And the steroids?'

'I don't know. In some ways I feel a little stronger, but generally I haven't noticed much difference. C.J. thinks I'm still getting worse. But that might be just because I've been lying about in hospital for so long. Don't you think that could be the reason, Harry?'

'Possibly.' But he doubted it. 'Sometimes the steroids can take a little while to kick in,' he added, more in hope than belief.

'I hope you're right'

'How are you managing, generally?'

'I must admit, Harry, it's a bit of a struggle, but I'm managing. I fell down the stairs the other day and now C.J. insists he's there before I try to go upstairs. If I listened to him it would make life pretty awkward – the loo's upstairs, you know. It's C.J. I'm worried about, Harry. I'm not sure how he's coming to terms with my illness.'

Harry was quite glad at that moment that C.J. and the kids were not at home. Knowing Julie as he did, he doubted if she would be so candid about her problems if they had been around.

'I'll get an occupational therapist out to visit you.'

'What can he do?'

'In the first place, *she* can have a look at your stairs. For example, how many stair rails do you have?'

'Just the one on the one side.'

'Well, maybe if she got one fitted on the other side as

well, you could manage the stairs on your own and then C.J. needn't worry so much. Or at the very worst she can get you a commode downstairs, so you don't have to struggle up and down all the time.'

'I suppose so.'

'And there's probably a lot of other aids and appliances that she can get for you.'

'I do *not* want a wheelchair.'

'Nobody said anything about a wheelchair, Julie.'

It was true Harry hadn't mentioned it. However, it was a real issue. One only had to chart Julie's deterioration over time to realise that her walking was likely to become seriously compromised. This, as Harry understood it, was often the natural history of this disease. It would start in an insidious manner, often so mild as to go unrecognised, but then over time it would take hold and progress with a relentless inevitability.

'Harry, I've got two young kids, for God's sake. How could I look after them from a wheelchair.'

Julie started to cry. The tears ran freely down her cheeks.

Harry's heart sank; he didn't know how to reassure her.

'I'm sorry, Harry, for swearing. It's just so damn unfair. Oh there, I've done it again.'

'I know, I know.' It was the best he could offer. Harry knew a little about MS and he knew a lot about the Julie of old, and he feared from deep within himself that the two were not easy bedfellows.

Harry heard a key turn in the lock, then into the room burst Becky, Julie's eldest. Three years of age and full of mischief, she charged into the lounge. The door banged noisily into the arm of the sofa and rebounded. Becky, arms outstretched, ran across the room, ignoring Harry's presence and disappeared into her mother's all-embracing arms before climbing up onto her lap. Julie's mother Dora, a distinguished-looking woman now in her early sixties, followed. Harry hadn't seen Dora since about the time of his graduation from medical school many years earlier. She looked tireder and greyer than he remembered her. Dora carried a sleeping Tom in her arms. Harry rose to his feet and Dora tried to shake his hand, but the baby prevented her. Harry kissed her gently on the cheek instead.

'Hello, Harry. I wondered whose car that was outside.'

They exchanged a few pleasantries and an update on the behaviour of the children that afternoon.

'Thank you for all you've done for Julie,' Dora continued.

'It's nothing, really.'

'Isn't there any more, though, that you or the neurologist can offer her? I hate to see her the way she is.'

It was already happening, Harry thought to himself. He'd witnessed it so often before, a person, a real person, an individual with a personality and a character of their own, develops a disability and all of a sudden the disability becomes all that others can see. The person simply becomes a manifestation of that disability, their former individuality and personality dissolved and invisible. Dora was talking to Harry as if Julie wasn't there and only the spectre of the disease sat in the chair across from him.

'We were just discussing things, Julie and I,' he replied. He wanted Julie to know that he, at least still regarded her as the complete person she had always been. 'I've had some thoughts about how we can help, Julie's thinking about them.'

'What sort of things?' Dora asked.

'Well, we talked about getting an occupational therapist to call out—'

'That's all very well, but isn't there some medicine, or an operation, or something, available that could make things better?'

'Mother, please. Leave Harry alone, he's doing the best he can.'

'Well. It's not good enough.' Dora's voice wavered with emotion. 'Look at you, you can hardly walk. You can't take proper care of your children any more and I'm getting too old to do everything for you . . .'

'Mother! Please! Just stop it, stop it now!' Julie started to cry again.

Harry felt useless. Although it was true he was doing the best that he knew how, Julie had a condition that modern medicine could not cure. He knew that. Julie knew that and even Dora deep down knew it. That didn't make things any easier. Dora was attacking him, but he realised that she was really just striking out, venting some of her pent-up emotions. Harry just happened to be involved and available. Funnily enough, he thought, even though he felt aggrieved at her assault, he agreed entirely with her sentiments. Surely there was more that he could do?

MS is sufficiently uncommon that a GP will only have perhaps one or two cases in his practice at any one time. No two cases are exactly alike and therefore a GP's experience of the disease is often quite limited.

Harry resolved there and then to try to find out more.

Early next morning, before his clinic started, he rang the hospital and, probably due to the early hour, got straight through to John Anderson. He too was about to start his clinic but with a bit of persuasion and both of them creatively juggling their commitments, he agreed to meet Harry at lunchtime in the ward.

His spirits raised, Harry called his first patient forward from the waiting area.

The Neurology staff room was of small proportions. In bygone days it had probably served as a side ward. Now it housed a motley collection of chairs, a small table, an assortment of coffee mugs, tea bags, coffee jars and a poor imitation of a cafetière. Seated around the walls were a number of junior hospital doctors intermingled with one or two medical students. Dr Anderson was seated directly in front of them, holding court. He was questioning the students on how to recognise an inverted supinator reflex, and its significance. Harry, catching the tail end of the discussion, thought to himself that he barely remembered its significance himself. Still, neurology had never been his best subject at med. school.

Noticing Harry's entrance, John Anderson broke off from his impromptu tutorial, much to the relief, it seemed, of many of the struggling medical students.

'Harry, how are you? It's good of you to come all this way to see me.'

'No, Dr Anderson, it's good of you to allow me to come and discuss things with you.'

'John . . . Please, call me John – less of the Dr Anderson. Help yourself to a cup of coffee and we'll go up to my office. It's a bit quieter there. I'm afraid I haven't that much time, I've a ward round starting at one thirty . . . Wait for me if I'm a bit late, Gavin, we need to discuss Mrs Young's anti-convulsants.'

The last remark was addressed to a bespectacled doctor, whom Harry took to be the senior registrar. With that, John Anderson was on his feet and striding off down the corridor towards, Harry presumed, his office. He bounded eagerly along in his wake.

On reaching the office, the two exchanged a few recollections of patients they had shared. Time was short, however, and Harry wanted to get as much information as he could. John Anderson opened the blue cardboard-covered file which contained Julie's clinical records. He went through her admission and the diagnostic process in his usual efficient manner.

'There is little doubt that she has multiple sclerosis.' He

pointed out the abnormalities on her MRI scan. These are the multiple nodular lesions so characteristic of the disease.

'We gave her a course of intravenous methyl predniso-lone while she was in with us. I had hoped that it might slow down or arrest the disease process.'

'From my visit to her yesterday, it hasn't had any such effect, unfortunately,' Harry added.

'It's disappointing to hear you say that. The condition is very variable and difficult to predict, but yes, from my own observations Mrs McCormick does appear to be suffering from quite an aggressive form.'

'Isn't there anything more that we can offer her, John?'

'You know as well as I do that MS is at present an incurable condition. Steroids have been our mainstay of treatment. Unfortunately, while they often help, sometimes, as it seems to be the case for Mrs McCormick, they may be of no benefit whatsoever. Call me an optimist, but I do remain quite hopeful for the future. Over the last few years we have seen the development of a new type of treatment for MS, one that actually may change the course of the disease.'

'What is this treatment?' Harry was suddenly curious.

'The most hopeful one at present is beta interferon. I hesitate to name it, because we have problems prescribing it at present, but basically it is one of a group of compounds that cells produce naturally in response to viral infection and which protect other cells from similar attack.'

'Now you mention it, I do seem to recall something to that effect being mentioned in the dim and distant days of microbiology. But how does it work in MS?'

'MS is an inflammatory condition a bit like an infection. It attacks different parts of the nervous system at different times. The problem we have, though, is that we don't know what triggers the inflammatory response in the first place.

Beta interferon alters the immune response and hence reduces this inflammation. In MS it is the beta-1-b and beta-1-a subgroups that appear to be the most effective.'

'Have there been clinical trials?'

'Oh yes. We're well beyond that stage now. The drug is licensed and can be prescribed.'

'I haven't heard of anybody on it yet.'

'No, and you're probably not likely to either.'

'Why not, if it's such a good prospect?'

'There are a number of reasons. Firstly, it's no wonder drug. It doesn't cure the disease but it seems that it can reduce the risk of relapse and probably of progression.'

'That must be worthwhile.'

'Yes, but it's not perfect. Overall results suggest about a thirty per cent reduction in relapse rate. Clearly, though, some patients do much better, some worse, but you won't know whether you're a responder or not till you've been on it a while.'

'So why aren't more people getting a trial of the drug?'

'Well, it has side effects. And it's awkward to use, the patients have to inject themselves with the drug, usually about twice a week, and they have to continue to inject themselves life-long.'

'That's not the problem, surely. Diabetics inject themselves twice a day.'

'Sometimes patients with MS can develop a rash at the injection site.'

'That's a small price to pay if the disease can be retarded.'

'Don't get me wrong, Harry, I hear what you're saying and tend to agree with your sentiments, but we have major problems persuading the health authorities to allow us to prescribe it. They are being increasingly squeezed for funds from all directions. The cardiologists want extra resources to carry out more coronary artery bypass surgery, the orthopods point to the length of the waiting lists for hip and knee replacement, the physicians want more beds to deal with the annual winter chest and flu epidemics.'

'But surely a drug that reduces the severe disability associated with MS must get some priority?'

'You'd think so, wouldn't you, especially here where we have some of the highest rates of MS in Europe.'

'So what's the problem?'

'Number one, the health authorities point to the low efficacy – thirty per cent reduction of disease doesn't compare favourably, for example, with a hip replacement. Number two, and this is the main factor, Harry, it's very expensive – at present approximately £10,000 per patient per year.'

'Phew, that is a lot of money. But again, in comparison with some of the new anti-cancer drugs or the anti-AIDS drugs that we are able to prescribe, it's still relatively cheap. Surely as well there must be massive savings to the health budget if disability is reduced, if people can remain at work and out of hospital or dependent on others.'

'You'd think that would be a factor, wouldn't you. The problem is we're dealing here with health service accountants. Any savings will be down the line. No savings at all for a number of years, yet an initial, and continuing, large outlay of expenditure. Also any savings in reduced disability are likely to benefit the social services budget not the health service budget, and it is the health service that has to fund the drug.'

'So you're saying it's basically a matter of money.'

'I fear so, Harry, I fear so. That's what it's all about in the health service these days. I do have a certain amount of sympathy with the health boards. They are in a difficult situation, working within limited budgets, trying to provide the best overall care for everybody. They're particularly twitchy about beta interferon, though, because of its potential to bankrupt the system. There are, after all, about two thousand people with MS in Northern Ireland alone. If all of them went on the drug, it doesn't take a genius to work out that there wouldn't be much left over for the other specialities.'

'There must be some groups of patients for whom the use of the drug would be justified?'

'Quite so, Harry, quite so. Most of the studies on the drug have been carried out on patients with what is termed relapsing/remitting disease.'

'That's the early stages where the disease flares up in one area and then may settle down and even go away, only to flare up somewhere else some time later?'

'Exactly so, Harry. You haven't forgotten all your neurology then.'

'Not all of it,' he joked.

'Given the results of the trials,' Dr Anderson continued, 'a sub-committee of the learned and good of the Association of British Neurologists, our governing body, have produced guidelines. They concluded that the drug is justified for patients in the relapsing/remitting stage of the disease, provided they have sufficiently severe and frequent relapses to justify its usage. About three relapses over two years is the cut-off point.'

'So why are there so few people on the drug here in Northern Ireland?'

'Two factors. One, so called "post code" prescribing. That basically means some health authorities provide sufficient cash to allow the guidelines to be used, others provide only a fraction of the amount required, so that we doctors have to ration the drug further. To be honest, here in Northern Ireland we do quite well compared to other areas of the UK. In many areas of Scotland, for example, the drug isn't being used at all. But we are all miles behind Europe and the United States in prescription numbers.'

'And . . .?'

'And secondly, many patients in the early relapsing/remitting phase feel perfectly well between attacks and don't want the hassle and bother of regular injections anyway.'

Harry's mind went back to the purpose of his visit.

'What about Julie – sorry . . . Mrs McCormick – would she be considered a candidate? I'm sure she wouldn't turn it down if it was on offer.'

'Alas, no, Mrs McCormick won't qualify.'

'Why not, for goodness' sake? I can't think of a more deserving case. She's young; her whole life is ahead of her. She has two lovely children who depend on her, a husband who dotes on her, and it's all going to fall apart as she goes steadily downhill into increasing disability and despair.'

'I share your frustration, Harry. That's why at the outset I said that I hesitated to discuss beta interferon with you, because I knew at the end of the day I wouldn't be able to get it for her . . . not yet, anyway. I mentioned it simply to demonstrate that there is some light at the end of the tunnel for this condition, at long last. Perhaps in a few years when the price comes down I'll be able to prescribe it for your patient.'

'It'll be too late for Julie by then. At the rate of her present decline, she'll be off her feet and in a wheelchair, or worse.'

'I know, you're right, of course. I was generalising. You, on the other hand, have an individual to look after. I'm sorry.'

'Can't I just prescribe the drug for her myself through the practice?'

'Unfortunately not. The health boards have insisted that all interferon prescriptions are written by a consultant neurologist and that supplies are obtained only through the pharmacy here in the hospital.'

'Why can't you prescribe it for her then, John?'

Dr Anderson consulted Julie's file. He flicked over the pages before replying.

'The problem is that Mrs McCormick's disease has moved on. She's now in a secondary progressive phase.'

'What does that mean?'

'Mrs McCormick's disease probably started a few years ago. She had a couple of bouts of numbness affecting her hands.'

'I remember seeing something in the GP notes about that. We diagnosed a trapped nerve, possibly a carpal tunnel syndrome at the time, but it cleared up completely each time.'

'Then more recently she had an episode where she lost the vision in her eye.'

'Yes, again it cleared up. She was seen at the hospital, though, because of it.'

'Yes, it was diagnosed as retro bulbar neuritis. Inflammation of the optic nerve.'

'I remember now.'

'All of those symptoms, with the aid of that most useful of medical instruments – I refer of course to, the retrospectoscope – were probably the early manifestations of Mrs McCormick's relapsing/remitting MS. Now, however, her disease has moved on and she has entered this secondary progressive phase, which tends to progress relentlessly. The health boards at present provide only limited funding for sufferers in the relapsing/remitting stage, they provide no funding whatsoever for the provision of beta interferon for people with progressive disease, whether, like Mrs McCormick, they have relapses superimposed or not.'

Harry felt even worse now. He and his colleagues had missed the early signs of Julie's condition and now she'd missed the boat.

'If we'd picked the condition up earlier would she have got the beta interferon?'

'In fact, probably not. Interferon has only become available so recently that it wouldn't have been around when Mrs McCormick was in the relapsing/remitting phase.'

Harry felt only marginally reassured by this response.

'Why won't the health boards provide monies for the drug in this phase. Surely these are the people who really need their disease retarded?'

'You're quite right, Harry. The health boards quote the lack of evidence to support its use in this group. But again, I suspect that there are financial considerations here. This is a group of patients who, as you rightly point out, are deteriorating and can see themselves deteriorating. If interferon was available, every one of them would jump at the chance of getting it. The health boards know this and therefore are resisting including this group in the prescribing guidelines.'

'You said that there is a lack of clinical evidence?'

'To the best of my knowledge there have been two published clinical trials on the use of interferons in secondary progressive disease. One had a positive result – the drug seemed to benefit the patients – and the other had a negative result – no gain demonstrated. Consequently the health boards conclude there is insufficient evidence to justify its prescription. I have heard, however, that a third definitive trial has just been completed in the United States but its results aren't yet published.'

'Any indications as to whether it has been positive or negative?'

'I don't know. I have heard, though, on the medical grapevine, that all those who took part in the study, whether randomised to drug or to placebo, have been started on beta interferon now that the study's completed.'

'Which kind of suggests that the study has demonstrated that the drug works, doesn't it? Or they'd all have been taken off it.'

'Possibly so, Harry. But I emphasise it's still only a rumour. The government has set up a group to examine the nationwide prescription of beta interferon, among a number of other new and expensive drugs.'

'Is that the NICE group?'

'Yes, the National Institute of Clinical Excellence. However, my own personal feeling is that they won't be too nice (if you'll pardon the pun) to beta interferon.'

'So you think that even if this third study is published sometime in the future, my patient still won't qualify for interferon, possibly simply due to financial constraints?'

'I'm afraid that's my current opinion, Harry.'

Harry sat back, somewhat frustrated by his lack of progress. From what Dr Anderson had said there seemed little prospect for Julie. Beta interferon did offer some hope. Not, it seemed, a lot, but still some sort of hope of retarding the disease at least, perhaps till something better came along. But just as some form of hope was offered, it was just as quickly snatched away again. Guidelines and financial constraints along with government bureaucracy and red tape had conspired against any chance that Harry had of obtaining the drug through the health service.

'I'm going to have to go now, Harry. I'm already late for the ward round.'

'Thank you very much for your time, John. You've been very helpful. At least you've given me a lot to think about.'

They rose in unison and made for the door.

'I'll be seeing Mrs McCormick again soon anyway,' said Dr Anderson. 'Feel free to discuss anything we've talked about today with her. I haven't gone into the pros and cons of beta interferon with her, as yet. She was already, I felt, a bit shell-shocked by the diagnosis and, to be honest, I didn't think it was justified to mention it if I can't get it for her.'

'If money wasn't a issue, could she get it?'

'You mean privately?'

'Well, yes.'

'I didn't get the impression that Mrs McCormick was in a position to lay out ten thousand pounds a year. Not many people are, you know.'

'But if the money was provided outside the health service, could she get the drug?'

'Basically, I don't see why not. It's really only the financial constraints placed upon us by the health boards that limit its use so drastically.'

As Harry turned to leave, he felt compelled to ask just one final question.

'John, can I ask you, if you were in Julie McCormick's shoes and could get an unlimited supply of beta interferon, would you take it?'

'Oh God, *yes*. I would, of course I would.'

'Thanks, John. That's all I wanted to know.'

Dr Harry Wallace,　　　　Albert St Health Centre,
　MB, BCh, MRCGP,　　　Albert Street,
　　　　　　　　　　　　Belfast.
　　　　　　　　　　　　BT2 4XY

BY FAX

For the attention of:　Mr C.J. McCormick
　　　　　　　　　　　The *Belfast Spectator*

Dear C.J.,

I have tried ringing a number of times but the line is
constantly engaged – the pressures of investigative
journalism I expect.

Do you fancy a game of golf on Sunday? I have
something that I'd like to discuss with you.

Can you fax me back quickly as I am going out on
some home visits soon.

Cheers

The Belfast Spectator
Est 1923

Facsimile Transmission

FAO Dr Harry Wallace
Albert Street Health Centre

Dear Harry,

Sounds intriguing

See you on the first tee Henry's Bay golf club,
10 a.m. Sunday.

With best wishes

C.J.

PS With regard to faxing back *quickly* – as I am unable
to alter the speed of my fax machine, I have faxed back
promptly instead.

6

Harry pulled the zip of his waterproof jacket all the way up to his chin, as the fresh morning breeze cut at his face and hands. Stamping vigorously to keep warm, he watched the steam of his breath merge with the surrounding air. To his right, C.J. puffed on the remains of his cigarette, before pulling another from the packet and lighting it from the dying embers of the first. Then he strode about vigorously flapping his arms across his chest.

They stopped and stood in silence as they watched the couple ahead drive off. Two reasonable shots, both balls finishing by lying in good positions on the fairway.

The first tee box at Henry's Bay golf club occupied an elevated site adjacent to the clubhouse, with which it shared a spectacular sweeping view down over the first fairway and on to Henry's Bay itself and Belfast Lough beyond. Henry's Bay was the name of the small coastal hamlet, about ten miles east of Belfast, and the popular beach that it surrounded. In the summer the beach would be thronging with holidaymakers and day-trippers from the city and beyond. Today, a cold, overcast, but still thankfully dry, November morning, the beach, which they could see in the distance, was all but deserted. Only a long-coated, scarfed and wellington-booted gentleman was walking briskly across its length, but halting and stooping occasionally to pick up a stick that he would toss ahead for the red setter that bounced along beside him. In the background beyond this solitary figure the wet sand glistened where the tide had recently receded and, further still, the white-crested waves broke and crashed down onto the shore. A pair of screeching seagulls whirled about in the light breeze above their heads.

Harry had asked C.J. to meet him today because he wanted a chance to discuss Julie's condition with him in the light of his meeting with John Anderson. But first he had a game of golf to play. Over the years C.J. and Harry had become quite close friends. Harry had tended to avoid the company of other medics when off duty, preferring as he did to discuss anything but medicine. C.J.'s quirky nature and slanted look at life appealed to his own somewhat oblique sense of humour, so they saw quite a bit of each other, and Harry thought that they both regarded the meetings as an opportunity to let off steam. At the moment Harry felt that C.J. needed taking out of himself.

C.J., impatient to get going, strode purposefully onto the tee box and glanced down the fairway to ensure that the other players were out of range. Observing them now to be walking towards the green after their second shot, C.J. pushed his tee into the ground, placed the ball on top and then adopted his stance. Swinging his 'John Daly Wild Thing' in a series of aggressive swipes, he suddenly ceased, took a half-pace forward to stand over the ball. Knees bent slightly, he affixed the ball with a determined stare, brought the club head back slowly and then slammed it forward in an arc, sweeping the ball a magnificent two hundred yards straight down the centre of the fairway.

'Super shot,' Harry said appreciatively.

'Thanks.'

'It's a pity, though.'

'What's a pity?' C.J. rounded on him.

'It's a pity that you didn't remember that I won last time

out. So in fact it was my honour to go first this time. You may want to try again after I've had the opportunity to drive. And not to put too fine a point on it, nor did you declare your ball before you struck it.'

'Titleist three.'

'Too late.'

'I think you'll find that it was an infringement of etiquette only,' argued C.J., rising to the challenge, 'not an infringement under the rules of golf. Let's get on with it before we hold others up.'

Harry marched up to the tee box, glancing at the ball in his hand before placing it on the tee.

'Pinnacle four,' he announced deliberately.

Harry's shot also ended up on the fairway and within possible striking distance of the green, though it was nowhere near as long as C.J.'s magnificent blow.

'I can tell what you're doing wrong,' offered C.J. helpfully.

'What's that then?' Harry asked.

'You're standing too close to the ball,' suggested C.J. '*after* you've hit it.' He laughed as he picked up his bag and strode off down the fairway.

'Very funny, I don't think.'

As they made their way along the tree lined fairway, C.J. was moved to ask; 'What do you think of the fairways, Doc? Aren't they in wonderful condition?'

It was true. Through the winter months many golf courses even had to close, or to supply players with little plastic mats from which shots had to be made, because of the poor state of the grass. Henry's Bay with its location on a hill sweeping down to the sea, had considerable geological advantage.

As C.J. spoke, Harry located his ball and swung at it. Then it happened. He allowed that most common of golfer's faults to occur – he lifted his head to observe the flight of the ball before he had even hit it. The result was that he missed the ball entirely. In its place he sent a divot the size of a small dog at least 100 yards down the fairway. Harry looked in disbelief and horror at the hole in the baize surface below his feet.

Quick as a flash, C.J. turned back and asked: 'And what do you think of the fairways now, Doc?'

After five holes C.J. was three up. Then Harry mounted a comeback, winning the next three holes. Thus, as they stood on the ninth tee box, waiting for the fairway ahead to clear, the match was evenly balanced. As they had decided to play only the nine holes, it was down to the final few shots.

The ninth tee box was at the bottom of the course. The fairway swept uphill ahead of them to the green, which was just to the left of the clubhouse.

Two shots each further on, the two were now in the area of the green. C.J.'s ball was on the front edge but Harry had missed the green entirely and was in an awful position in a gully to the right and about twenty feet below it. His ball was lying in the light rough. Although the flag was virtually directly above his head, his approach was shielded by a large bunker. C.J. was up on the green but Harry couldn't see him, such was his position. Harry's only hope was to get under the ball, hit it as high as he could and then bring it down quickly with as little forward motion as possible. A little ambitious, he thought to himself. Oh well, here goes nothing.

Harry swung the club and up went the ball, high in the air, clearing the bunker and then landing with a gentle thud somewhere on the green, just above his head.

'Nice throw,' came the shout from above.

Harry clambered up onto the green. 'I beg your pardon?'

'Nice throw,' C.J. repeated.

'Are you accusing me of cheating?' said Harry.

'Merely complimenting you on your sleight of hand, that's all.'

Harry was furious, but he quickly realised that C.J. was simply trying to distract him from his putt. He didn't reply.

C.J., being furthest away, putted first.

Three feet short, there is some justice in the world, Harry thought to himself.

'Aw! I never hit it!' exclaimed C.J., with obvious annoyance.

'I think you'll find you did.' Harry suppressed a smile. 'Otherwise it wouldn't have moved at all. Do you want to putt again while you're still angry?'

C.J. paced the green. He squatted down behind his ball. He squatted behind the flag. He went over to the edge of the green and looked at the path of the ball from a different angle. Finally he stood over his ball. He tapped the ball. It ran in an arc following the contours of the green, homing in on the hole. The ball rolled up to the side of the hole and stopped, hovering over the edge. It didn't fall. C.J. regarded it for a moment or two and then strode over to tap it in.

'I'll give you that,' said Harry, with feigned generosity.

'Thanks for nothing.'

It was up to Harry. One putt to win the game. Two to draw. Three or more to lose. Nine holes it may be. Two mediocre golfers they might have been. But this was a contest, make no mistake.

Harry strode over to where he'd marked the ball and replaced it. He looked at the hole, he looked at the ball. He tapped the ball. It rolled towards the hole. Harry closed his eyes.

Ker-plunk! Unmistakable. The sound of dimpled cover striking metal cup.

*

'Let's get the drinks in, Doc.'

'Two pints of Guinness, please, John.'

John had been the barman in the club for more years than even he could remember. When they had first played at Henry's Bay he was always seen resplendent with a fine head of very black hair. On this occasion, the apparently fine head of hair had suddenly and completely disappeared.

Harry was immediately shocked by John's sudden altered appearance and secretively inquired of C.J. what could possibly have happened. Harry detected from C.J.'s smile that he had missed something.

'Surely you knew it was a wig,' C.J. whispered.

As John delivered the drinks, C.J. piped up with: 'That's a fine head, John.'

John, still a little self-conscious, only recently having made the decision to dispense with his hairpiece, swivelled round to confront the speaker – only to find C.J., glass raised, head to one side, gazing intently at the white foamy top on the pint of Guinness. John, not a little bemused, receded (in much the same way as his hairline had some years previously, Harry supposed).

C.J. lit a cigarette and they raised their glasses.

'Sláinte.'

As C.J. and Harry relaxed in the warmth of the bar, Harry knew that the outing had done them both the world of good.

'Thanks for asking me for the game, Harry.'

'No problem, I always enjoy taking money off you. But I did have an ulterior motive.'

'Which is?'

Harry told C.J. about his visit to the hospital and about beta interferon. He was acutely aware of the risk of raising false hope, and this had been the main motivation for wanting to talk to C.J. by himself well out of Julie's earshot.

'You mean that this new drug might help Julie?'

'It *might.* But we wouldn't know for sure till she tried it.'

'But I can't get it for her?'

'Not at present. Unless we can raise the money to buy it.'

'I don't have the kind of dough that you're talking about, Harry. Even if we sold the house, by the time we paid off the mortgage it still wouldn't be enough and then we'd be homeless as well.'

'That's why I wanted to talk to you, C.J. Couldn't you write up a story in your paper to try and raise some support? Or alternatively could we try and organise some sort of fund-raising event? What do you think?'

'Or both.'

'Or both, indeed.'

'I'll have to talk to Julie about it.'

'Do you want me to come round when you do?'

'That would be great if you would, Harry, to explain about the new drug. I'm not sure that I can remember all the details. In the meantime, we can go away and think about what sort of fund raiser we could organise. It'll have to be a good one if it's going to raise the sort of money we need.'

C.J. was visibly lifted by the conversation.

The arrival of one of the club's waitresses interrupted further discussion.

'Good afternoon, gentlemen. How nice to see you here again. Would you like to order something to eat?'

'Just a bar snack would be sufficient, thanks.'

As the waitress left to fulfil the order, C.J., leant forward and whispered in Harry's ear.

'Lovely girl. Beautiful long blonde hair. But tell me why, Harry, does she go to all that bother of dying her roots black?'

'Oh dear, oh dear. A saucer of milk over here, please.'

7

C.J. sat at his desk, finishing the day's copy. As he did so, he ruminated over yesterday's conversation. After the recent dark days, here perhaps was a small glimmer of hope, but he was not blind to the many difficulties ahead – not the least of which was if and when he should tell Julie and, if he did, how to find the necessary cash to secure a supply of the drug.

The other journalists who shared the communal office were all either busy with their own copy or were not at their desks. Out, perhaps, thought C.J., on the hunt for that one big elusive story, the one that would make the nationals and would secure their place in journalistic history. So few of their kind, though, ever did secure a story of that degree of magnitude. In the end most settled to eke out their existence hacking out regular pieces for whichever local tabloid would publish them.

C.J. was thirty-two years of age. He had felt that he was getting too old still to harbour hopes and aspirations of national recognition but too young to abandon them completely. His mind went back to Patsy Harte and the story he had related. Since the peace process had begun, the newsworthy happenings in Northern Ireland had considerably diminished. No longer were there the daily violent episodes, not even the threat of civil unrest existed. The world's media, once so prevalent, scavenging for new stories or

84

even new angles on old stories, that former scrum had receded now to a few residual stragglers continuing to hope for a new insurrection, a recommencement of hostilities. But as time passed with the peace holding, even they would concede that the violence of former years was unlikely now ever to return. Even Northern Ireland's politicians were behaving less like flag-waving cheerleaders and more like the political representatives that they always should have been. For C.J., therefore, the peace process had been a mixed blessing. Brought up during the 'troubles' and cutting his journalistic teeth, he, like many of his colleagues, had found it difficult to adapt to the changed circumstances. Nevertheless, as a long-term pacifist, C.J. welcomed whole-heartedly the Good Friday Agreement and wished for its continued success.

Only recently, though, the process had stalled. The old distrusts between Unionism and Nationalism had once again started to re-emerge. The problem on this occasion was the 'two Ds' – devolution and decommissioning. The Unionists were refusing to sit down in the new Assembly with representatives of Nationalist groupings who still held onto their weapons, whilst Sinn Fein were refusing to give in to any preconditions regarding the decommissioning of the IRA's arms, especially preconditions set by a Unionist agenda. So it was that one side wouldn't sit in government with the other unless they handed over their guns, and the other wouldn't hand over their guns unless and until they sat in government with the Unionists and everybody else. Northern Ireland politics, wondered C.J., could anybody figure them out?

He completed the article that he had been writing on his computer and sent it down to the print room, then pulled a cigarette from the half-empty packet on the desk and, leaning back, lit it and inhaled a lungful of the warm, relaxing, nicotine-laden smoke. As he allowed himself to relax, he blew smoke rings up towards the ceiling. He lazily watched them enlarge and merge with the surrounding air, gradually dissolving from view. He recalled his meeting with Patsy. It seemed like an age ago but in reality it had been less than two weeks previously. He had heard nothing since. Neither the police nor George had come to him and told him of the final outcome of his reporting of the arms cache. Neither had they given Patsy's version of why the information had been imparted in the first place any credence. They had also ignored C.J.'s own protestations on the matter. Patsy was his informant, he had known him for years, and although C.J. had his own reasons for taking Patsy's information with a pinch of salt in the past, he felt that the way that his editor, on the advice of the police, had simply disregarded and even dismissed out of hand what he had to say had been unfair and unjustified. They preferred to believe their own version of events.

That was why Patsy's story had appealed to him so much. What if the information was true? Then Sinn Fein were trying, albeit in a secretive manner, to advance the peace process. Surely that possibility was of too great importance just to overlook. But overlooked it had been, and that made C.J. annoyed. Even if Patsy's story had only been partially true, that there was an arms dump where he had said it was, and that the dissidents were, as the police thought, going to liberate the arms for themselves. That Patsy had told him, or had been ordered to tell him, the location of the guns, surely meant that the IRA felt that it was better to give up the arms rather than have them in the hands of those who would have no hesitation in using them. Surely, rationalised C.J., that must mean that Sinn Fein had persuaded the IRA army council that the peace was worthwhile preserving. Given the IRA's reluctance to decommission arms previously, it must also indicate a massive sea change of opinion within the organisation. The more C.J. thought about it, whatever the truth was, surely there was a story here worth reporting – a story with a potential to be huge. A big story could net him thousands of pounds from the nationals, and if ever there was a time when C.J. needed a break this was it.

It was already getting dark outside. The nights were drawing in as winter approached. C.J. made up his mind what to do. He rose, stubbed out the butt of his cigarette and left the office without a word to anyone. He descended by the back staircase and came out two flights down in the photographic department. Two of the paper's photographers glanced up lazily at C.J. as he entered the large open-plan office. Showing them scant attention, C.J. walked down the length the office towards the darkroom situated at the far end. The two photographers returned to their coffee and conversation unperturbed.

Knocking on the darkroom door, C.J. waited patiently for a response. The door was guarded by a red light, below which was emblazoned the message: DO NOT ENTER WHEN LIGHT IS ON. The light was on, indicating that film processing was in progress.

'Hang on a minute,' came the reply from within.

C.J. recognised the voice immediately, it was who he thought it would be; beavering away in the darkroom until a better offer came along.

'Oh, hi, C.J. What can I do for you?'

'Can we have a talk ... alone.' He glanced over his shoulder at the other two photographers, neither of whom appeared to be paying any attention to them. Appearances can be deceptive, thought C.J., people in this building were paid to be nosy. These were professional busybodies and he did not want word of his plan getting back to his editor. Not just yet, anyway. Ben Sharpe he could trust, the others he couldn't vouch for, and he didn't know everyone on this floor. The other two photographers he recognised, but he didn't really know them. Discretion is the better part of valour, he thought.

Ben Sharpe had been with the paper when C.J. joined and they had frequently worked together on stories. Ben was probably in his late forties, but he looked much older. The weather-beaten and haggard visage had been sculpted by years of waiting around, often in the worst of Irish weather conditions, for that single moment when his quarry would appear and then almost as quickly disappear from view and from viewfinder. His quarry could be a politician on a holiday with his secretary, or a celebrity of the musical or sporting variety paying a brief visit to the Province, or even some rare ornithological species making just as brief an appearance. Ben Sharpe was equally as happy with one as with the other. He was at his happiest behind his lens ready to shoot. If not out in the field he could invariably be found in the darkroom, developing or printing picture after picture until he was satisfied that he had selected just the correct angle or view that he wanted. It was in this retreat that C.J. had located him today.

'Come on inside,' said Ben. 'We'll not be disturbed in here.'

Ben led the way back into the darkroom, C.J. followed obediently. It was warm and clammy inside and it smelt of acidic chemicals that bit at and irritated C.J.'s nasal passages. Ben was immune, his exposure to the selfsame chemicals over the years meant that he was no longer even aware of them. Ben pulled on a cord somewhere in the gloom and a red light suffused the small room. The room was cluttered with exposed film, most of which hung from the ceiling in long strands, like rolls of flypaper. There were trays of chemical on the shelf against the wall and the rest of the room was nearly filled by a large desk completely covered in photographs and cuttings from photographs.

'Okay, we're alone. Why the secrecy?'

C.J. went on to explain about the meeting with Patsy and his revelations. He, however, omitted to tell Ben about the involvement of the police, preferring to explain the secrecy as the result of C.J.'s editor's reluctance to pursue the story and indeed his animosity to the idea of being used as some sort of political intermediary.

'So, he's ordered you to forget about it. Is that what you're saying?'

'Yes.'

'But you don't want to drop it. In fact, you want to pursue it, and you want me to help, despite the fact that we could both end up sacked. Is that it?'

'Basically, yes.'

'All right, you're on. But just this once, right? What's the plan?'

C.J. had known that Ben would be up for a bit of undercover work. He was, like C.J., a 'the end justifies the means' man.

'I want to see if the information that Patsy gave me is correct. Firstly, I want to find the arms cache and make sure it actually exists. I need that evidence to run with the story. And I need you to come along to photograph whatever we find, that's the sort of proof that I'm going to need.'

'Why don't you just borrow a camera and leave me out of it?'

'Number one, because I'd be afraid of mucking it up and number two, we're going to have to get the photos undetected. I can't afford big flashes going off.'

'Ummm, so you want me to take pictures in the dark, without a flash.'

'If you can, or at least keep it to a minimum. We can't afford to be found poking about an IRA arms dump.'

The threat was real enough. If detected by the terrorist group, it could mean a beating, a kneecapping or worse. It was certain that there would be summary justice dispensed.

What C.J. of course left out was that the threat of detection was increased by the possibility of police surveillance. He suspected that the arms would not necessarily be protected twenty-four hours a day by the terrorists but that any police surveillance could well be continuous.

'I'll see what I can do with some low light film. When do you propose having a look?'

'Later tonight, under cover of darkness and when everyone else is tucked up in bed. I'll pick you up at your place about two a.m.'

With that C.J. took his leave. He was glad that Ben was coming along, not just because of his technical skills as a photographer, not just because two pairs of eyes and ears would be better than one in spotting any unwelcome observers. C.J. had specifically sought out Ben as Ben had served his time as an investigative photographer and he knew better than anyone in the building how to get in and out of places undetected. With the unseen threat of both terrorist and police out there, he welcomed Ben's expertise. C.J. did not underestimate the danger in what he was proposing to do

With the arrangements made, C.J. made his way back to his own office and rang Julie to tell her that he would be very late getting home that night.

At five minutes past two C.J. turned into the cul-de-sac where Ben lived. His was the only house with a light still on. As he pulled up outside, C.J. could see Ben seated in his living room, drinking from a can of beer and watching television, the glow from the set illuminating his features. He looked round as he heard C.J.'s car pull up. Peering out through the living room window, he spotted C.J. starting to clamber out of his car. Ben gave a brief wave, in order to prevent C.J. from rapping on the door and waking his sleeping family in the rooms above. C.J. reseated himself in the driver's seat and closed the car door against the biting cold of the night. He watched as the light was extinguished and Ben emerged from the front door, pulling it carefully, but silently, shut behind him. A moment later and Ben was easing himself into the passenger seat beside C.J. A few cursory murmured greetings and C.J. set about turning the car around and heading off in the direction of West Belfast.

At this time of the morning the streets were generally deserted. The orange fluorescent street lamps lit up and glistened off the dark and damp road surface ahead. A light drizzle suffused the air. En route, apart from an occasional drunk weaving his way inexpertly home from a late-night drinking den, Belfast was asleep. Passing over the Albert Bridge, they witnessed some of the most obvious changes brought about by the peace process. The route that they followed was one of the main thoroughfares into the city centre. Up until a few years previously, the road had been bordered by Victorian working-class terraced housing. This was still the case as one approached the bridge. However, as one crossed, so the new developments swung into view. The older two-storey terraces had been cleared to give way to new waterside apartment blocks. These were intermingled with new, modern pubs and restaurants, of a type usually found adhering to a minimalist furnishing philosophy. These public houses boasted inflated prices, as did the apartment blocks they served, which only further drove the few remaining original inhabitants closer to a real sense of alienation.

An occasional 'For Sale' sign adorned the window of these fashionable apartments, but such was the demand that these signs never remained in the same place for long. Behind the apartments, the waters of the Lagan reflected the purple lights from the newly constructed barrage, which had been considered essential to maintain a constant water level upstream. This meant that the recently installed residents of the riverside dwellings were no longer exposed to the scenes of oil-laden silt dotted with mounds of decaying rubbish and the occasional abandoned shopping trolley so frequently uncovered by the receding tide in earlier days.

Passing over the bridge, C.J. swung right then left to travel up May Street, behind the City Hall, then straight ahead up the Grosvenor road. Ben and C.J. both puffed on cigarettes as they reached the top of this road and sat and waited for the traffic lights to change. To their left sat the Royal Victoria hospital, situated between the Grosvenor and Falls roads, whose proximity to the scenes of much of the violence of the seventies had gained it an international reputation in the management of trauma cases. C.J. remarked that the 'Royal' marked the boundary between a staunch Loyalist area and the Nationalist Falls. He grinned as he remembered the wit of the people who lived in this area even at the height of the troubles. Before the peace process had begun there had been previous attempts at resolution of the conflict. Among these had been the so-called Anglo-Irish Agreement; it, however, had been bitterly opposed by the Unionist population, who had largely been excluded from its formation. It had eventually crashed under the weight of a resistance campaign entitled 'Ulster says No'. This slogan had been emblazoned everywhere. In support of the campaign posters had appeared depicting Ulster's red hand portraying a 'thumbs down' sign. 'Ulster says No' also featured as graffiti, among countless other sites throughout the city, it had appeared emblazoned in large letters along the perimeter wall of the hospital. Seeing this and probably because this was an area of mixed religious alliance, someone had inscribed below 'But the man from Del Monte, he say Yes'. Below this again a further wag had written 'And he should know, because he's an Orangeman!'

C.J. related his thoughts to Ben and they both laughed. This humorous recollection seemed to help ease the tension that C.J. knew they shared. Then Ben recalled a similar incident during the same era.

'Do you remember when the Unionist city councillors in City Hall put a huge banner around the dome of the building again proclaiming "Ulster says No"?'

'Weren't there protests about that?'

'Yes, there were but they couldn't persuade the Unionists, who were in the majority at the time to have it removed. But then one of the Nationalists realised that to erect such a hoarding in fact needed planning permission. So the Unionists, portraying themselves as the upholders of the law, were compelled to have it removed.'

'But they didn't, did they?'

'No, they found a loophole, you remember. It was coming up to Christmas at the time. So instead of taking it down they just added a bit on. They made it into "Ulster says NO-EL". A Christmas decoration doesn't require planning permission.'

'Very clever.'

They both laughed at the absurdity of the situation that had prevailed not so many years previously.

Across from the lights they could see the Belfast headquarters of Sinn Fein, now locked and barred against the night. As the lights changed to green, C.J. revved the car to get it up the short incline onto the Falls road and then turned left to travel down the road itself. The car's headlights illuminated the more intricate examples of graffiti that adorned what seemed like every gable wall. These wall paintings left no one in any doubt as to the political persuasion of the inhabitants of the area through which they travelled. They depicted and celebrated the presence and former triumphs of the IRA or its individual members. Bobby Sands, the first hunger striker to die in the 'H' blocks of the seventies, was a frequent representation. C.J. recalled the scenes in this very area the night he had died. The inhabitants were awoken by the sounds of dustbin lids being banged, calling them out onto the streets. The army had been quick to respond, having been prepared for this eventuality for days. They moved in and tried to disperse the crowds but were beaten back by volleys of stones and petrol bombs. The rioting had lasted night-long. Now things were so different but the past was not yet, and could not yet be, forgotten.

Travelling cautiously along the Falls road, they reached the lights that marked the junction with the Whiterock road. Turning right, they followed this road past the cemetery on the left and the heavily fortified police station on the right. Further up the road they turned right into the maze of back streets. Here the Victorian terraces persisted and had not been the subject of developers' ambitions. Many of the small two up, two downs bore the scars of earlier years of civil conflict. As they passed deeper into the labyrinth of houses, more and more appeared abandoned, many had their doors and windows bricked up.

Deciding that they were close enough to their goal and not wishing to attract attention to themselves by driving any further, C.J. pulled the car over to the side of the road and parked. C.J. and Ben sat for a while, watching and listening for anyone or anything that could signify that there were others about who also watched and listened. Having sat in silence for several minutes, both were satisfied that they were alone apart from each other. They got out of the car, closed and secured the doors quietly behind them, and proceeded to walk the last few hundred yards to their target.

Neither spoke as they made their way along the deserted and only partially lit street, for many of the street lamps were either defective or damaged. In this part of the city repairs were at best haphazard. C.J. wrapped his coat tightly around himself as protection against the damp cold air that seemed to get into his very bones. He could see Ben's breath rise as a cloud as he exhaled. They reached the end of the street together. They glanced up and down the next street, which, apart from a few parked cars, was also deserted. This was the street on which the arms cache was allegedly located. They walked the length of the road, passing by the house in which it was supposed to be found, neither outwardly giving that house any more attention than any of the others, but inwardly noting every detail. Number 24 was the eighth house on the right-hand side from the end of the street where they now stood. It looked as if it had been empty for a long time. Its front door and all its windows were sealed up with cement blocks. The house adjacent to it on the near side appeared to be still occupied, but there was no noise from its inhabitants, all the lights were out and the upstairs curtains were drawn. The house on the far side was derelict and boarded up. Given the proximity of the next-door neighbours, C.J. realised that they would have to be very careful. If number 24 did contain an arms cache, then those in number 26 might well know of it and be ideally placed to act as sentries for its protection.

Moving along the gable at the end of the row of houses, they located the narrow entrance to the small laneway that ran along behind the houses for the full length of the street. Off this were the back gates to the small cobbled yards at the rear of each house. This entry allowed the council refuse collectors access to the rubbish bins during the day. At this time of the morning, it was dark and uninviting. C.J. and Ben felt their way along the wall that was one side of the narrow walkway, picking their way carefully along, trying to avoid the abandoned bags of rubbish and the broken bottles that lay littered along their route. They attempted to make as little noise as possible, so as not to wake the sleeping inhabitants of number 26 and to avoid detection. Counting each gate as they reached it, it wasn't long before they stood silently, side by side, outside the back gate of number 24.

The house had been bricked up for a few years, but as C.J. pushed gently on the gate, it opened with surprising ease. If no one had been through this way in years then the gate would have stiffened on its hinges and piles of rubbish would have accumulated behind it as people discarded it in the yard of the abandoned building. This gate had clearly been opened recently. It swung freely and noiselessly on its hinges. There were no impediments to its path. Slipping quickly through, Ben and C.J. shut the gate behind them. They explored the back of the house through the gloom that engulfed them; the moon briefly broke through the clouds and afforded them a glimpse of the house and its neighbours. There was still no noise, no sign of alarm from those next door. C.J. examined the back door. It was heavily and securely bricked up, there was no way in through it. He looked over at Ben, who in turn was trying his luck at one of the downstairs windows. Ben motioned to him. C.J. approached the window. It was sealed by a large piece of decaying plywood. The wood moved when pushed upon. Together, C.J. and Ben were able to pull the plywood cover free from its fastenings and reveal the window that it covered. This window had clearly, like the other windows and the doors, been bricked up when the original inhabitants left. But the bricks or blocks that had sealed this window had been removed and the window carefully resealed with the less secure plywood barrier. With a quick final glance to the upstairs windows next door to ensure that their exertions had not alerted anyone to their presence, C.J. and Ben climbed in through the now open window and crouched together to listen and to regather their thoughts.

The light coming through the aperture which C.J. and

Ben had created to ease their entry only scantily illuminated the interior of the room in which they found themselves. Squinting around him, C.J. inspected the space in which they crouched. It clearly had been the sitting room in better days. Now, apart from a dilapidated sofa through whose covers the stuffing protruded at regular intervals and an empty fireplace with tile surround, though many if not most of the tiles were broken or chipped, the room was devoid of any furnishings. Crumpled up newspapers and many of the broken tiles from the fire surround were scattered around on the floor where in the days of occupation the carpet would have lain, covering the now dirty and dust laden floorboards.

Edging their way carefully and deliberately forward together, C.J. and Ben crossed the living room area. They eased open the door that still hung, though precariously, from its hinges and stepped out into the hallway. This was a narrow corridor; straight ahead were the cement blocks that sealed the front entrance. To their left, as they faced the front entrance to the house, and rising from the front door to above their heads was the stairway. Beneath the stairway and behind them was the door to the kitchen. C.J. motioned with his index finger, to indicate that they should proceed upstairs.

Feeling their way forward in the dark hallway, they reached the foot of the staircase. Confident that they were, by now, suitably encased within the sealed premises and that their presence could not be detected from outside, C.J. and Ben produced the flashlights that both had concealed in the pockets of their anoraks. C.J. led the way. He shone the beam of light onto the stairway ahead. The exposed, and in some cases broken, stairs stretched upwards to the next floor. C.J. felt each individual step carefully with his foot, before transferring his full weight onto it, while feeling the next step in turn with the other foot. Many stair boards protested their unaccustomed usage with creaks and groans. Ben eased his way up the stairs behind C.J. As they reached the top, one step cracked loudly under the weight of the intruders. Both men froze, listening for any external sign that their presence had been discovered. None came.

Off the landing there were three doors, two leading to the bedrooms and one to what had, in earlier times, been the bathroom. Now only a few jutting pipes betrayed its former utility. Patsy had suggested that the cache was hidden in one of the bedrooms, but had been unable, or unwilling, to be more specific. C.J. moved to enter the bedroom on the right and motioned to Ben to try the one on the left.

As Ben disappeared into the bedroom behind him, C.J. pushed open the door in front of him and shone his torch around the space beyond. This room was again devoid of any furniture. The remains of some wall covering hung limply from the wall at intervals and there was dust and rubbish everywhere. Everywhere, except the far corner of the room. Here the floorboards had been crudely lifted, fracturing many and leaving their jagged ends to guard the hole created. C.J. advanced, slowly, to examine the crevice. Getting down onto his knees so that he could see more clearly into its recesses, he shone his torch back and forth into the gaping hole. Nothing. Only the exposed pipes and wiring that ran along beside the rafters. Then: 'What's that?' he whispered to himself.

At the far reaches of the exposed rafters, just beyond arm's reach, he had detected a momentary glint, reflected from the beam of his torch.

C.J. bent down, his head virtually on what remained of the floorboards. Reaching into and along under the floorboards ahead of him, he felt his way with his fingers, examining each object they brushed against in the darkness beyond. Finally his fingers touched his target. But it remained at the extremes of his reach. Try as he might he could not get his fingers around it to retrieve it. The harder he tried, he only succeeded in knocking it further out of reach. Exasperated, he sat up, breathing heavily. He tried again, this time he used his torch, now extinguished and plunging the room into total darkness, to extend his range. He manoeuvred the end of the torch beyond the object and then scraped it back towards him. In so doing he dragged the prize a few inches in his direction. Relighting the torch and again scrambling about under the floorboards, he could now reach it . . . just. He eased it gently towards himself and then with a sudden grasp of glory seized it within his fist. Holding the torch in his left hand, he opened his right fist slowly and carefully as if not to let anything drop or escape, and revealed the object it contained. There was no doubt what he had found, for shining back at him from the palm of his hand was a .22 bullet, live and unused.

Ben had joined C.J. after a fruitless search of his own bedroom. There were no other arms or ammunition to be found. They stood back and examined the room with their torch beams. The dust on the floor had been disturbed in areas. Footprints, although many had been at least partially obliterated, could be clearly delineated in several areas, particularly around the uplifted floorboards. C.J. and Ben examined these prints with the care of two scenes of crime officers.

'Those look like the tread from Caterpillar type boots,' declared Ben. 'Let's see what size they are.'

He compared his own size eight shoes with one of the clearest prints. The print was probably at least one or two sizes larger.

C.J. carefully placed the bullet in the gaping hole in the floorboards and Ben took a couple of hasty photographs. He followed this with an equally hasty couple of shots of the footprints. C.J. retrieved the bullet and the pair eased their way as quietly as possible back down the stairs to the room through which they had entered the building.

As they left through the window that had afforded their entry, a light shone out briefly from the upstairs window of the house next door. They froze momentarily. But the light was quickly extinguished. Probably just somebody rising to go to the toilet, they thought. Having been reprieved, they scampered through the back gate, down the alleyway, onto the road and back to their waiting car. Firing up the engine they beat a hasty retreat, disappointed with their find but relieved, at least, to get away and evade discovery.

Having returned Ben to the bosom of his family, C.J. returned to his. He entered the house quietly so as not to disturb the sleeping occupants. Rather than going straight up to bed he sat down in an armchair, pulled a cigarette from the pack, lit it and sat back blowing smoke rings towards the ceiling. He tried to assimilate the events of the last few hours. The evidence certainly supported Patsy's report. The house had been empty for some time. Yet there was evidence that it had been entered more recently. The boarded window and the footprints in the dust bore witness to that. He reached deep into his pocket and retrieved the bullet that he had found. He held it up in front of his face between finger and thumb. So there had been some kind of arms cache in that house, of that there could be no doubt. But when had it been removed? And by whom? The footprints had been those of adults. Patsy's claim about the concern of children entering the building and accidentally finding the arms was not borne out by those prints. No, the arms were gone. But had they been retrieved by the police, and if so why had they not come back to the paper to report the story? After all, it was the paper that had tipped them off. Or had the terrorists who had placed them there already removed the arms, and if so why had Patsy tipped the paper off?

Tossing these imponderables over and over in his head, C.J. imperceptibly drifted off to a welcome but troubled sleep.

When he awoke, the few remaining hours to the morning had passed. He wearily opened his eyes. His neck ached, his left arm was numb. He blinked to take in his surroundings. He found himself still seated in the armchair, still fully dressed from the night before. He shook his left hand back and forth to relieve the pins and needles sensation that suffused it. Grudgingly he rose and stumbled across the room still half asleep. He lit his first cigarette of the day as he did so. As he inhaled he started to cough loudly and copiously. He stood at the bar counter in the kitchen, still smoking, still coughing and waited for the kettle to boil. Then he took a cup of tea up to the still sleeping Julie. Sneaking into the room, he sat on the edge of the bed for a moment and just watched her. She looked beautiful as she lay there, he thought back to all the happy times they had shared and wished for them never to end. Then he silently cursed himself at his failure of the night before. He had fallen at the first attempt to lift them from the abyss which opened before them.

Julie stirred and opened her eyes.

'C.J., where have you been? I waited up for you.'

'Sorry, I was really late and I fell asleep in the chair downstairs.'

'I expect you came back smelling of alcohol and cheap perfume.'

'If I had been out with another woman, I can assure you, the perfume would not be cheap.'

They laughed as they had so many times before. Julie knew and trusted C.J. implicitly and C.J. knew she did and would never have betrayed that trust.

Two cups of black coffee later, C.J. had summoned up the energy to pull off the clothes soiled from the night before's exertions and replace them with cleaner, though on C.J. even new clothes looked shabby. Calling his good-byes he pulled the door behind him and he set off for the *Spectator* office, the issues of number 24 still unresolved.

C.J. sat at his desk pulling on yet another cigarette, all the while, his gaze fixed on George Thompson's office. His editor had not as yet at arrived at his desk. C.J. waited, ready to pounce the moment he did.

At 9.15 a.m. George, briefcase in hand, attempted to push open his office door. Before he could enter, he was aware of someone standing immediately behind him. He turned around quickly.

'C.J.? What's up?'

'I need to talk to you, in private . . . now.'

C.J. pushed his editor into the office, closing the door behind them. He had decided to raise his concerns with George.

'That arms cache we discussed last week.'

'The one you got the tip-off about?'

'Yes. What's happened about it?'

George Thompson regarded C.J. curiously. 'What do you mean?' he asked.

'What's happened about it, since we discussed it last week?'

'I haven't heard anything. I presume the police will let us know if there are any developments.'

'Developments? Like it gets moved or discovered or something?'

'Yes. That sort of thing. The police said that they'd let me know.'

C.J. glared at him. The lack of a full night's sleep had made him irritable and the level of frustration he felt made him not in any mood for easy appeasement.

'It might interest you to know then that it's gone.'

'Gone, what do you mean gone?'

'Disappeared, moved, shifted . . .'

'How do you know it even really existed in the first place anyway?'

'I know that it was there and I know that it's been moved.'

George Thompson sat down behind his desk and regarded C.J. curiously.

'How do you know that it's been moved?'

'I just know,' said C.J. defensively.

'How?' asked the editor. There was now some steel behind the question.

'I went there.'

'When?'

'Last night.'

'You were specifically told by the police, and myself, not to interfere. You were told to let the police do their job and that they would let us know.'

'It was my story and nothing was happening, so I went to investigate. That's what you pay me to do, to investigate. When I investigated, what did I find? That things had happened and that nobody had told us a damn thing!'

'You were told to keep away from that house, you were told not to . . .'

George Thompson's final rejoinder fell on deaf ears. C.J. was already halfway out of the room. He carried on till he was outside the building, where he stopped, leant back against the outer wall, pulled another cigarette from the seriously depleted pack and puffed furiously on it.

8

'So, I could get this drug if we were willing to pay out £10,000.'

'Unfortunately, £10,000, *per year.*'

'We haven't got that sort of money, Harry.'

'I know, but C.J. and I have had an idea.'

Harry went on to explain about the possibility of a fund-raising exercise and the need for Julie's support in the venture if they were to proceed.

'. . . and, of course, there's no guarantee of success.'

'No, we realise that Harry, but I'm definitely in favour of it anyway. Anything that might help Julie. We have to go for it,' added C.J.

Julie was less sure. She wanted to discuss the pros and cons of the drug further. Harry did his best to answer her questions but in the end had to suggest another appoint-ment with the neurologist. He said that he would arrange this, he wanted to discuss the idea of raising money for the drug with him, in any case. Julie also had grave concerns about C.J.'s idea of publicity. She had never been one to seek the limelight and she did not relish the thought of doing so now, especially for the purpose of announcing her disability to the world.

As they discussed things further late into the evening, Julie, while still not totally convinced about beta interferon and even less convinced about being the subject of a publicity exercise, started to see the wider injustice of withholding a potentially useful medicine purely on the grounds of cost. She felt this injustice not just for herself and not just because she had MS, but because she realised that there were probably many hundreds if not thousands of people in the British Isles who were being subjected to similar decisions, and that these decisions were being made not necessarily by doctors but by accountants. Having recognised the merits of publicity and a campaign to highlight the problem, they turned their attention on just how they were to go about raising the necessary cash.

'It means raising a lot of support, though, doesn't it? said Julie. 'How much did you say it cost again?'

'Approximately £10,000 per year.'

'And how many years' supply would we need to provide?'

'That's less certain, but according to the neurologist two things are likely to happen: one, the drug will get cheaper and two, the health service will start to supply it more widely.'

'But when are these things likely to happen?'

'I don't know, but an educated guess would suggest that sometime over the next five to ten years.'

'So we would need to raise at least £50,000 and maybe as much as £100,000 or even more. I know I keep saying this, but that's an awful lot of money, Harry.'

Harry could sense C.J.'s mind working overtime to come up with ways round the problem. C.J. could at least sense a story, one with a strong human interest element in which he was close up and personal. He could immerse himself in it and use it to generate support. At the same time it was a story that was unlikely to get him on the wrong side of his editor and might even help to mend some bridges.

'Our paper could run an article on Julie and then widen the issue, even mount some sort of national campaign.'

'Now just hold on a minute, C.J. I'm still not totally

convinced about that aspect of all this. It's too much to take in all at once.

'Okay Julie, I accept that. But can't you see the advantage to others in the same predicament if we can publicise the issue?'

'Yes of course I can, but I need to come to terms with it, that's all.'

C.J. was in full flow but Harry could see that Julie needed more time. He changed the subject.

'So, what about a fund-raiser? Any thoughts on that?'

'What about a charity dinner?' asked Julie.

C.J. was momentarily distracted from his publicity campaign.

'Sure, a charity dinner could be part of it, but we need some excuse for the dinner. Something bigger, something much bigger and more memorable.'

Harry coughed nervously.

'What is it, Doc?' asked C.J.

Harry blushed slightly. 'Well, since we last met, and since C.J. first suggested doing something, I've had an idea.'

'What idea?' asked Julie suspiciously.

From experience Julie and C.J. realised that Harry was probably the least likely of the three to come up with an original idea.

'I thought that perhaps we could write to a bunch of celebrities and ask them for their favourite joke or their favourite recipe.'

'And . . .?'

'And then we could compile them into some sort of a book, which we could sell for charity.'

Harry reached into his pocket to produce a piece of neatly folded paper. As he did so he spotted out of the corner of his eye C.J. and Julie exchanging glances.

'What have you got there?' asked C.J.

'To see if celebrities would reply, I sent off a few letters as a sort of pilot study. I've received one reply already . . . Look.' Harry carefully unfolded the sheet of A4. This is the reply I got from Ally McCoist.'

'Who?' asked Julie.

'You know,' Harry added helpfully, 'the former footballer. He's on that quiz show now. You know the one . . . it's . . . it's . . .'

'*A Question of Sport*,' butted in C.J.

'Look, here it is. I think it's quite good.' Harry offered the recipe around.

Succulent Soccer Stew or Humble Pie

(Ally McCoist's favourite stew)

Serves 11 (plus two substitutes if required)

Seated in 4. 2. 4. formation

Ingredients

* 5 fluid ounces of Gazza Tears
* One packet of Salt & Lineker crisps (for crusty top)
* 1/2 pint of Cantona gravy for Gallic flavouring and to add some kick
* 1lb of Lineker sausages
* 10 butter fingers (David Seaman brand)
* Plant 4lb of Celtic potatoes (so they have something to lift this year)
* 2 ounces of Best Flower of Scotland
* 5 ounces of Rangers Blue Cheese
* 1 ounce of Celtic Green Cheese
* A sprinkling of Coleman balls

Method

This recipe should only be tackled on a Saturday to ensure the best results. Pass all the ingredients into a red hot cauldron (any football stadium); mix together in any formation and stir until the cooker shows the red card. Serve in a pair of Gazza football boots for added flavour.

'Aye, aye Captain, changing course to thirty-eight degrees, speed five knots,' murmured C.J.

'I'm sorry?'

'He's implying that we're fishing for red herrings. He think's he's funny.'

'I'm sorry C.J., I'm not with you,' replied Harry, fixing C.J. with a stare. 'I thought that when we'd got enough for a book, we could organise a big launch party to raise more funds.' Harry became a little more confident and enthusiastic over his idea. 'Maybe we could even get some of the celebrities to come.'

'Well, yes, Harry, I see what you're trying to do, but . . .' C.J. struggled to find the words.

'But?' Harry asked, sensing that perhaps C.J. was not quite as enthusiastic as he himself was.

'But it's just not original enough,' added C.J. bluntly. 'Every bloody charity has already done something similar. Anybody in the least way famous now keeps a recipe on their word processor, just in case somebody writes to them on the pretext of producing a cook book.'

'I don't think C.J. meant it the way it sounded.' Julie glared at C.J. 'I think he just meant that—'

'It doesn't matter, it was just a thought,' replied Harry, somewhat crestfallen.

'Okay, I'm sorry, Harry. Let's try and work something out.'

'I thought at first of some sort of sporting event, even

one that we could partake in, but it has to be something . . . different.'

'If we're going to play in it then it has to be something relatively sedate. We're not getting any younger, you know.'

'Well, you boys always enjoyed your golf. What about something with a golfing theme?'

'I know,' said Harry, trying again, 'what about trying to break the record for the fastest round of golf. The quickest time for eighteen holes.'

'You'd have to have teams of people at every hole to hit the ball each time it came to a standstill.'

'We couldn't play in that then,' Harry added.

'Why not?'

'Because neither of us could hit the ball straight enough to keep it on the field of play, that's why not.'

'True enough,' replied C.J. 'But although it would be great to take part, just organising the event would probably be challenge enough. Anyway, what *is* the record for the fastest round of golf?'

'No idea.'

'Pass me that *Guinness Book of Records*, it's over there in the bookshelf beside you, Doc.'

C.J. flicked through the pages, before finding the one he was looking for.

'Well?'

'Twelve minutes.'

Doesn't really seem any point in that then,' said Harry. 'There would be no pleasure if it was all over that quickly.'

'Hold on, Doc that's given me an idea, one which just might appeal. If it only takes twelve minutes to do 18 holes how long do you think it would take to do thirty-two?'

'Probably about twenty minutes.'

'So you definitely think that we could get all thirty-two holes done in a single day then?'

'Of course, but I don't quite see what you're getting at.' Harry was intrigued.

'What if all the holes were on different courses?'

C.J. knew he had their undivided attention. He continued to play with them for just a little longer.

'Different courses, one hole per course. Instead of a team of players playing their way round eighteen holes, we get one player to play his way round thirty-two holes of golf.'

'Yes, but why thirty-two holes?' Harry asked. 'And why at different venues? You've got me this time, C.J.'

'You're not your usual quick-witted self today, Doc, are you? What about you, Julie? Any thoughts? No? Want a clue? 'Come on, it's quite easy really. What are there thirty-two of in Ireland?'

'Thirty-two? Of course, I've got it,' Harry said triumphantly. 'Thirty-two counties! I see it now. You're suggesting that somebody tries to play one hole of golf in each of the thirty-two counties of Ireland in the space of one day.'

'Precisely so, Harry. Well, what do you think?'

Harry considered the proposal for a few seconds and then, 'Brilliant, quite brilliant. I don't think anybody's thought of something like that before. What do you think, Julie?'

'I don't understand golf but if you guys think it's a good idea then it must be.'

'But can it be done?' quizzed Harry.

'To be honest, I don't know. That's what makes it such a challenge. We probably won't find out if it can be done unless we try.'

'So how do we do it?'

'I haven't got the first clue, but if we all agree that this is to be the project then I propose we give it some thought and then get together again to plan it out.'

'Sure C.J., but time is of the essence. If we are going to do it then we need to get on and get it sorted a.s.a.p.'

'Agreed.'

9

As Harry turned into C.J and Julie's driveway the following weekend, he clutched a copy of *Golf Courses of Ireland*. Harry had been filled with a renewed sense of optimism and was really looking forward to the prospect of developing C.J.'s idea and turning it into a reality. Harry, however, was immediately surprised to find a Black Porsche Boxter parked behind C.J.'s six-year-old Ford Fiesta and impeding his progress.

'Doc, I'd like you to meet Emma Duncan,' said C.J. as he ushered Harry into the living room. 'Emma works for a public relations company that I came across through the *Spectator.*'

Emma rose to her feet and flashed the whitest of smiles at Harry.

'Pleased to meet you, Harry. C.J.'s been telling me all about you.'

Harry noted immediately and with some satisfaction that Emma appeared to possess those two features that, C.J. and he held, made up the lowest common denominator of beauty in a woman. Harry glanced at C.J. and, from the wink he returned, Harry detected that he was in broad agreement. His mind went back to the innumerable smoke-laden bars they had frequented during their years of obser-vation and research before finally formulating their thesis. Their careful and selfless study had led them to the inevitable and unanimous conclusion that if one needed to rely on just two features from which physical attractiveness could be gauged, then these were undoubtedly straight white teeth and a thin upper arm.

A cursory assessment of the newcomer's brilliant white smile and lissom figure in no way appeared to challenge their earlier results. Harry estimated her to be in her mid-twenties and, he mused, of immediate attractiveness in an upfront gorgeous sort of a way. Her age and her beauty were tempered, however, by the neat business suit she wore, which suggested, as Harry suspected that she intended it should, an edge of decisiveness and determination.

Harry returned the greeting, feeling himself flush as he did so.

'. . . I thought Emma and her colleagues would be useful to our project . . .'

Harry was only half listening to C.J.

'. . . Particularly if we want to publicise it widely.'

'Absolutely,' he replied, attempting to suppress his own enthusiasm just a little and appear as professional as possible.

Harry shook Emma's hand. He noted that it was warm and soft.

'Welcome to the strategic planning committee, Emma. You know, however, that we are in the very early stages and, perhaps more to the point, we haven't got any money. Certainly not enough money to employ a public relations consultant.'

'No, of course you don't.' Emma smiled sweetly. 'C.J. has explained the whole thing to me. I overheard C.J. discussing the venture one day when I was over at the *Spectator* offices and I just knew then and there that I had to get involved. My aunt had MS and through my mother I've been involved with the MS charities for years, so I have personal experience. When I told C.J., he thought that my professional expertise might prove useful. So here I am, I've come along today simply to offer my services and, of course, there will be no charge – though I can't pretend it won't do me or my firm any harm at all to be associated with such an ambitious venture, especially if you can actually pull it off.'

'So shall we get down to business then, now we're all here?' said Julie, who was sitting in an armchair by the fire. She had been carefully observing Harry's ineffectual attempts to stop himself staring at Emma's many other attractive features.

'Who is actually going to attempt the record?' asked Emma. 'Have you anyone in mind?'

'Actually, yes,' said C.J. 'I've been doing a bit of thinking over the last few days, though I haven't spoken to any of you except Julie, of course, about it before today. Harry, you remember that Pro-Am we were involved with a few years ago? Well, I got quite friendly with Philip Watson then. You've heard of him, haven't you?' He turned to Emma. 'He's the current Irish number one. He plays on the European circuit, in fact he's near the top of the money list at the moment and he's played in the Ryder Cup.'

'Didn't you write an article about him when he was last over?' Harry asked.

'That's right. In point of fact he quite liked it. Did you read it? . . . No, of course not. Anyway, when I was writing it I met him at his father's house – his dad still lives over here. So I looked up the address and gave him a call last week. He's a decent old spud and he and Philip are still quite close. So, to cut a long story short, once I'd explained the whole thing to him, his father thought that Philip would definitely be up for it.'

'That's great, C.J.'

'He promised that he would talk to Philip and get back to us, though I haven't heard anything yet. I gather Philip's still away on tour somewhere.'

'If Philip Watson would do it, then it's bound to be a winner even if the challenge fails,' exclaimed Harry.

'That doesn't sound quite right, Harry, but I think I know what you mean,' said C.J.

'So, how do you think it should be done?' asked Emma.

'First of all, it's going to have to be held sometime around midsummer.'

'To maximise the daylight hours,' Harry suggested.

'Exactly. To get round all thirty-two counties, we'll need some form of transport, and the only feasible one that could possibly get us round within the twenty-four hours would be a helicopter.'

'So we would need to hire a helicopter?' Julie asked.

'In point of fact we would need to hire two, to allow for refuelling stops.'

'Sounds expensive.'

'Well yes, but you've sometimes got to speculate to accumulate. In any case, I would propose that we try to attract some sort of sponsorship or backing to cover these sort of costs. What do you think, Emma?'

'I think that should be possible.'

'With regard to the other practicalities, we need to identify thirty-two golf clubs, one in each of the counties, willing to participate. We need to think about that, and how to get the clubs actively involved. Philip, or whoever, will land and only play one hole before leaving again. For practical reasons it will also only be a par three each time. We also need to think about a finishing venue and ways of raising money.'

'How many hours of daylight do you think there would be at that time of year?' Harry asked.

'Sun up at, what three thirty a.m.' C.J. replied. 'Sunset

114

about ten p.m. What's that? About eighteen and a half hours?'

'Okay, say eighteen hours, for argument's sake. Thirty two counties, therefore just over half an hour for one hole of golf and to get to the next county.'

'On a par three it will only take one drive and one or two putts. Ten minutes maximum.'

'So twenty minutes to get to the next course. How fast do helicopters travel?'

'A hundred miles per hour?'

'So a range of about thirty-odd miles between courses.'

'Seems reasonable if we plan it right.'

'Thirty miles between courses and thirty-two courses in all means a total distance of just under a thousand miles. Ireland's about a hundred miles wide and two hundred long.'

'We'll have to sit down with your golf book, Harry, look at some maps and plot the shortest route around the counties, but it does sound possible . . . just.'

'I hope so, C.J., I hope so. There's a lot riding on this.'

Their planning was interrupted by the telephone. C.J. got up and took the call in the hallway and when he returned he announced that it had been from Philip Watson's father. Apparently Philip was playing in some tournament in Spain but his father had explained the challenge to him, and the good news was that Philip had said that he would do it, as long as the dates suited. C.J. explained that as professional golf competitions were usually held Thursday to Sunday, with Wednesday to practise and Tuesday for travel, the proposal was for a day around midsummer, and after a consultation with respective diaries the date of Monday the twenty-sixth of June had been agreed as the preferred date.

'That's great news, C.J. Well done.'

C.J. went on to explain that a Monday was likely to suit

participating clubs best as well anyway, as it wouldn't interfere with any of their pre-arranged tournaments.

'It looks like it's all systems go, then,' Harry said. 'So what do we need to do next?'

'We need to try to plot out the shortest possible route between the thirty-two counties and identify suitable golf clubs, then contact them and persuade them to participate.'

'How are we going to convince them to co-operate?' asked Harry. 'Golf clubs can be funny places.'

'Maybe I can help there,' suggested Emma. 'What if we offer them an inducement?'

'What sort of inducement?'

'Two come to mind,' she explained. 'One, we could offer the club captain a couple of places at the dinner. You do intend having a dinner at the conclusion of the day, don't you?'

'Absolutely,' said Julie, and added, 'That was my idea, any excuse to get dressed up.'

'Well then, offer them one or two places at the dinner with the option of buying more, perhaps even taking a table. Secondly, you could offer a club member the opportunity of playing the hole with . . . what's his name?'

'Philip Watson.'

C.J. thought for a moment and then added, 'Actually, that's a great idea. The club could offer one member the opportunity to participate in the event by playing the one hole at their club with Philip. They could raise money within the club through a ballot or as a prize in one of their own golf competitions and any monies collected would go into the fund.'

'That's a super idea,' Harry echoed. He thought out loud. 'Say five pounds a head to enter. Golf clubs have what? about two to three hundred members? If only a hundred took part, that's £500. Times thirty-two, that's £16,000 straight off.'

116

'Then of course there would be sponsorship.' Emma was again demonstrating her business acumen. 'I would recommend corporate sponsorship – that's where the big money is. The inducement would be to provide places at the dinner and perhaps the opportunity to travel on a leg of the journey by helicopter with your man. Plus, of course, the publicity. Again, that's where my firm and I can help. I believe that this is a newsworthy event; and it's not only on behalf of a good cause, but also highlights a national scandal. Don't you agree, C.J?'

'Naturally.'

'Well then, it's up to us to get this into the public domain. If we can do that then the fund-raising will be a piece of cake.' Her business plan presented, Emma sat back.

'But there is still a lot to discuss and still a long way to go,' said C.J. 'I'll draft a letter to the golf clubs, if we can identify likely candidates today.'

'Okay, where are you going to start and where are you going to finish?' Julie asked.

'It must start in Belfast and finish in Dublin,' offered C.J. 'Besides, we have to consider the party afterwards. We need a venue large enough to hold a dinner dance for about two or three hundred people minimum, as this is also going to be a major source of income, through sponsorship and the selling of tickets . . . and it has to be beside a golf course.'

'With a helipad,' added Julie.

'What if we laid a carpet down Landsdowne road and put a flag at one end, then we could hold the dance in Jury's hotel,' Harry butted in.

'Oh, yeah,' said C.J., 'Can you imagine the bounce the ball would take off that, or off the road, if it landed there. That would fairly scupper the event. No, Doc, sensible suggestions only please.'

'What about the Kildare County Club,' suggested Emma.

Harry knew of the club, though he'd never been able to

117

afford to stay there. He recalled that it was a luxury golf and country club encompassing a five star-hotel just outside Dublin. With a championship golf course . . . and a helipad.

'Done,' said C.J.

The four spent most of the rest of the afternoon making plans and drafting letters: letters inviting clubs to participate, letters asking potential sponsors to cough up financial support and letters to the media informing them of the forthcoming challenge and welcoming their support in publicising it and the reasons behind it. A general air of enthusiasm suffused them all. What had, at first, been just a vague idea was quickly metamorphosing into a potential reality. Although each approached their tasks with an attitude of guarded optimism and each of them operated within their own individual area of expertise, the four seemed to be drawn closer together by their newly found shared sense of purpose.

10

A few moments before it had all been going like clockwork. The car had been parked virtually beside the door of the building. The building in question was a cold impersonal structure with a grey concrete facade. The outer wall boasted only a heavy wooden door and a row of small rectangular windows, high off the ground, affording no clear view of the interior. Its purpose was revealed only by the red sign with the words 'Post Office' in yellow lettering which hung high above the door and by the large red pillar box on the pavement outside. The post office was one of the larger district headquarters. Ignoring the double yellow lines, the driver had manoeuvred the car against the kerb and extinguished the engine. The car was of a popular and nondescript type, it did not attract any more attention than that of any other early afternoon shopper.

This car differed from the others parked about solely in the fact that it had been stolen a couple of weeks before and had had its number plates changed in readiness for today's operation. It had also been thoroughly checked over by a mechanic loyal to the cause. Fortunately, it had been certified to be in good working order and would serve the purpose in hand. That it hadn't needed any special attention was a bonus, as its usefulness to the cause would in any case be short, destined as it was to be found burnt out in the hills above the city in a few hours time.

The four men exchanged steely glances. This was not the first time any of them had been on a similar operation. All had become hardened to such activities over the years of conflict during the armed struggle. This was the first time, however, that they had combined as a team. In recent years each man present had risen through the ranks and been rewarded with control over a small number of their own 'volunteers', who were normally employed to perform menial operations such as the one they were now engaged upon. Each had known of the others, as much through reputation as from personal contact. Each man seated in that car felt that they had earned their due respect and reputation. As each year of conflict had passed, each member present had become more powerful within the organisation to which they had formally sworn allegiance.

Suddenly times had changed. The peace process had isolated the likes of these men. Others in the organisation now seemed convinced on a policy of peaceful negotiation, headed by the politicians in Sinn Fein. Those men sat in offices, smoked cigars and congratulated themselves on their perceived success. The men who sat in the car saw themselves among the foot soldiers, those who had first-hand experience of internment, interrogation and imprisonment, and those who now found it difficult to accept that this new and peaceful regime could deliver results. Worse still, far from being regarded as heroes among their own people, they were now looked upon as dinosaurs. The four had suffered a fall from grace and could only see a life of ignominy and rejection looming before them. Now, they had agreed it was time to fight back. Time once again to stand up and be counted.

They had planned this afternoon's operation meticulously during many covert meetings held over the last few weeks. To re-launch the Nationalist military offensive, they had quickly realised the need for publicity to promote their flagging cause. Much as they rejected the propaganda war that their former commanders were now pursuing, they acknowledged the importance of the publicity it had generated. Hence, a daytime raid audacious enough to attract media attention, a target simple and easy enough to guarantee success. The result, a focus for disaffected Nationalists, embarrassment for their former commanders and the added bonus of a pot of money with which to re-arm and re-train. Simple, yet effective.

The leader of today's operation was Brian Maguire. He sat grimly in the front seat, beside the driver, Francis 'Frankie' Molloy, and carefully surveyed the surrounding area. Brian Maguire was a name well recognised in Republican circles. He had first come to the attention of security forces when, as a sixteen-year-old, he had been arrested for being in possession of a revolver at a Republican funeral. The fact that the pistol had been slipped to him by an older and more experienced Republican quartermaster when the police had suddenly and unexpectedly appeared, he had never revealed, preferring to suffer the arrest, interrogation and subsequent imprisonment in silence.

This stoical acceptance of the Republican code, especially at such a young age, and his lack of capitulation under police interrogation, had brought Brian quickly to the attention of the local IRA commander. The prison sentence – the prosecution insisted on a spell behind bars because of his refusal to co-operate – was relatively short, largely because of his age, his previously unblemished record and the prosecution's reluctant acceptance of the fact that he was a mere go-between. On his release he had been recruited as a volunteer into the West Belfast brigade of the Irish Republican Army. Brian was determined that jail term would be his last. Since then, throughout his rise through the Republican ranks, he had been suspected of many terrorist offences, with some justification, and although he had been detained for questioning several times, he was never again charged or imprisoned. This fact owed as much to good fortune as it did to good planning and, not least, the very real threat that Brian and his colleagues posed to potential informers or prosecution witnesses.

Brian's early experience of incarceration had not been pleasant. He had found himself to be one of the youngest inmates held at Her Majesty's pleasure in the infamous Maze prison. As such, he became the object of attention of a number of older, manipulative prisoners. One inmate in particular had preyed upon him. The man was in his fifties and had sought out Brian from his arrival in the prison. Initially, Brian had thought that the older man was simply being protective and supportive, but then during one rest period he had forced himself on the naive teenager. He was larger and stronger than Brian, who could make only ineffective attempts at defending himself. Alone and over-powered, Brian had been raped and abused. When the man had satisfied himself and left, Brian lay curled up on the floor, bleeding, frightened and ashamed. That assault had been repeated at intervals, though Brian had learnt over time to stay in the company of others as much as possible and to know just who he could trust and who he could not. Nobody had ever learned of Brian's humiliation. Brian had never talked of it, too ashamed to confide in another. He had bided his time. He waited for several years until finally he learned of his persecutor's release. One dark night he had visited that man in his dirty, lonely flat. He had taken him at gunpoint from that flat and forced him to drive high into the hills above Belfast – and there he had shot him dead. One neat bullet hole just behind his right ear. Somebody out jogging, the following morning, had discovered the body. It had been discarded at the roadside, hooded and bound just like any other ritual paramilitary shooting.

The police had made futile attempts to find the perpetrators. But just as with so many other similar murders, there were no clues, no witnesses, and no results. It had been assumed that the murder was just one of many paramilitary punishments.

In recent years, more junior members under Brian's command would have carried out the like of today's operation. He would not have expected to have been directly involved himself, but those junior members had been removed, no longer under his direct control. Brian, who could not accept the new order, had found himself marginalised. He was not, however, alone in his views. Many former colleagues shared his scepticism of the new regime. Whilst some, though dismissive of the peace process, remained loyal to their commanders and held the peace, Brian had not found it difficult to recruit others, who, like him, preferred the more direct approach to politics in Ireland. Now he wished to mobilise his small army, he felt that the time was right to push them into the limelight, in order to attract other disaffected former IRA men. This operation, by securing the necessary publicity and extra cash, would, he felt, be instrumental in achieving this goal. It was goal he felt important to achieve, and quickly, particularly before other independent disaffected groups arose and became too powerful to consider bowing to his command.

The driver and occupants of the rear seat had been recruited from IRA cells in other areas. Gerry and Liam were from Crossmaglen, that border village notorious for its Republican links. Frankie, the driver, came from North Belfast. He was younger than the rest but had come with all the necessary credentials; reared on car theft and joyriding, he had eventually attained insufficient adrenaline buzz from these activities and had graduated to more dangerous pursuits, but ones in which his driving skills could be maximally employed. He had taken part in a number of similar raids in the past and also been the driver for a least two drive-by shootings in Loyalist areas. He craved the excitement generated by such former involvement. When Brian had offered him the opportunity to once again utilise his skills, he had jumped at the chance.

Brian Maguire glanced round at the occupants of the back seat. As he did so, an elderly woman pulling a wheeled tartan shopping basket emerged from the post office and made her way slowly down the street. Across the road two boys of about eight years of age kicked a football against the gable wall of a row of terraced houses. The ball was punctured. It refused to bounce, landing with a dull thud on the pavement each time it was kicked. As the pensioner made her way down the street she remained oblivious of the four pairs of eyes carefully monitoring her progress. Brian nodded to Liam and Gerry. The old woman turned the street corner and disappeared from view. Gerry reached into the holdall which sat between his feet on the car's floor. He pulled out two sawn-off shotguns and a Browning revolver. The two boys across the street were now wrestling with each other, bored with the football that wouldn't bounce. Gerry passed the revolver forward to Brian. Keeping one of the shotguns himself, he handed the other to Liam. Nobody spoke.

The four sat quietly in the car for a few more minutes. All four surveyed the surrounding streets. Seeing nothing out of the ordinary, Brian produced a black balaclava from his pocket and pulled it over his head. Those in the back seat copied his action immediately. The balaclavas had been sewn up so that now all that was visible of their faces was their eyes, which glared with an exaggerated menace.

A further nod. The car doors opened and the three men bounded across the pavement and thrust the post office door forcibly and brusquely aside. Frankie remained in the

124

car. Gripping the steering wheel tightly, he watched the three enter the building and disappear from view.

As Brian, Liam and Gerry crashed into the interior of the post office, those behind the cashier windows suddenly looked up. The three uninvited guests fanned out across the floor. There were two customers in the room on their side of the counter. One was an elderly woman collecting her pension; the other was a younger woman who a moment before had been just about to hand a bulky parcel to the assistant behind the counter. Now the parcel slipped from her grasp and fell noisily to the floor. Its owner, having turned to see what the noise was, took a step backwards. Her mouth opened, but no noise emerged from her throat gripped with fear. Both of the customers were quickly rounded together by Liam moving swiftly to their side. He pushed them roughly away from the counter. The old woman stumbled in her haste to move as bidden. She regained her balance as she and the younger woman were then forcibly made to lie down on the floor, flat on their stomachs, and told in no uncertain terms to keep quiet. Gerry quickly approached the counter and thrust the end of the shotgun at a terrified assistant. He barked the order to open the door that led to the area behind the counter. The counter assistant's arm moved slowly and shakily to a small button on the counter. A buzzer sounded and the door catch was released.

As Brian stepped through to the space behind the counter he could hear the sobbing of the women on the floor behind him. The three counter staff swung round on their chairs to face him. Brian pointed the revolver towards them. He hadn't needed to speak, their hands automatically rose. Gerry followed through the door behind him. Brian waved the revolver, indicating that the staff members were to lie down. Again noiselessly, they complied. As they did

125

so, suddenly and unexpectedly, a man in his early thirties wearing a shirt and tie, with the sleeves rolled up tightly, appeared through a door behind Brian. He was evidently the branch manager and had emerged from his paperwork to see what the rumpus was about. He came to an abrupt halt just outside his door when he stumbled on the two intruders directly in his face. He seemed to be about to say something, but the words never came; Gerry struck him on the side of his head with the butt of the shotgun. The manager's knees buckled and he sank unconscious to the floor. There he was to lie for the duration of the raid, blood oozing gently from the wound on the side of his temple.

Now Brian started to shout his orders at the terrified staff. One young woman was pulled forcefully to her feet. While Gerry guarded the staff and Liam continued to menace the customer, Brian and his young victim made their way into the locked back room of the post office. There, Brian pushed his guide roughly against the back wall, where she slid slowly down, her legs crumpling. She cried and sobbed with fear. Brian ignored her. He opened the canvas bag that he had been carrying and filled it systematically with money, stamps and postal orders, everything of value that he could lay his hands on.

Gerry was getting impatient. He called to Brian to hurry up. Brian, however, was enjoying the feeling of power and the excitement it induced – feelings he hadn't experienced for some considerable time. This raid was his idea, he was in charge. He wasn't about to let Gerry dictate to him. He continued to search the shelves for more notes. Then with a final flourish he turned and pointed the revolver at his helpless victim cowering against the wall. Any remaining colour drained from her face, which was already frozen in a mask of terror. She stared wide-eyed at the gun, seemingly mesmerised by the mouth of the barrel. A gush of urine emerged from between her legs and grew as a pool on the floor beneath her. Brian laughed cruelly. Then he turned, gestured to Liam and Gerry and all three plunged out through the front entrance. As they did so they pulled off their masks and blinked in the daylight outside.

Brian had expected to hear the roar as the car's engine come to life. But they were greeted only with an eerie silence. The car was sitting where they had left it, but the driver was gone. Worse still, from each of the wheels a small wooden match protruded above the air inlet valve, wedged in to allow the tyres to deflate. The matches had done their job and all four tyres were by now completely flat.

He looked quickly up and down the street. He was just in time to witness Frankie being bundled around the corner at the end of the street, the same corner that the old lady had rounded a few minutes earlier. Frankie's arms were being forcefully held by two men, unknown to Brian, who dragged him along. Their backs were to the group that had just emerged from the post office, but they revealed all the information that Brian and his fellow conspirators needed. For each of the men, though dressed casually, wore shirts which were covered by a black bulletproof jacket across the back of which, in white fluorescent letters, was emblazoned the word POLICE.

Anger flashed in Brian's eyes. It was a trap, somehow they had been betrayed. All three men turned as one to run. But as they did so, they became aware of others in the street around them. From behind the parked cars across the street, heads appeared, faces turned towards them. There was another head at the second floor window of the house across the street, behind the parked cars. Then three heavily armoured police Land Rovers appeared from side streets, two above them and one below. The vehicles' tyres screeched as they came to a sudden halt, blocking the roadway at either end. Doors opened and then slammed shut as the occupants leapt out and retreated to the far side of the vehicles. More heads appeared over the armour, and the barrels of numerous guns bore down on the three post office raiders.

Liam and Gerry froze in their tracks. Brian looked back and forth for a means of escape.

'ARMED POLICE, DROP YOUR WEAPONS,' rang out around the otherwise deserted street. It came from a megaphone held by one of the police officers cowering behind the bonnet of one of the two Land Rovers.

No response.

'ARMED POLICE, YOU ARE SURROUNDED. DROP YOUR WEAPONS.' The voice grew in confidence.

Brian heard the clatter behind him as Liam and Gerry, white and now frozen in fear, dropped their shotguns. He still clung to the hope of escape. Brian had long before resolved never to return to prison, at least not without a fight. The fact that it was a fight that he could never win – the odds were too heavily stacked towards those that surrounded their little group – did not matter. All that mattered was that he would go down, as he had lived his life, fighting for the cause.

'ARMED POLICE . . .'

As the final warning came, Brian raised his pistol and pointed it towards the sound. It was his final act of defiance. He never got to pull the trigger. The world around him exploded.

In a sustained burst of gunfire from three sides, the police opened fire on the terrorists. The fact that two had dropped their arms was negated by the one who had raised his weapon in a threatening manner. The police were not in a forgiving mood. Chances, on this occasion, were not to be taken. A successful conclusion to the affair was all that mattered. Within seconds all three terrorists lay in a bloody mess on the pavement.

As the smell of cordite drifted slowly away on the breeze,

a sergeant cautiously approached the bodies and examined each one in turn to ensure that life had been extinguished. Satisfied, he gestured to his colleagues, who rose from their fortified positions. As they did so, one of the female customers made her way, shakily, out of the post office. She stopped in the doorway and, spying the three bodies spread out before her, started to scream uncontrollably, until ushered away in the arms of a police constable.

The officer in charge barked instructions into his radio and simultaneously, in many different areas scattered across the city, doors were broken down, houses forcibly entered and occupants arrested. The contents of the houses were then carefully and systematically searched. The whole operation had been carefully planned and co-ordinated. The officers involved had moved quietly and quickly into position outside their respective targets and awaited the signal to go. As the officer in charge gave orders to those others further afield, the area around the post office was being carefully and systematically cordoned off with long lengths of blue and white police tape. The bodies were left where they had fallen but hidden from view by black tarpaulins. Finally, the remaining staff and customers from the stricken post office were assisted from the building and helped into waiting ambulances.

As the clear up began, the scene of crimes officers carefully sifted through the site. Simultaneously and as if from nowhere, members of the press began to gather. Hungry for a story, having been denied such activity since the onset of the peace process, they strained behind the lines of tape. Some called to members of the security forces in the hope of a comment or even a picture. Among their number was C.J., who had got news of the raid from other excited journalists in the *Spectator*. It had been shouted over to him during the scramble for notepads and pens as his colleagues headed off in the direction of the incident. The paper had been tipped off virtually immediately that there had been a major incident.

Standing amongst his colleagues at one end of the street, C.J. raised himself up onto his tiptoes in order to see over his fellow journalists who had reached the scene first and also to see over the incomplete line of police that stood behind the tape. Over the right shoulder of one such policeman, C.J. could glimpse the aftermath of the shoot out. Three tarpaulin covered mounds lay just outside the entrance to the post office. Below one tarpaulin there oozed what appeared to be congealed blood and lumps of another unidentifiable substance. C.J. felt nauseated. He had attended murder scenes before, but he had never quite become acclimatised to the sights that greeted him there. He always felt ill at ease, no matter how many times in the past he had been in a similar situation. He looked away, regained his composure and then resurveyed the scene. Beyond the tarpaulin mounds, four men wearing white overalls and plastic surgical type gloves crouched over the pavement. C.J. knew that these were the scene of crimes officers searching the area and carefully documenting any findings. Between the bodies walked two others; they wore ordinary street clothes. One carried, loosely held in his right hand, a bulky camera with flash attached. Periodically the other would lift one of the black tarpaulins and the photographer would fire off a few shots at the corpse exposed beneath.

Further down the street, well away from the area now being documented and photographed, stood another group. All the members of this group were kitted out in black bullet-proof jackets and peaked police caps. Some still carried their rifles, though these hung loosely by their straps slung over their bearer's shoulder, their day's work now completed. This group milled around. Some chatted amongst themselves, some smoked cigarettes, others kept to themselves and just leant up against one of the parked Land Rovers. All were waiting to be picked up and whisked away from the scene, presumably back to police headquarters for a de-briefing and then, C.J. guessed, probably on to some pub, to celebrate a job well done.

Among this latter, flack-jacketed, group, C.J. squinted and looked closely at one of their number. He pushed his way forward for a closer view. The object of his attention stood chatting to a group of others and then moved off to another figure, who stood apart and alone. He engaged this individual in a brief conversation, before patting him on the back and then passing on to yet another small group. It appeared to C.J. that this man had been in command of the operation and was now congratulating his troops. C.J. screwed up his eyes again in an attempt to discern his features. He wasn't sure, but then the officer turned to directly face C.J.; he was probably saying something derogatory about the massing press presence to his colleague and had turned to indicate the growing scrum behind the police tape. When he turned, C.J. saw his face clearly, there was no doubt now. The policeman spotted C.J. among the throng, quickly turned back and with one final pat on the back for his fellow policeman made off further down the street to a waiting police Land Rover. C.J. was sure now, and the policeman seemed to have recognised him too. He knew exactly where he had seen that face before: in the offices of the *Spectator*. The two men had bumped briefly into one another at the water cooler. The officer had been one of the two who had been given the information about the arms dump.

Was it just coincidence? Were the two events unrelated? Certainly a Special Branch officer would be involved in many different investigations at any one time. But C.J. was

131

troubled. He watched the Land Rover with the officer inside move off. It turned up a side street and disappeared from view. C.J. calculated that if it was returning to the local police station, then it would probably, on reaching the end of the street, double back to pass behind the crowd which now engulfed him.

C.J. started to disentangle himself from the melee of journalists and general Nosy Parkers that, by now, stretched right across the street. He pushed his way to their rear and finally stepped clear. As he did so, he glimpsed the bonnet of the Land Rover emerging from the side street beyond him. It was momentarily obstructed by a car which, prevented from proceeding down the road by the crowd ahead, was attempting to do a three point turn. C.J. grasped his opportunity. Breaking into a jog, he approached the stationary police vehicle. As he neared it, he could clearly see his quarry seated in the front passenger seat. C.J. rapped on the window beside him. The officer turned to face C.J. He held him in his stare for a moment and then opened the Land Rover door a few inches.

'What do you want?' barked the police officer, clearly annoyed by C.J.'s presence.

'I think we've met before,' replied C.J.

'I don't think so,' said the officer.

'Perhaps at the offices of the *Spectator*?' offered C.J.

'No comment.' He attempted to close the door, but C.J. held tightly onto it.

'Any comments on how the police got here so quickly?'

'No comment.'

'Has this anything to do with our tip-off to you?'

'NO COMMENT! Now go away, or I'll have you arrested for obstruction.' The officer was becoming visibly more agitated by C.J.'s continued presence and line of questioning.

'Did you know—'

C.J. got no further. The other car had completed its manoeuvre and the Land Rover, its path no longer impeded, sped off down the road, the door slamming shut as it did so.

Despondently, C.J. turned and made his way slowly back to the *Spectator*.

There was an audible buzz in the office when he entered. Journalists, excited by the breaking news were dashing back and forth comparing notes. Others were gathered around a television screen that had been hastily acquired and set up in the far corner of the room. C.J. moved slowly towards this latter group and, sitting on the edge of a desk, watched with them the events unfolding on the small screen.

There was a series of pictures of the scene at the post office, a brief shot of the three tarpaulin-covered bodies, then a fresh-faced reporter filled the screen, recounting the passage of events before interviewing an elderly woman whom he introduced as an eyewitness. From that interview it was back to the studio and then a collage of political reactions. A Unionist spokesman – C.J. recognised him as one of the first minister's chief advisers – stood outside the parliament buildings. He stated that the day's events had reinforced and given justification to his party's reluctance to allow Sinn Fein into a power-sharing executive. He had no doubt, based on information received, that the perpetrators were IRA terrorists. This act of armed terrorism, in his view, proved to the world that the threat of bloody insurrection had not yet lifted. Nothing, he turned to face the camera and said, could persuade him or his party to sit around a table and negotiate the future of Northern Ireland until the IRA surrendered and voluntarily gave up all its arms and weaponry. He then launched into a preamble about the morality of democracy versus holding the state in constant fear of reprisal if decisions didn't always please. C.J. had heard these arguments a hundred times before. The senior Unionist politician followed up by praising the vigilance of the RUC in aborting this outrage so successfully, without loss of innocent life. He finished by reinforcing his party's support for that organisation and vowed to continue to reject Nationalist calls for its disbandment.

Next up was the deputy leader of Sinn Fein. Not surprisingly, he had a quite different view of events. He stated categorically that the raiders were not of the IRA. The IRA, he asserted, maintained its cease-fire, which still stood, despite Unionist intransigence towards the peace process. The men involved in this raid were, he alleged, on the basis of information received, dissident Republicans dissatisfied with the progress made towards a peaceful resolution of the conflict. He stated that his party in no way condoned the carrying or use of arms, but he said that he understood these men's frustration. He blamed this frustration squarely on the Unionist parties. They, he said, had not kept good faith with the Good Friday Agreement, and further, he prophesised, if the peace process did not continue to advance, then he and his party could not be held responsible for further reckless acts, such as that which had occurred today. That blame lay roundly with the Unionist politicians. He went on to outline his party's continuing aims, which included a society where guns played no part. However, he proclaimed, if the Unionists talked of disarmament, then this must include the disarming and indeed disbandment of the RUC, which was perceived in Nationalist circles as a Loyalist army, simply there to preserve the privileges afforded to Unionists in the current society.

Towards the end of the interview the Sinn Fein spokesman became more vitriolic in his condemnation of the RUC's role in the affair. He claimed that the police had ambushed the raiders, that they could have been arrested

134

and not shot, or murdered by the state, as he preferred to call it. He said that he had eyewitness accounts that the men involved were in the process of surrendering when they were mercilessly gunned down. He had kept his powder dry, and brought this most damning indictment right at the end of the interview when there was no time for a cross examination of these claims by the reporter.

C.J. sat back. He thought, as might have been expected from Ulster politics, there was a dichotomy of opinion. The peace process, which he and apparently seventy-two per cent of the population had been in favour of, had brought people closer together, but the recent stalling of progress had allowed the old adversities to be rekindled and now, listening to the reactions to what had happened today, any hope of reconciliation seemed to be in ruins.

A buzz of heightened activity at the other end of the office caused C.J. to leave the television and move off to investigate.

'Apparently the police are holding a press conference in about half an hour,' one of the other hacks informed him.

The editor was delegating jobs to his troops, one to source eyewitness accounts, another to seek quotes from opinion leaders, others to gauge political response. C.J. didn't want to get involved, he preferred to make his own enquiries in his own way. Besides, he was determined to attend the police press conference and couldn't be sure that this task would be allocated to him, so quickly and quietly he slipped out of the building to make his own way to police headquarters, where the conference was due to be held.

Having left early, C.J. was one of the first to arrive. He offered his press card to the officers at the gate. They examined it carefully, but did not ring the *Spectator* to verify his identity. C.J. was glad of that. Word of his whereabouts might have got back to his editor and then questions would have been asked.

A uniformed officer escorted him to a large conference room in the main building. The room was laid out with rows of chairs facing a small platform stage on which two tables had been pushed together. Behind the table, in front of a backdrop on which hung an oversize RUC badge, a royal crown atop an Irish harp entwined with shamrocks, five chairs awaited their occupants.

C.J. moved along one of the rows at the rear of the room and sat down in a seat near the corner. It wasn't long before the rest of the journalists from the world's press started to arrive. C.J. recognised many of them from previous similar conferences over the years. He nodded greetings to some, but sat quietly, not speaking to any, engrossed in his own thoughts. Before long the room was full to overcapacity. All the chairs were occupied. A few extra were found and added to the already cramped rows. Many late arrivals, however, finding no room to sit down, were forced to squeeze in and stand along the back wall of the room.

The hubbub that now filled the room suddenly died with the arrival of five uniformed policemen. They entered through a side door at the front of the room and moved quickly to take up their positions behind the table on the stage. As they gained their seats an explosion of flashbulbs went off. The officers blinked in the dazzling lights. Taking the opportunity before the conference proper began, camera crews adjusted the focus of their cameras, by now positioned on tripods down the centre aisle. Soundmen pushed forward to place microphones, brightly labelled with their company's logo, in prominent positions in front of the main speakers.

The most senior of the police officers took up the centre seat; he was clearly going to conduct the conference. On his right were two other high-ranking officers, both of whom stared in a businesslike way straight at the assembled journalists. On the left were two other officers of lesser rank. They shifted uncomfortably in their seats, less at ease at their exposure to the world's media.

The press conference started with the central officer giving a brief statement and handing out a press release.

'Good afternoon, ladies and gentlemen,' the senior officer began. 'For those of you who don't know me, I am Chief Inspector Geoffrey Armstrong. The other officers here are members of the RUC who were directly involved in today's terrorist incident, whether through planning or on the ground. I have no intention of naming these officers, however, for fear of terrorist reprisals.'

C.J. surveyed the group. The officer in the centre was the officer commanding; it was he, C.J. was sure, who would steal the limelight and take the plaudits for the success of the operation. The officers on his right were probably the planners, the back room men behind the exercise, and the officers on the left those who were actually at the scene. C.J. surmised as much, but was the more convinced by the fact that the officer on the far left, the one who shifted position repeatedly in an ill-at-ease and restless manner, who stared constantly at his feet and continually wrung his hands, was the very officer that he had recognised at the scene of the foiled raid – the officer who seemed to be in charge of the others and the one who had earlier refused to talk to C.J.

C.J. quickly scanned the press release that had been handed to him. It started with a summary of the day's events, highlighting the successful outcome with no loss of innocent life. There was a short statement regretting the terrorist fatalities, but emphasising that the officers involved had issued warnings according to laid-down guidelines, but had been left with no alternative but to open fire when their own lives had been threatened. The final paragraphs

137

were devoted to the continuing need for vigilance, as clearly a threat from terror groups, whether IRA dissidents or Loyalist groups not on cease-fire, still existed.

The senior man read out the statement to the hushed room. Then, placing the sheet of paper down on the table, he raised his head and addressed the room.

'That summarises our statement. We are prepared to answer a few questions.'

There was an immediate frenzy of activity as hands were raised, others called out questions, as much to attract attention as to get an immediate reply.

'Gentlemen, gentlemen. One at a time, please. You in the second row.' He pointed to a middle-aged hack wearing a suit that had seen better days. His hand had been raised from almost before questions had been sought.

'Inspector Armstrong, who were the men involved?'

'We have one man in custody, three as you are aware died at the scene. We believe we know their identities, but I cannot divulge these until they have been formally identified and all the next of kin have been informed ... You, near the back.' He pointed at an eager young journalist in a sharp suit.

'Do you believe that the raid was paramilitary related?' the young man asked nervously.

'Yes, we do. Our information leads us to believe that all the men involved were part of a paramilitary organisation.'

'Which one?'

'We believe that all four are, or were, members of the IRA.'

An audible murmuring grew in the room. Hacks scribbled furiously in notepads.

'But the IRA are supposed to be on cease-fire. Do you believe that this is a breakdown in that cease-fire?' shouted somebody that C.J. couldn't quite see on the far side of the room.

The inspector ignored the fact that the questioner had raised the point unbidden and answered anyway.

'We don't know the answer to that one, I'm afraid. Whether these men were on active service for the IRA, or whether, as may be more likely, they were part of a breakaway group, perhaps the so-called "Real IRA", remains under investigation. Either way, I think it simply highlights the need for continuing police vigilance.'

C.J. rose to his feet, his arm aloft. The movement caught the inspector's eye.

'You, yes you, at the back.'

'Inspector,' C.J. asked, though he looked directly at the officer on the left of the group, who sensed C.J.'s stare and looked up from his feet for the first time since the conference had begun. 'How did the police manage to get there so quickly? Did you have prior information that the raid was going to take place?'

'We were acting on the basis of a tip-off, yes.'

'Where did that tip-off come from?'

One of the stern men on the right of the commanding officer butted in: 'You don't honestly expect us to reveal our sources, do you?'

'Inspector Armstrong.' Another uninvited call from the floor.

The inspector turned to face the new questioner, who was a small, stocky man whom C.J. recognised as a reporter from one of the Dublin papers.

'Yes?'

'Inspector Armstrong, what do you say to the accusation made earlier today that the men were in the act of surrendering when they were gunned down?'

'That accusation has no grounding in fact. My men acted in accordance with published and well-known guidelines. Any attempt to say otherwise is simply an affront to my officers.'

139

'You deny that the RUC still has a shoot-to-kill policy?'

'I deny emphatically that the RUC *ever* had a shoot-to-kill policy. Now, gentlemen, I think we have covered everything. If you'll excuse us.'

There were a few more calls and attempts at questions but these were steadfastly ignored as the five men rose and filed out of the room.

The press conference ended and the world's press started to leave. The hacks filed out, some already on mobile phones to their editors, others playing back the contents of their hand-held Dictaphones. The soundmen retrieved their microphones, the cameramen disassembled the tripods and lifted the heavy cameras out to their vehicles. C.J. sat quietly, deep in thought. He reached into his pocket and pulled out his cigarette packet.

Only three left. Better stop and buy another packet on the way home, he thought, looking down at it. Then, ignoring the sign proclaiming NO SMOKING directly above him, he lit one and inhaled the warm smoke deep into his lungs.

Finishing his cigarette and stubbing it out on the floor, C.J. was the last to leave the conference room; everybody else had deadlines to meet. He, on the other hand, was simply following his own agenda. He made his way slowly back along the corridors towards the exit. As he turned the final corner into the entrance foyer, there ahead of him, resting back against the wall one leg up behind him, was the officer he had earlier recognised. He seemed to be waiting for someone.

As C.J. approached, the officer looked up.

'In here,' he ordered, opening up the door to an interview room.

'Why?' asked C.J. a little fearfully. The policeman was much bigger than he was. And C.J. didn't know who or what was in the room into which he was being ushered.

'Just get in there, and quickly,' came the reply.

Somewhat reluctantly, C.J. did as he was bid. Gingerly entering the small room, he glanced nervously around. He was relieved to find it deserted except for a small wooden table and two plastic chairs.

'Sit down,' came the command.

'What do you want?' asked C.J., some of his self-confidence starting to return.

'You seemed to want to talk to me earlier,' said the policeman. 'Now's your chance.'

C.J. sat down in one of the chairs. The policeman pulled out a pack of cigarettes and proffered it in C.J.'s direction. C.J. accepted and the officer took one also and then lit both.

The policeman was again first to speak.

'Now listen, whatever I tell you is strictly off the record. Is that understood?'

'Whatever you say.'

'I'm only telling you this because I think that you have a right to know, okay?'

'Okay.'

'You're suspicious that your tip-off about the arms dump was in some way connected with today, aren't you?'

'Well, was it?'

'Yes, it was,' came the reply.

C.J. had dreaded as much. What had started so promisingly as a means to reduce violence had resulted in the deaths of three people.

'So tell me what happened.'

'This goes no further, is that absolutely understood?'

'Absolutely.'

'Okay, so your paper gives us the tip-off about the arms dump. Fairly routine, normally, we just move in and clear it, nothing dramatic. But this time, before we do anything, word comes down, from another informant, that there is a group of dissident IRA men out there about to rearm and revitalise terrorist activities. The powers above, given the alleged source of your information . . .'

'Sinn Fein?'

'Sinn Fein/IRA. Our commanders reckon that the IRA don't want this group to get their hands on any arms. Probably in case they start to draw support away from the current leadership. So this arms dump is most likely an old one, known to one of the dissidents. Rather than let the arms fall into their former buddies' hands – and they can't move the guns themselves in case they're caught and the cease-fire is blown out of the water – they come up with the idea of having them found by the security forces. Then, to maximise the publicity, they come up with the cock-and-bull story about kids finding them and getting injured, or the alternative subterfuge of some kind of secretive and initially unacknowledged decommissioning exercise. That one was probably going to be exploited, and you along with it, later down the line, when the political going gets tough.'

'So what actually happened?'

'We received orders not to discover the arms, but to keep the building under close observation.'

'I went to that house a few weeks later and the arms were gone.'

'You did what? That was really pretty stupid. Do you know what could have happened to you if the IRA had caught you? You could've been shot.'

'I realise that, but nothing seemed to be happening.'

'A lot was happening, believe me. You obviously entered the house after the guns had been collected. They were taken about a week after you told us where they were.'

'Who took them?'

'The same gang who raided the post office today. We've been tailing them ever since. The guns were stored in a house in West Belfast for the last few weeks. We maintained surveillance on it and on everybody who came to that house. At the time of the raid, colleagues of mine conducted pre-planned searches on that house and on the homes of every visitor to that house ever since the guns were stored there. There have been a number of arrests and I believe that we now have all the guns under lock and key.'

'But why didn't you just move in and arrest everybody earlier? Why let the attack happen?'

'That's precisely why I'm talking to you now. I don't hold with everything that has occurred . . . and also to warn you. When the dump was entered, we had it, as I've said, under close surveillance. I was there myself. We radioed for advice, fully expecting to be told to arrest the terrorists on the premises. But, no, we were told to hold back, to follow and observe but not to arrest. This we did, until today. When they entered the post office we watched them, when they came out we were ready and waiting for them.'

'But why hold back when you could have arrested the gang without bloodshed?'

'I've since found out the reasons for that.'

'Which are?'

'As you are aware, the peace process has stalled. But the politicians are jockeying for position. One side wants the IRA to give up its arms immediately, the other wants political power and status before it can recommend such a move.'

'Yes, so?'

'Well, the RUC is piggy in the middle, or at least that's how it feels to most of us in the force. We are being used as a political football at the moment. There is a lot of pressure on us to disarm, reduce in numbers, or even be disbanded. With no terrorist threat to counter, the arguments against such moves are weakened. Chief Inspector Armstrong, who you met today, is an ambitious man. He has visions of being Chief Constable one day. But with the threat of disbandment or even reorganisation along politically correct lines hanging over the force, the chances of a former Special Branch officer making Chief Constable seem somewhat remote, to say the least.'

'Are you saying that he let the raid go ahead, even though he could have prevented it, just to preserve his own aspirations within the force?'

'I'm not saying that, but you can draw your own conclusions. What Unionist politician is going to let the police be disarmed now after today's activities? The official line is that there is a renewed terrorist threat, which we were lucky enough, due entirely to good police work, to abort on this occasion. But the public will feel threatened again. We have to be there to protect them.'

'So those men were sacrificed, in your view, for the greater good.' C.J. felt the bile rising in his stomach; he just wanted to get out. He rose unsteadily and started to make for the door.

'I brought you in here because I wanted to warn you,' said the officer, now standing in his path.

'Warn me?' asked C.J. 'Warn me about what?'

'Those guys that got shot, they may have broken away from the IRA, but they still have a lot of friends in that organisation. Those friends are going to be very unhappy with what went down today. They are going to start asking questions, and it won't be long before your role in all this comes out.'

'My role?' C.J. felt his voice quiver and the nausea increase.

'You gave us the information about the whereabouts of the arms. They won't like that.'

'But . . . but it was on their instructions.'

'Don't count on any of the membership owning up to that now. Be careful. Be very careful.'

*

C.J. left police headquarters. He sat for a long time in his car before driving off. The tyres squelched over the newly deposited pile of warm vomit that C.J. had left beside the vehicle. He turned the wheel and headed for home.

11

C.J. spent the next morning in bed. Tucked up, under the warm duvet, he had little inclination to rise and face the increasingly uncertain world outside. The events of the previous twenty-four hours revolved in his head. Julie had left him to lie in, recognising his restlessness of the previous night. The fact that he had been in some way responsible for the deaths of three human beings C.J. found difficult to assimilate. It did not help to know that these human beings were armed terrorists engaged in an act of criminal activity. He continued to toss and turn, unable to disengage his mind from the recurring nightmare. Eventually, though, he dragged himself wearily out of bed and dressed slowly and laboriously, before bidding Julie and the children farewell and making his way to the *Spectator*, to belatedly begin his working day.

Reaching his desk, he noticed a yellow Post-It stuck to his phone. '*Ring Patsy*', followed by a telephone number, was all that was written on it. C.J. sat down at his desk and dialled the number. It rang four times and then an answer machine cut in.

'There is no one available to take your call . . .' came the bland tone.

'Hello, hello, Patsy . . . it's me, C.J. McCormick . . . If you're there, lift the phone . . . Hello? . . . Hello? . . .'

Finally, C.J. heard the receiver being lifted and Patsy Harte came on the line.

'We're in big trouble, you and me. We need to talk. Meet me in Ormeau Park. Near the bandstand.'

'What time?' asked C.J. He could tell from Patsy's tone that he was in no mood for a discussion on the subject.

'In fifteen minutes.' The phone went down and the dialling tone returned.

C.J. rose and was about to leave the office, when George Thompson emerged from his office.

'C.J., where the hell are you going? I've been looking for you since yesterday.'

'Sorry, George,' replied C.J. He was in no frame of mind to even attempt to placate his editor. 'No time to explain.'

With that, he turned his back on the editor and made for the door. George Thompson, momentarily taken aback at being dismissed so blatantly, quickly recovered his composure and shouted something after C.J., but it was too late, the words rebounded off the swinging door through which C.J. had already left the office.

As he walked through the park, the sun glinted through the trees. Although it was mid-winter and there was a frosty breeze, the sunshine warmed C.J.'s spirits. He rounded the corner of the narrow footpath and spied the bandstand ahead. Unused for several years, it had been allowed to slip into a state of disrepair. The stage was littered with empty cans of imported lager mingled with those of an equally strong cider. Strewn about with the cans were plastic bags heavy with a congealed substance from which, just the evening before, the glue sniffers had been inhaling solvents. The wind had not as yet gathered sufficient strength to disperse these bags further afield.

At this time of day, the drinkers were on the streets trying to beg borrow or steal enough money to purchase more booze, and the glue sniffers were, most likely, still in bed. The bandstand area was therefore deserted. As C.J. approached, he could see Patsy Harte seated on a bench in the shade on the far side of the bandstand. He sat legs wide apart, his head cradled in his hands, his elbows supported on his knees. He appeared deep in thought. Initially he seemed unaware of C.J.'s arrival. When he did finally note his presence, it was with a sudden surprised start.

'Jesus!' he exclaimed. 'You gave me fright there. Don't sneak up on me like that.'

'I didn't mean—'

'It doesn't matter,' Patsy said hurriedly, looking wildly about him all the while. 'Sit down, will you. We have to talk.'

'What's the matter, Patsy?'

'You mean you don't know?' exclaimed Patsy, almost shouting the question.

'Is this something to do with that raid yesterday?' C.J. asked.

'Of course it bloody is. Don't play the innocent with me, you know it bloody is.'

'What's your problem, Patsy?'

'What's my problem? What's my problem? What's *our* problem, more like.'

'Calm down, Patsy, and tell me what you're on about.'

'What I'm on about, what I'm fucking on about, is those three guys that were murdered by the fucking RUC yesterday. As if you didn't know.'

'They were in the middle of an armed raid, for Christ's sake.'

'They were set up. The pigs were waiting for them when they came out of that post office and they cut them down in cold blood.'

'That's not the official line.'

'Quite frankly, I don't care what the police say. All I know is that those guys had connections. Word on the street is that the leader of the group was a guy called Brian Maguire.'

'Brian Maguire? I've heard that name before.'

'Sure you have. He was a big man in the organisation, a regular hero. In and out of trouble.'

'If he was in the IRA, what's he doing with a gun when they're supposed to be on cease-fire, and what's it got to do with us?' C.J. asked the questions but he already knew the answers.

'Oh, use what little imagination you have, will you. Look, those guns came from the dump that I told you about. Those guys that got shot may have broken ranks but they still have a lot of friends. Now the organisation wants revenge. An eye for an eye, a tooth for a tooth, is their standard philosophy . . .'

'But any information that you gave me was on their instructions.'

'Don't count on anyone from the hierarchy owning up to that now. No, if there has to be a scapegoat then the buck stops with you and me.'

'But we didn't deliberately set those guys up.'

'Do you think that really matters now? Look, I just came to warn you. I'm getting out. I intend being on the ferry to Liverpool tonight. At the moment the organisation don't know exactly where I am, and what's more I intend to keep it that way till the heat dies down. More importantly from your point of view is that they don't yet know that it was you I talked to. They just know that it was a journalist from your newspaper. But don't underestimate them. They have informants everywhere. If I were you, I'd lie low for a while . . . and keep your fingers crossed and hope that they don't get hold of your name.'

With that, Patsy Harte rose and made to leave. C.J.

regarded him as he turned to go. It appeared as if he'd aged ten years; he looked weary and haggard, the lines on his face were more acutely drawn, beads of sweat gathered on his brow.

'Thanks, Patsy. Thanks for the warning,' he said it to Patsy's back as he shambled away.

'See you around,' came the mumbled reply.

C.J. made his own way slowly back to his office. He wasn't in the mood for work but he didn't know where else to go. He wasn't in the mood for a confrontation with George Thompson either, but that was precisely what he got when he entered the office.

George was still fuming at being cut off by C.J. earlier and was not in a forgiving mood.

'My office. Now!' came the bellow from the editor, half in and half out of his office doorway, as C.J. arrived.

C.J., also in no mood to compromise, pushed his way past the other desks towards George's office. Slamming the door shut behind him, C.J. was quickly on the offensive.

'Do you know where I've been these last couple of days?' he growled at the editor, leaning forward over his desk, both hands planted firmly on the desktop.

'No, I don't,' came the, slightly defensive, reply from George seated behind his desk and somewhat taken aback by the normally placid C.J.'s aggressive attitude.

'Hell. That's where I've been. I've been to Hell and back.'

'What do you mean?'

'Those guys that were shot . . .'

'The ones on the post office raid?'

'Yes, the ones on the post office raid. We are responsible for their deaths. You and me both.'

'Don't talk daft.'

'I'm not. The police knew about the raid in advance. You and I told them.'

'Told the police? When?'

'When you told them about my tip-off about that arms dump back in November.'

C.J. went on to expand on the connection between the two events. George Thompson remained silent throughout the explanation. He turned slightly pale when C.J. revealed the potential threat that now loomed over him. George paled even more when C.J. made sure that he realised he was likely to be included in any possible punitive reprisal actions of the IRA.

Reaching the end of his story and his anger still not assuaged, C.J. turned on his heel to leave the small office.

'Don't you walk out on me,' shouted George. 'I haven't finished with you yet.'

C.J. turned round to confront his editor, who by now was up on his feet. C.J. fixed him in an icy stare, before replying.

'You may not have finished with me, but I've finished with you. If you had listened to me, those three men would be alive today . . .'

'They were armed terrorists . . .'

'They were still human beings.'

With that, he stormed out of the editor's office. As he slammed the door behind him, he had just time to add the words, 'I resign,' and, inaudibly under his breath, 'you can stuff your paper where the sun don't shine.'

12

Harry had heard of C.J.'s departure from the *Spectator* within a few days of its happening. In respect of news and gossip, Northern Ireland is essentially a small village, everybody knows everything about everybody else's business, especially when something unusual occurs. Although he had known of C.J.'s resignation, Harry had not been fully appraised of the reasons behind it. On subsequent meetings with C.J., Harry found him to be somewhat unusually sullen and morose, and generally unwilling to discuss the matter further. So Harry had not pushed him on the subject. He simply accepted the fact that he had had some form of a disagreement with his boss, and left it at that.

C.J. was firmly of the belief that every cloud has a silver lining, for him this meant that his newfound freedom had enabled him to devote himself more completely to the task of money raising. He spent long hours sitting at his desk at home drafting and sending letters all round the island of Ireland and beyond. He wrote to potential golf clubs, he corresponded with firms that might offer sponsorship and he worked out deals with helicopter companies and other businesses that could provide technical support. Emma was also rapidly proving herself to be a valuable member of the team. Harry suspected that C.J. was probably driving her mad with requests and ideas to be followed up now that the record attempt was his only source of interest. But she never complained, she worked on the publicity machine, securing articles that C.J. readily drafted in a number of local and even some national journals and newspapers.

By early January, and the dawn of a new year, much of what they felt was required was already in place. They had a purpose and a desire. They had located a firm willing and able to provide two Ranger type helicopters and, due largely to C.J.'s persistence, to supply them for only the price of the fuel used. The pilots would also waive their normal fee as C.J. had persuaded them that they and their firm would benefit from the ensuing valuable publicity. The publicity machine also, under Emma's guidance, was going well. Each day, they received letters and calls pledging money or support. One problem still remained: they were still short of some venues. In some of the more rural counties, it had proven difficult to identify and sign up golf clubs willing to participate in the event. Some of the difficulty was that many felt overshadowed by their larger urban rivals. Others had pre-arranged club competitions on the day in question and were unwilling to disrupt these with the arrival of a helicopter and all the paraphernalia that the event encompassed.

With the bulk of the organisation in place, Emma had persuaded the team to have an official launch of the project. This, she explained, was to maximise any potential media coverage. What she proposed was that they announce a press conference and media launch party scheduled in the next week or so. This would permit sufficient time to attract interest, sponsorship and, above all, the support of golf clubs in the missing links of the chain. It would not, however, be too far ahead of the event to allow public interest to wane in advance of the project itself.

Emma was forceful in her persuasion and this was backed up by the obvious logic of her argument. It was difficult to resist. Nevertheless, the idea of such a public spectacle did

153

present its own difficulties. If there was to be a media circus then Julie, for whose benefit, after all, the event was being run, was going to have to be present and would be the centre of media attention. Harry wasn't sure just how she would react to that prospect. Dr Anderson would also, he felt, need to be enrolled; whilst Harry was a doctor, this was John Anderson's area of expertise and, he argued, he needed to be present, personally, to advance his case.

Harry rang John Anderson the following day. The consultant seemed genuinely pleased to hear from him. Harry was able to update him on Julie's condition and, with only a little persuasion, cajole him into giving a media interview.

Harry met Julie and C.J. Medically, Julie's condition had remained essentially unchanged – something that he was grateful for, because even if they succeeded, at best he could simply hope that things would stabilise and further deterioration be prevented. There would be no return of that which had already been lost.

It was immediately evident to Harry that although Julie was keen to be closely involved with the event, she remained much less enthusiastic about the idea of going public with her problems. C.J. was much keener, in this respect, to push ahead.

'You've got to do it, Julie; you've just got to,' pleaded C.J. 'We've all been working so hard to set this up and now, just as it looks that it really might go ahead, it needs your input to keep it on track. You can't let Emma and Harry down.'

'To be fair C.J.,' Harry interjected, 'we don't really matter in this. To us it's been a challenge just to get it this far. If we have to pull out now, it doesn't matter. Nobody's lost anything; nobody will get hurt or be disappointed. At this moment all we're operating on is a bunch of loose promises.'

'But we'd be disappointed, wouldn't we, Julie?' replied

C.J., turning again to face his wife. 'We discussed this last night and you agreed to go ahead, didn't you?'

'Yes, but ... I'm scared. I've never been on television before and going into a studio to sit in front of a whole load of reporters and just moan about my illness and then to beg for money ... Well, it's just not me, you know that. I just don't know if I could do it.'

'To be honest, Julie,' butted in Emma, 'I don't think that's what anybody wants you to do. As I understand it, the plan is for a reporter to do a one-to-one interview with you, here at your own house, if that's what you want, and then for you just to be at the press conference.'

'What'll I have to say?'

'Just the truth. He will probably just ask you how your illness has affected your lifestyle—'

'That's easy, I don't have a lifestyle any more!'

'There you go. It's that simple. What the reporter will probably be most interested in is not the fact that this event is to raise money to help your particular case but rather the wider issue of other people like you being deprived of a potential treatment owing to lack of resources.'

'I'm sure you have some views on that, don't you, Julie?' asked Harry.

'You bet, Harry, you bet.'

'I've lined Dr Anderson up to do a parallel interview to cover these issues as well. So you don't need to worry about facts and statistics and stuff – he can do all that.'

Julie sat quietly deep in thought for a few moments. Then she looked up, straight at C.J., and said in a resolute manner, 'Okay guys, sign me up. I'll do it.'

'That's my girl,' exclaimed C.J., gripping her tightly by both hands and kissing her strongly on the lips.

*

Emma had hired a small conference room in the new Belfast Hilton for the official launch. As Harry entered the foyer, he took in the minimalist furnishings and the row of desks behind which the receptionists were dealing with incoming guests. To the left of the large spiral staircase was a notice board on which was written in bold type '**ROUND IRELAND CHALLENGE – First Floor**'. Harry's heart leapt at seeing the words emblazoned in a public place for the very first time. He made his way up the staircase, to the open reception area. There he found Emma, who had arrived earlier. Harry smiled with satisfaction as he noted that she looked simply stunning in a black linen sleeveless dress and a single row of pearls strung around her neck. She was directing operations. Bar staff, dressed from head to toe in black, appeared behind the bar counter, aided by a group of waitresses, also in black. This, Harry understood, was the modern Hilton uniform. Waitresses were also manning a large table, covered with a white linen tablecloth, in the centre of the room. On it were arranged rows of glasses of red and white wine, and a few even contained orange juice. The bar manager ordered his staff about, as they lingered haphazardly around the foyer, in order to have them in readiness for the guests.

Emma smiled in Harry's direction. 'Thank goodness you're here, Harry. It's been hectic. The hordes are expected soon. But at least it's marvellous just to see things coming together at last.'

'It certainly looks as if you've done a good job.'

Around the walls of the foyer were a number of posters and banners proclaiming the local firms which were in some way supporting the venture. Those firms that had contributed most had their advertisements inside the main hall where the conference was to be. There they had more chance of appearing in photographs or even on television. People were starting to drift in, usually in ones or twos, some in larger groups. Many carried cameras or micro-phones or both. Some just brought small Dictaphones. Some of the older paparazzi seemed only to have notebooks and pencils. On arrival all made their way directly to the bar, where they gathered in small groups, chatting away, oblivious of Emma and Harry's efforts to try to herd them towards the conference area. Whilst the glasses containing the red and white wines had rapidly been claimed and there were frantic attempts to replenish their contents, Harry noted that the glasses holding the orange juice remained largely undisturbed.

C.J. emerged from the elevator. Julie, looking nervous, was on his arm. C.J. chatted animatedly, trying, Harry guessed, to put her at her ease. The crowds continued to swell and, by the allotted hour of the conference, the area round the bar and the drinks table in particular were totally congested. Others continued to try to edge their way through the crowds to get at the serving areas. The bar staff rushed back and forth trying, often in vain, to placate the thirsty would-be drinkers.

Emma gesticulated for the four of them to move into the conference room.

'Emma and I have set up a video playback of the inter-views that have been done, with copies for the television companies. We're going to show that first,' C.J. explained, trying unsuccessfully to suppress his own excitement. Harry knew that C.J. was well used to press conferences, but this was different. This time he was not on the receiving end, this time he and, more importantly, Julie were to be the focus of attention, and Harry guessed that C.J.'s nervous excitement stemmed at least partially from his anxieties about exposing her to the media scrum.

On the other hand, Emma was definitely in organisa-tional mode. 'We've also set up a video link with Philip Watson – he's somewhere in Texas. I hope it works because it's set to go live in about thirty minutes, so we'd better start to get these guys into the hall.'

'Texas,' said Harry, looking suitably impressed. 'That's a long way away.'

'You certainly have the knack, Harry,' replied C.J., 'of stating the completely bleeding obvious. Go and start ushering people in, would you please.'

It had been decided that all four of them would be onstage but that Emma and C.J. would lead the discussion. Harry was to be there to field any medical-type enquiries and Julie had reluctantly agreed to answer questions about her condition.

'I hope I don't say anything stupid in front of all these journalists,' she said, her voice quivering as she did so.

'I've every confidence in you, Julie,' Harry replied in what he hoped was an encouraging tone.

As the crowds were prised away from the bar and entered the hall, C.J. and Harry helped Julie to clamber up onto the small elevated stage area. Above and behind them was a large video screen. At present all it was showing was a large Hilton Hotels group logo.

When most of the crowd appeared to have squeezed in and even though some were still searching for a free seat, Emma rose to her feet.

'Ladies and gentlemen,' she shouted over the buzz of the background conversations.

C.J. banged hard on the tabletop with his fist.

'LADIES AND GENTLEMEN, . . . Thank you.'

The crowd became silent except for the occasional almost inaudible whisper. Emma continued.

'I'm sorry to rush you all away from the complimentary bar . . .'

Boos and hisses pervaded the room.

'. . . but we have a deadline for a live video link up with

the United States. So we have to stick to a fairly rigid timetable, I'm afraid.'

More boos.

'However, the bar will be open and continue to serve after the conference is concluded.'

The crowd cheered.

What she didn't, of course, tell them was that it would only stay open for a short time afterwards. They didn't want to waste all their precious funds on the gentlemen of the press, who in any case they wished to encourage to return to their places of work and write about the project in hand.

Emma proceeded to introduce herself, C.J., Julie and Harry to the audience. Harry shuffled with embarrassment, Julie looked decidedly uncomfortable.

'Today,' C.J rose to his feet and reported, 'is the official launch of our Round Ireland record attempt. First things first. We've made a short video explaining the reasons behind the attempt and exactly what we propose to do. It only lasts ten minutes or so and your full attention would be appreciated. For those of you who want copies from which you may make cuttings for your own broadcast purposes, we have ample supplies . . . Could you dim the lights, please.'

The lights were duly dimmed and the video screen came to life. There was an opening montage of a helicopter flying across a sunset, interchanging with Philip Watson playing a few golf shots. Then a title 'The Round Ireland Challenge' across the screen. Following the montage a reporter – Harry recognised him from local television but couldn't remember his name – appeared on the screen and gave a reasonably concise overview of the project. He then went on to expand on the *raison d'être* of the event. This led into the interview with Julie, who, as Emma had promised, was interviewed at her home. In fact the scene opened with her

159

in her garden with her children. She sat on a garden seat with the baby in the buggy beside her and watched Becky playing. Then Becky fell over and the camera followed Julie's attempts to come to her aid. The camera angle seemed to accentuate her walking difficulties. As Becky lay crying it seemed to take Julie an age to get to her. After comforting her daughter, Julie was interviewed briefly about her illness and the course it had taken. Harry glanced over towards Julie, who was seated at the far end of the table. She gripped tightly onto C.J.'s hand, her head bowed as if embarrassed by the scene that played out above her. Then the scene switched to Dr Anderson's office. He was seated behind his desk, wearing a pristine starched white coat and looking every inch the professional.

Emma leant over towards Harry and, shielding her mouth with her hand so as not to distract any of the audience, whispered that she had organised the video through some of her publicity contacts.

John Anderson was able to recount facts and figures regarding the consequences of MS. He gave, also, an outline of the effectiveness of the new drug beta interferon in treating the disease. It was expensive but it had been shown to reduce the number of relapses and slow disease progression. Quoting recent medical literature, he reported that from a cost of illness study conducted in the United States it had been estimated that the annual cost of MS was $34,000 dollars per year (over £20,000), and clearly the hope was that this cost to society might be reduced considerably if the drug was more widely available.

From Dr Anderson, the video moved to an interview with the chairperson of The MS Awareness Society, a well-spoken and extremely forthright woman whose husband had died of the disease some years earlier. She was able to expand and develop the components of cost that John Anderson had alluded to. The major monetary costs were due, she said, to inability to work and the cost of providing care. However, she was at pains to point out that much of the cost of the disease was intangible and immeasurable. These costs were the reduced quality of life, due to a mixture of pain, grief, anxiety or social handicap, and that these costs could impinge just as much on the carers as on the person directly affected with the disease.

Then it was back to the studio for a brief resumé of the project by the unnamed reporter: its aims of providing beta interferon for Julie and highlighting the wider issues surrounding the disease. The video closed with a few acknowledgements and a view of the helicopter turning and flying off into the sunset.

Harry had to admit that the video had been professionally produced and had effectively summed up the project perfectly in ten short minutes.

'Ladies and gentlemen,' began C.J., once more on his feet, 'I hope that video gives you some idea of what we are about, what we intend to attempt and, more importantly, the reasons behind it.'

He looked down and studied his watch intently.

'I was going to ask for some questions at this point, but as I said earlier, we have a live link-up with the United States, where Philip Watson, the current Irish number one golfer, is waiting to speak to you and, fingers crossed, will be able to answer a few questions. It is Philip, of course, who will be making the record attempt of playing golf in every single county in Ireland within a single day.'

He turned to address the TV screen.

'Hello, Philip . . . Hello, Philip . . . Are you there?'

The screen remained blank. C.J. looked uncomfortable, Harry felt embarrassed for him. Then just as he was about to give up and turn to apologise to the audience, the screen opened up and was filled with the ample, sun-tanned visage of Philip Watson.

'Hello, Belfast. Can you hear me?'

'Loud and clear, Philip,' replied C.J. 'This is C.J. McCormick speaking, on behalf of the organising committee. I'm here with a posse of the press. What's the weather like out there in Texas?'

'Fine, just fine, C.J. It's quite early in the morning here at the moment, though. It gets a lot hotter later on.'

'Congratulations on your recent tour success. I believe you're in the middle of another competition at the moment. How's it going?'

'Well, thanks for asking, C.J. I just got knocked out, actually . . .'

There was some muffled laughter from around the room.

'Yeah, I didn't make the cut this time. Still you can't win 'em all.'

C.J. appeared a little shame-faced after his last question. He decided to move things quickly along. He invited Philip to talk about his role in the forthcoming project.

Philip Watson had clearly prepared a set answer to this invitation and went into a preamble about how honoured he was to be invited to make an attempt at doing something that had never been done before. The scheduling had fitted in perfectly with his plans, as the Irish Open was later that same week and all in all he'd be able to spend a bit more time than usual in Ireland visiting his family and renewing old friendships. He said that he was particularly pleased to be involved in raising money and awareness of multiple sclerosis. A former school friend of his wife's had had the disease and he knew what a devastating illness it could be. He hoped that, with all the publicity, something good in the longer term would come out of this record attempt.

When he had finished his short monologue, the audience broke into spontaneous applause.

'Thank you . . . thank you,' came from the TV speakers.

Philip Watson looked genuinely moved by the show of appreciation.

'Philip,' said C.J., facing the screen, 'thank you for that. Can I ask you what you think are our chances of success?'

'You are probably in a better position than me to judge that, C.J. You must have all the facts and figures worked out by now.'

Again muffled laughter from the audience, many of whom knew C.J. well.

'Mind you, the one big variable is my putting,' he continued. 'It's not been going too well recently . . . Perhaps you ought to add in an extra few minutes on each hole to allow for the additional putts.'

The audience applauded.

'You'd better keep practising then,' replied C.J., 'because by our calculations it's touch and go whether we can do it as it is.'

'Okay then, C.J.'

'One final question, Philip, because we are going to lose the link up very soon. Who do you think . . .?'

Before he could get any further, the screen dissolved into a snowstorm. The satellite link was lost.

The audience roared and clapped.

The lights came on again. C.J., still in control of the meeting, though perhaps only just, informed everyone that copies of the original video presentation were available to those that wanted them, after the press conference had concluded. There then followed a question-and-answer session, in which members of the press fired questions at those on-stage. Harry fielded most of the medically orientated ones. Happily, he thought, the questions were neither so probing nor so difficult that he couldn't address them properly. In any case, the video and satellite link-up had gone a long way in satisfying the journalists' curiosity and providing them with sufficient facts to draft their copy.

163

The meeting ended and the guests filed from the conference chamber. Many paused briefly at the bar to top up their alcohol levels and to compare notes. Others left directly to return to their offices and, Harry hoped, start to work on their report. A reporter from UTV, the local television news company, buttonholed C.J. as he was about to leave the main room and manoeuvred him off to the side for a private interview. Emma, Julie and Harry made their way back into the bar area. There they sat down at one of the tables and a waiter brought a round of drinks over. As they drank, Harry could see C.J. was now in full flow in front of the television cameras.

'It's good to see C.J. back to his old self,' he remarked.

'He's been very down lately,' Julie confirmed. 'I'm glad now that we went ahead with the whole thing. It seems to be giving him a whole lease of life.'

It seemed to Harry somewhat of a paradox that C.J. and he had set out to help Julie and here she was thanking him because it was actually helping C.J. out of his recent doldrums. He was about to remark on this, when they were interrupted by the arrival of a newcomer.

Emma was on her feet. Julie and Harry exchanged glances

'You've met Julie McCormick, of course, but this is Harry Wallace, Julie's GP and one of the instigators of—'

'Hello, Harry.'

'Hello, Olivia.'

'You know each other?' Emma looked inquisitively back and forth.

'You could say that,' Harry replied. 'To what do we owe the pleasure, Olivia?'

'Olivia works with the company that produced the video and organised the live link-up,' explained Emma, still a little taken aback.

As Olivia had reverted to her maiden name as quickly as

was socially acceptable following their break-up, there was, of course, no way that Emma could have made the connection. However, if Olivia's company had filmed the interview with Julie, then C.J and Julie must have known, but not seen fit to tell him, he mused.

'Really?' Harry looked hard at Julie, who averted her gaze.

'Looks like I'll be seeing a bit more of you then, Harry. Especially now Emma's signed over the TV rights for your challenge to our firm.'

With that, Olivia turned on her heel and made her way back to where her film crew were struggling to pack up their equipment. Ignoring their efforts, she strode past them and on out of the hotel, hailed a taxi and was gone.

'Thanks a lot, guys,' Harry said, looking alternatively from Emma to Julie.

'I'm sorry, Harry, I didn't know there was a history there,' pleaded Emma.

'I think you'll find that with Olivia it's less a *his*tory and more a *her*story.'

Emma looked puzzled.

A few moments later, C.J., interview concluded, rejoined the group in the bar.

'I thought that went quite well,' he offered.

'Did you ever hear of the expression, self-praise no recommendation?' Harry returned, still a little tetchy.

It was C.J.'s turn to look puzzled.

Emma decided to change the subject. 'What were you going to ask Philip Watson just before the video link went down?'

'Ah yes. Well, you know he's in Texas – I told you that, didn't I? Well, he's actually just outside Dallas. So, I was going to ask him who he thought shot JFK.'

Julie and Harry held their heads in their hands.

'Why, C.J., . . . why?'

'I thought it would help to lighten things up a bit.' C.J. looked from one to the other defensively.

'Then it's probably just as well the satellite link failed when it did,' said Harry.

'Well, who do you think shot JFK then?' asked C.J. He wasn't about to be deflected. 'There are two currently held theories. One, that Lee Harvey Oswald did do it. Or two, that it was a CIA set-up. The first theory, of course, relies heavily on the existence of "the magic bullet".'

'The magic bullet?'

'There were three shots heard, and for Lee Harvey Oswald to have been the lone marksman he had to fire all three in rapid succession. One missed, one killed JFK outright but then there were other wounds to JFK and also to his minder. If these were caused by a single shot then this bullet had to travel through both of them. Implausible as that might be, what makes this bullet "magic" was that it then ended up being found apparently completely undamaged on the floor of the limo.'

C.J. had clearly shaken off any remnant of his former malaise as he continued unabated.

'Personally, I find "the magic bullet" theory difficult to believe. My own preference is to believe that he was the victim of triangulated fire, emanating from among other places the famous "grassy knoll" and further that the perpetrators were from the CIA—'

'You mean then,' interrupted Harry. 'that he was shot by somebody from outside Texas?'

'Well,' replied C.J., a smirk breaking across his face, 'that would have been a hell of a good shot then, wouldn't it.'

13

When the call came through, at first Harry thought it was about the progress they had been making on setting up the record attempt. He quickly realised that he was mistaken.

'Hello Harry, sorry to bother you, but could you call out to see me?'

'Sure, Julie, of course I can. Nothing wrong, I hope?'

'I don't know, but there might be.'

Julie was no more forthcoming. But Harry knew that she wouldn't have asked him to call unless something was up. So as soon as the morning clinic was over he drove round to her house.

Julie and the baby were alone in the house when he arrived. C.J. was out and Becky was with her grandmother. Tom screamed loudly as Julie ushered Harry into the living room.

'Sorry about the noise. He's in very bad form today. I think he might be teething or something.' Julie picked up the sobbing infant and cradled him in her arms. The crying quickly ceased, and as Julie rocked him gently back and forth it wasn't long before he was sound asleep. She laid him gently down on the sofa.

'I came around as soon as I could. What's wrong, Julie?'

'Thanks for coming, I'm sorry for dragging you round here and it's probably me fussing about nothing, but it's my right hand, Harry.'

'What's wrong with it?'

Julie went on to explain that since the day before she had been aware of a feeling of pins and needles in her fingers and that today her hand wouldn't do what she wanted it to do. It was clumsy, she dropped things and she couldn't even write her name.

'Honestly, Harry, my writing's now worse than yours.'

'I can't believe that.'

But he got her to write her own name and address on a piece of paper and there was no doubt, it was. She gripped the pen tightly but there was an unaccustomed awkwardness to her movement and her hand shook violently as she tried to form the words.

'I'm glad C.J.'s not here to see this. I've been trying to hide it from him. He's got enough on his plate without worrying about me as well.'

'Okay, put the pen down and let me try some tests on you.'

Julie dropped the pen and Harry proceeded to examine her strength. It seemed perfectly normal. Next he tested her sensation by jabbing her with a small pin.

'I can feel it, Harry. It's just that over my right hand, particularly across my fingertips, I don't know . . . it just doesn't feel right somehow. Do you know what I mean?'

'I think so. Try this . . . Touch your nose with your finger . . . good. Now touch my finger with yours.'

Harry held his finger out for her to touch, but sufficiently far away from her so that she had to stretch for it. Julie's hand shook uncontrollably as she neared his finger.

'That's terrible, isn't it?'

'No, no, it's okay, well done.'

'So what's wrong with me?'

'I think you know the answer to that question, Julie.'

'It's this old MS thing again, isn't it?'

'Look, there's no point in beating about the bush, I think

you're having what's called a relapse. It's clear to me that this problem that you've developed is part of your illness and that for whatever reason that illness has flared up again.'

Julie started to sob. Harry guessed that she'd known what he was going to say before he said it. But that didn't reduce the impact of the confirmation.

'The question in my mind, Julie, is what I can do to help?'

'There's nothing you can do, is there? You haven't found a cure for this awful thing yet, have you?' The tears swept down her face as she spoke. 'I'm stuck with it, like it or not, aren't I?'

The sadness and despair that was slowly breaking down Julie's former resolve tore at Harry's heart, more so than any of the physical manifestations of the disease itself.

'I can't cure this disease, that's true, but I might, just might, be able to help you get over this relapse.'

'How are you going to do that?'

Harry reached for his prescription pad. 'I'm going to prescribe a short course of steroids.'

'But I had those in hospital in a drip and they didn't do a thing for me.'

'That's true, but this time I'm going to give you them in tablet form over a longer period – say, two to three weeks. They may not have worked in hospital but then you weren't in a relapse. You are now and steroids work best against an acute relapse.'

'So there is some hope of recovery then?'

'I can't promise anything with this condition, Julie. But yes, there is a fair chance that with the steroids and plenty of rest things will settle down and improve again. However, it is going to take time. These things tend to come on quickly but resolve much more slowly.'

'How long will it—?'

169

They were interrupted by the sound of a key turning in the lock. Tom heard it too. He opened his eyes and then, remembering his former discomfort, started to bawl again.

'Hey, hey, big fella, what's the problem?' said C.J. as he entered the room and immediately reached down to pick up his son. Then, noticing Harry's presence, 'Harry! What are you doing here?'

Julie shot Harry a glance.

'Oh, just a courtesy call, you know.'

Harry noted that Julie was frantically trying to wipe her face. She didn't want C.J. to notice that she'd been crying.

'Don't try to kid a kidder,' replied C.J. as he made his way over, Tom in his arms. to sit down beside his wife. Harry didn't know to which of them the remark was addressed but he suspected it was quite rightly directed at both of them at one and the same time.

C.J. reached for Julie's hand and squeezed it tightly. He looked directly into her tear-smudged face.

'Do you really think that I hadn't noticed something was wrong?'

'Oh C.J., I didn't want to tell you, you've enough to worry about at present . . .'

'If you think that I wouldn't want to know if you've got a problem, then after all these years together, you don't know me at all, do you?'

Julie started to cry again. Harry offered her his handkerchief. He was pretty certain that it would be more hygienic than C.J.'s. She took it gratefully and started to wipe away the second flood of tears.

'Okay, are you going to tell me what's wrong?' C.J. asked gently.

Harry butted in and let Julie sit and entertain Tom while he explained Julie's recent symptoms to C.J.

'So this course of . . . what did you say it was?'

'Dexamethasone – it's a steroid.'

'This dexa— whatever, it will take away this new problem, won't it?'

'C.J., there are no guarantees, I'm afraid. We'll just have to try it and see.'

Harry wrote out the prescription and handed it to Julie, with instructions on how to reduce the dose every third day till the course finished eighteen days hence. C.J. escorted Harry to the door.

'She is going to be okay, isn't she, Harry?' he whispered as he let him out.

'C.J., I'm sorry, but to be honest I just don't know. What I do know is that each relapse when it comes will take more out of her, and the more relapses there are the less likelihood there is for a full recovery.'

'So basically you're saying that we need to get hold of this beta interferon stuff as soon as we can.'

'Well, according to Dr Anderson it offers the best hope of protection against any more relapses, so basically . . . yes.'

'Thanks, Harry.'

Harry looked C.J. straight in the face. The face that looked back no longer bore the happy and carefree features that so characterised C.J.'s former attitude to life. Those features had been cruelly transformed into a look that reflected only hopelessness and despair.

14

It was nearly Easter and C.J. had been working as a freelance journalist for some months. He was, for the first time in years, able to regulate his own day. He felt somehow more fulfilled now that once more he seemed to have regained a degree of control over his professional life. Financially, though, he and Julie were struggling a bit, but they had cut back, reduced their outgoings, and they were at least coping. C.J had managed to sell a few stories to some of the nationals, which had helped, and then he had been offered and accepted a part-time post with one of the smaller local papers, ostensibly filling in for one of their own journalists who was recovering from a recent heart attack. All in all things were not going too badly. The extra time his new status afforded him allowed him to concentrate much of his energies into the planning of the forthcoming record attempt. Things in this area also were moving forward very satisfactorily. Since the press conference, interest and support had grown. Many of the bigger companies had been approached regarding sponsorship of the venture. Some had freely given contributions but most, while full of promises, were holding fire to gauge the success or otherwise of the venture. With expenses mounting up, things were still far from certain.

There were other, non-financial problems also to be resolved. The starting venue had been suggested as King

William golf club, situated on the outskirts of Belfast, and the finish at the Kildare County Club outside Dublin. The Kildare County Club had been relatively easy to convince, even about hosting the evening dinner dance. One aspect which was strongly in their favour, was that, although when they started negotiations with the owners of the club they were unaware of it, some two weeks after the proposed record attempt, the Kildare County Club was hosting the European Open and the club's owners were keen to attract as much publicity as they could get. The Kildare County Club management had wished to ensure as big a crowd as possible at this Open event, which traditionally was not a major crowd-puller, because they felt that the size of the audience would reflect favourably or otherwise on the Kildare County Club's bid to host the forthcoming Ryder Cup. The management, in fact, perceived the Round Ireland Challenge as a very useful, and even relatively cheap, means to that end.

The committee of King William golf club in Belfast had been less easy to persuade. C.J. and Harry had been summoned to present the case before the council. They had arrived, as requested, at the appointed hour but were still kept waiting impatiently in an unwelcoming corridor outside the committee room for a further thirty minutes, ostensibly whilst the members debated an emergency motion. This motion, C.J. found out later, centred on whether the club would permit ladies into the gentlemen's bar area on the evening of Captain's Day, traditionally the highlight of the club's social calendar. The motion to do so, C.J. also found out later, was roundly defeated. As it had been, C.J. surmised, in every other year that such a radical proposal had been raised.

Eventually summoned forth, C.J. and Harry found themselves confronting the entire club council, all of whom were seated solemnly around a large and equally forbidding dark mahogany table. Glancing around, Harry estimated there to be approximately twenty council members present. Having been ceremoniously ushered to the only two vacant seats, at the far end of the table, they sat down. The councillors focused their attention on the proposals set out before them. Occasionally one of the group would glance up briefly in C.J.'s direction. Harry could sense their distrust of C.J. and his occupation. Journalism was, Harry guessed, not among the favoured professions of the membership of King William golf club.

'Dr Wallace, Mr McCormick, you are most welcome.' The oppressive silence was finally broken by a grey-haired and distinguished-looking gentleman who wore a dark pin-striped suit and was seated at the very top end of the table. Although the words bade welcome, the tone in which they were said actually suggested the opposite.

'Thank you for the invitation,' replied C.J. in his most courteous manner.

'You've come to tell us about this most interesting proposition, I believe?' The speaker continued to regard C.J. in a manner which suggested that he was something unpleasant which he had just spent several minutes scraping from the sole of his shoe.

'Yes,' replied C.J., first to take up the gauntlet.

Harry made a conscious decision to leave it to him.

'I'm sure that the committee will be most interested in the project we have in mind . . .'

As C.J. spoke, Harry took in the surroundings. He observed that the man who had spoken and whom he presumed to be the club captain was not alone in being smartly dressed in a dark suit. Indeed, all those present were similarly attired. All also appeared to be of similar age – late fifties or early to late sixties – and all seemed totally comfortable and relaxed in their own sense of self-importance. They came across as a group content in their position, both within and without this, their club. Harry guessed that all were, or had been, highly successful men in their own occupational fields and, having secured that level of local importance, were now devoting much more of their time to golf, or perhaps more correctly, to the golf club, because he suspected few of them, if any at all, played the game on anywhere near a regular basis. Rather, he assumed, they got their pleasure from drafting, amending and finally enforcing the many rules and regulations associated with membership of a golf club. Harry half suspected that many of the committee members of this particular club harboured political views which might appear as somewhat to the right of Hitler.

The room in which the interview was taking place was no less forbidding than its membership. It was heavily wood-panelled in dark mahogany, adding to the gloom within the chamber, which was only slightly lessened by the pale streams of dappled sunlight that filtered through the heavily leaded windows. Harry sneaked a glance sideways at C.J., who by this time, although still talking, was now sweating profusely and tugging intermittently at his collar. Things were not going entirely well.

'But, Mr McCormick,' interrupted the club captain, 'much as we can sympathise with the altruistic aims of your project, to be blunt, what does our club get out of agreeing to participate in your event?'

C.J. tried to explain that agreeing to participate simply meant allowing Ireland's top professional golfer to play one hole of golf, probably at around 4 a.m., and then leave by helicopter. The disruption to club life would be minimal and, C.J. went on to expand, the club would receive valuable publicity.

Harry quickly realised the mistake. C.J. noted it too. As

175

he later described it in his own inimitable way, at the word 'publicity,' the club captain had reacted as if he had just found a turd in his pocket.

'Publicity, publicity, Mr Anderson? This club does not crave publicity. This is a private members' club. Within these walls the members, many of whom hold positions of high office encompassing many professions within the Province, seek quiet and respite from the world outside. Publicity is *not* an attractive proposition.'

The other members around the table nodded and murmured their agreement.

'If I may interject at this point,' Harry interrupted. 'I don't think that Mr McCormick has quite got the full picture across. We desperately want your club to participate in this event simply because this is to be the start of the challenge, and where else to start but the most prestigious club in Ireland?'

Flattery will get you everywhere, he thought, and it seemed to be working. The club captain was nodding to the council member on his right and was looking much less aggrieved than he had only a few moments earlier. Harry decided to press home the advantage.

'One of your members will have the opportunity of playing the hole with Philip Watson and another the chance to travel in the helicopter with him to the next venue.'

'A helicopter ride, eh! Jolly good show, eh!' The voice came from a small man who sported a sergeant-major moustache, two places to the left of the club captain. Again there was a murmur of general approval. The club captain remained unmoved, however.

Harry faced the captain and addressed his next remarks to him directly.

'Then, of course, Mr Captain, there is the gala dinner in the Kildare County Club at which you and your good lady wife will be guests of honour. On behalf of our committee,

I would wish to formally invite you to share the top table with the other celebrities without whom this event could not take place.'

There was an immediate though barely perceptible change in the captain's facial expression. There was a hint of a smile, or at least as close to a smile as Harry presumed the captain ever allowed himself when considering weighty matters such as those before him. Just as quickly, however, he suppressed any signs of approval or pleasure and adopted his former expression of ambivalence.

'Well, Dr Wallace, Mr McCormick, on behalf of King William golf club, I thank you for your attendance today. You have made your position very clear. As is the usual procedure, the council will appoint a sub-committee to consider your proposals and liaise with you—'

'Could you give us some indication,' interrupted C.J., desperate to get things moving along as quickly as possible.

Harry kicked C.J. hard on the shins in order to shut him up. The captain was in full flow and unused to interruptions. Besides, he felt that that smile had betrayed a done deal.

'As I was about to say, Mr McCormick, I think that I can speak for the council in that, in principle, at least, we have no objection to your proposed event.' He glanced around his colleagues as if assessing their level of support, though he knew that their support, or lack of it, was irrelevant. His, and his alone, was the decision.

There were once again general murmurings of approval.

'Therefore, Dr Wallace, Mr McCormick, you may proceed with your plans and we wish you every success. You may liaise with the sub-committee when the details are finalised.'

'Thank you, sir.' Harry added the 'sir' sycophantically and made to leave.

Outside in the car park, Harry and C.J. analysed the events in the council chamber.

'I didn't think they were going to buy in,' said C.J.

'Yes, it's amazing what a little flattery and bribery can achieve. They just needed a little reminding of their own self-importance, that's all.'

'As if.'

15

Returning to his place of employment C.J. sat at his desk and found himself torn between his commitment to the Round Ireland Challenge, his continuing concerns for Julie's well-being and trying to finish the local newsworthy story on which he had been previously engaged. Resting his head on his hand, he stared absent-mindedly into the middle distance. His new office was much more spartan and much less busy than the larger *Spectator* offices. In proportion it boasted only three desks, which were more than sufficient for the current workforce. Not only had C.J. experienced a downsizing in the actual building but there had also been a seismic shift in his work pattern. Formerlly rushing around pursuing stories, the main emphasis of his working day was now to attract advertising from which the newspaper derived the bulk of its income. This pursuit involved C.J. in an endless round of begging phone calls to many locally based companies, a chore that he generally detested and felt a total waste of his skills. When his new boss had finally offered him the chance to write a report on the expulsion of a boy from the local grammar school on the basis of a drugs find, he had initially jumped at the chance. But he had soon become so bored by the mediocrity of the subject that his mind had started to wander over his other areas of concern.

So preoccupied was he with his thoughts, that he didn't at first notice Billy approach his desk.

'Penny for them, C.J.'

'Oh, hi Billy. I didn't see you there. What do you want?'

Billy was what in earlier and less politically correct times would have been termed the office boy, about seventeen, not long out of school, shaven-headed, baggy trousered and always wearing a fleece, even in the summer time. He clutched a package.

'Delivery for you, C.J.,' he announced, proffering the package in CJ.'s direction.

'Thanks, Billy.'

Billy turned and wandered off down the office. C.J. examined the package. It was a nine-inch by six-inch Jiffy-type padded envelope. Scrawled crudely across its cover was C.J.'s name in black biro but there was no address or postage stamp. It was well past the time for the normal postal deliveries, in any case. It bore no clues as to its source.

Remaining seated at his desk, he tore the package roughly open and reached inside. There was no letter or note, but down at the bottom recesses of the bag his fingers closed on a small, hard, cylindrical object.

C.J. stared at what rested on the pink creases of his hand. For several minutes, his eyes remained totally fixed upon it. His face, too, was immovable; pale, frozen as if a mask. There was no mistaking what the object was, nor its meaning. For there in the palm of his hand lay a single rifle bullet.

After several more minutes . . .

'BILLY!'

Billy turned round from his position at the end of the office, somewhat startled by the sudden summons. He ambled back towards C.J., who had leapt up from his seat as he shouted and now stood hopping from foot to foot in an agitated manner.

'What's up, C.J.? You look like you've seen a ghost.'

C.J. ignored the remark. 'Where did you get this package?' he said, waving the opened Jiffy bag under Billy's nose. He had already slipped the bullet quietly into his pocket.

'A guy gave it to me to deliver to you. Did I do something wrong?'

'No, no. What guy?'

'Just some guy at reception.'

'Look, this is important, Billy. What did he look like? Where was he from?'

'He was just the usual sort.'

'What do you mean, the usual sort?' C.J. was becoming more irritable by the minute. He felt himself shouting the last few words and struggled to contain himself.

'The usual sort of courier, that's all. Black leathers, motorcycle helmet, usual stuff.'

'What firm?'

'Funny thing, that. Didn't seem to be any logo. Not one I noticed, anyway. He didn't even bother to take his helmet off, just marched into reception, saw me, stuffed the envelope into my hand and beat it. Not a by your leave, just disappeared off up the street on his bike.'

'Oh, okay, Billy. Look, thanks. Sorry to shout at you like that, just wasn't expecting a delivery, that's all.'

'Bad news, was it?'

'You could say that, yes.'

Without a further word C.J. picked up his jacket and headed home.

At home, Julie greeted him in the usual way but immediately noticed his worried expression. He had ignored her, he had ignored the children, clearly preoccupied in his own thoughts. C.J.'s anguish was now, he felt, complete; he'd lost the only job he'd really liked, financially he and Julie were starting to struggle, the fund-raising exercise had

181

been proving a nightmare, a constant uphill battle to keep the whole thing going, and then in the background were the all-pervading effects of Julie's illness. And now he had received a death threat. His mind raced. Julie needed his presence and his physical and emotional support now more than at any other time in their lives together. He felt the real danger behind the message he had received, and his first instinct had been to run and to hide. But how could he? He was needed here, there was nowhere he could go. Julie's condition could be made worse by stress, Harry had told him that. He determined that he had no other option but to ignore, as best he could, the message from the bullet, hope and pray that it was just some sick joke and, beyond everything, he would not tell Julie about it.

The issues and implications continued to rotate and revolve around and around in his troubled mind. Julie could see that he wanted to be left alone. Eventually his disturbed thoughts were brought to a close by the ringing of the telephone.

'Hello, is that a Mr McCormick, a Mr C.J. McCormick?' enquired the caller. A female voice.

'Yes it is,' confirmed C.J.

'Mr McCormick, this is Staff Nurse O'Connell, I'm calling from Surgical Ward Two in the Mater hospital. I've been trying to track you down. The *Spectator* gave me your home phone number – I hope you don't mind.'

'That's okay, you've found me now,' replied C.J., not quite certain of the nature of the call.

'We have a patient here who is asking to see you.'

'A patient? Who is it?' enquired C.J., his curiosity banishing his earlier pain.

He heard the nurse fumble with some papers to retrieve the details.

'It is a . . . Mr Patrick Harte,' said the voice at the other end of the phone.

Patsy! thought C.J. So he's back in Belfast.

'Where did you say he was?'

'Surgical Ward Two in the Mater hospital,' repeated the nurse. 'He's been asking for you since he regained consciousness . . .'

'Regained consciousness?' echoed C.J. 'Why, what's happened to him?'

'He was quite badly injured and he's been in surgery.'

'Surgery . . . why?'

'I'm sorry, Mr McCormick, I'm not at liberty to discuss Mr Harte's condition over the telephone. All I can tell you is that he's been asking to see you.'

'Okay, Nurse, can you tell him that I'm on my way.' And then as an after-thought C.J. added, 'I will get in to see him, won't I?'

'Normally it's just close relatives, but if you ask for me, Staff Nurse O'Connell, when you arrive, I'll make sure that you get to see him.'

'Thanks, I'll be with you in about fifteen minutes.'

C.J. did not hang about. He had already decided that he wanted to see Patsy and to find out what the hell was going on. He guessed that Patsy would probably already know about his warning. He determined to question him, to see if he knew just how serious the threat to his life really was. Also, he had determined to get in and out of the Mater hospital as quickly as possible and certainly well before dark. In his mind C.J. was not absolutely sure that what he had just heard was not, or could not be, an elaborate trap. The Mater hospital is situated on the Crumlin road and to get there from his flat C.J. would have to travel through some of the staunchest Republican areas. Anyone observing him and following him would most certainly have the opportunity of kidnapping him along the route, where the police were few and far between. Even those police who did venture along those roads very rarely did so after dark, and even in the daylight hours remained cocooned within their heavily armoured Land Rovers, unwilling to venture out onto the uncertain streets.

Leaving the house with only a brief and mumbled explanation to Julie, C.J. paused at the front door and looked up and down the street. Where he and Julie lived was a dormitory area for Queens University. Most of the buildings, which were tall Victorian terrace houses slightly set back with narrow front gardens and short driveways, had by now been converted into flats, with the exception of his and one or two others. As he looked from left to right the street was largely deserted. At this time of day there were few people about. Most of the students would be in lectures or in one of the many specialist libraries in the area, preparing a dissertation or just revising for forthcoming examinations. Nothing struck C.J. as being out of the ordinary. He climbed into his car, a six-year-old, but older-looking, Ford Fiesta. C.J. was not in the habit of cherishing his motor vehicles, and it showed. The car was off-white and greying in colour. It had probably, in its former life, sparkled in a brilliant white gloss, but that was before C.J. had purchased it. It was adorned with a surfeit of small dents, usually obtained from the doors of other cars, due to C.J.'s habit of parking too closely or squeezing into spaces too small. Nevertheless, to C.J. appearances mattered little, and if anything the dishevelled looks of his car acted as a deterrent to car thieves or joy riders, who would derive little pleasure in stealing such an uncared for vehicle.

   C.J. backed the vehicle cautiously out of the driveway and drove carefully and deliberately up to the Mater hospital. Unusually, for him, he found himself repeatedly checking his rear view mirror and was more acutely aware than at any time in his life of the traffic around him. As he came to a halt and parked outside the hospital, the car that he had been watching behind him for the latter part of the journey pulled out to pass and sped off up the Crumlin road. C.J. noted that the driver was a nun in her fifties and her front seat passenger was older and of a similar calling. They paid no further attention to C.J. once the driver had manoeuvred her car past his. As C.J. left the car and crossed the road and advanced towards the hospital, he was certain, in his own mind, that he had not been followed.

He asked the girl behind the reception desk for directions to Surgical 2 and was pointed towards the main body of lifts at the far end of the foyer. As he stood to wait at the lift others slowly formed a queue beside him. For the first time in his life C.J. noted that he felt decidedly uncomfortable in the company of others. He felt the heat building up under his collar and detected the beads of sweat which started to emerge on his brow. Without explanation he suddenly broke away from the crowd and moved off, back down the foyer. But nobody gave him a second glance. Seeing himself go unnoticed, he tried to pull himself together and was about to rejoin the queue, when he spotted the sign 'STAIRS' to his right. He decided that, discretion being the better part of valour, he would walk. The ward was only on the second floor, after all.

When he reached Surgical 2, C.J. was already out of breath. He gasped and breathed hard and swore to himself that he would reduce his cigarette consumption. He was panting as he sought out the nursing station. There were three blue uniformed nurses seated there.

'Nurse O'Connell?' he enquired.

'That's me,' said a plump dark-haired girl in her mid-twenties. 'Mr McCormick, is it?'

'Yes, I've come to see Patsy.'

'Patsy? Oh Patrick ... yes. Come with me and I'll show you to him.'

She led him down the ward, past the rows of beds, all of which were occupied, C.J. noted, by individuals in varying states of distress. None appeared particularly comfortable. A scene from a *Carry On Nurse* film, Surgical Ward 2 was not. This was the reality of the modern-day NHS.

At the bottom of the ward, Nurse O'Connell stopped and indicated a bed to her right. The occupant was, at first, not at all visible, being curled up under a mound of pristine starched linen sheets. The mound that confronted C.J. remained quiet and still.

'You mustn't stay too long,' ordered the nurse. 'He's still quite weak and he needs his rest. If he hadn't been so agitated and anxious to see you, we wouldn't have let you in at all.'

With that, she turned on her heels and disappeared off back down the ward, leaving C.J. to face the unmoving pile of sheets.

He stepped forward close to the head of the bed and closer to the linen mountain. Now he could hear a soft snoring emanating from beneath the mound. A small tuft of oily black hair protruded from the edge of the sheets. C.J. bent over and reached for where he imagined Patsy's shoulder to be. Gently he grasped it and shook. A sudden tremble of awakening was accompanied by an annoyed yelp of pain. Patsy emerged slowly and carefully from his cover and with the aid of both arms pushed himself gently up into a sitting position.

At first C.J. didn't recognise his former friend, such was the change manifest in him. When he finally did, he took an involuntary step back in horror. His face must also have portrayed his anguish, because Patsy looked at him and said: 'That bad, eh?'

'No, no. Just a bit of a shock, that's all,' C.J. replied hurriedly.

Patsy's appearance had certainly shocked C.J. to the core.

186

His face was swollen asymmetrically and was covered in blue-black bruises. One eye was hideously puffed up and completely closed over, the other, through which Patsy could still view the outside world, was only partially open – and the part that was visible was bright red and bloodshot where the white of the sclera should have been. On one side of Patsy's head some of his hair had been shaved off, to allow for the repair of a 9-inch gash still visible on his scalp. The metal staples that had been used to close the edges of the wound could now just be seen glinting through patches of dark congealed blood, which further contrasted vividly with the surrounding pallor of the freshly exposed scalp. Patsy's appearance could have been almost comical if it hadn't been so real and so grotesque. As Patsy opened his mouth to speak, C.J. could see that his front teeth were missing, replaced only with bloody sockets, giving rise to a maniacal grin.

'What the hell has happened to you?' whispered C.J., recovering a little.

'Punishment beating,' replied Patsy starkly, slurring his words somewhat, due, thought C.J., to a combination of painkillers, the bruising and the missing teeth.

'I thought that you were still safe across the water. Why did you come back?' asked C.J.

'I got word that my mother was sick. She had breast cancer a few years ago, she had to have the breast off and we thought that it had been cured, but it came back. She's been in Belvoir Park hospital on and off since.'

'Radiotherapy?' offered C.J.

'Chemo. Anyway, she's pretty ill. The quacks don't think she's got very long. The cancer's spread to her liver. So you see, I had to come home, when I got the word.'

'Yes, I understand. But who did this to you?'

'I think you and I both know the answer to that question, don't we, C.J.?'

'So this was to do with post office raid?'

'Of course. The boyos have long memories and an unforgiving nature. Keep your voice down, though. The official line is that this punishment is all to do with drug-dealing rather than anything else and I'd like to keep it that way.'

'You mean, you'd rather be thought of as a drug-dealer than an informant?'

''fraid so, it's a lot safer in the longer term.'

'How did they get hold of you?'

'Obviously, the word got out fairly quickly that I was back, even though I tried my best to keep it quiet and kept a low profile. My guess, though, is that they probably knew that I was coming back before I'd even bought my ferry ticket.'

'How?'

'The IRA have connections everywhere. It could even have been a member of my own family that let them know. Anyway, it doesn't matter now, it's over and what's done is done. Or, at least, it's over for me. That's why I needed to see you. They beat your name out of me, and it's probably why I'm still alive. They'll be coming after you next.'

'I know that already,' replied C.J.

'How?' Patsy looked quizzically at him through his one good eye.

'I got a warning, just before the hospital rang to tell me you were here.' C.J. reached into his pocket and held out the bullet for Patsy to see.

'Jesus, put that away,' spat Patsy, looking wildly up and down the ward. 'They don't hang about, those bastards, do they? If I was you I'd try and get out of the country and stay out.'

'Can't do that, I'm afraid. Too many commitments, too much going on.'

'Then C.J., be careful, very, very careful.'

'What did they do to you, anyway?' C.J. asked.

'I was sitting in my mother's house – she was in hospital,

thank God. There was a knock at the door. My brother Brendan answered it and three fellas burst in past him. They were wearing balaclavas, but to be honest I have a fair idea who they were. You don't live in this area all your life and not get to know who is up to what.'

'You know the men who did this to you? Are you going to tell the police?'

'The police? You are joking, aren't you?'

C.J. hadn't been, but he understood the futility of the suggestion.

'Anyway, they dragged me kicking and screaming out of the house and bundled me into a car. Two of them stood on me in the back until we reached a derelict house, somewhere in the north of the city, I think. "The man" was waiting for me there.'

'Did you recognise him?'

'He was wearing a balaclava as well, but when he talked I definitely didn't recognise the voice. He did seem to be in charge, though, and he did all the talking from then on. When we got inside the house the three fellas produced baseball bats and set about me. To soften me up, I guess. It was after they had finished that the lead man started to ask me questions. Mostly they wanted to know who my contact was. Basically they wanted your name.' Hurriedly Patsy added, 'But I swear, C.J., I didn't give it to them, not straight away anyway. Not till after the guy in charge did this.'

Patsy pulled up the arms of his pyjamas to reveal what C.J. estimated to be about a dozen punctate circular wounds on the underside of each forearm. The wounds each had a central ulcer and were surrounded by a ring of reddened flesh.

C.J. flinched at the sight. 'What did that?' he asked.

'Cigarettes,' came the reply. 'I'm sorry, C.J., I held out as long as I could but in the end I had to give up your name.'

'No, Patsy, I'm sorry that it's turned out like this. What did they do after they'd wrung my name from you? Did they let you go?'

'Not quite. I reckon giving up your name saved my life, but they hadn't finished with me yet. Once he'd got your name the leader fella left, but not before he'd given the nod to the other three guys.'

'The nod?'

'Yeah, to tell them to go ahead and kneecap me – you know, that old traditional paramilitary thing, a bullet through each kneecap.'

'They did that to you?' C.J. felt physically sick.

'Yeah, but I was unlucky.'

C.J. couldn't imagine just how much more unlucky Patsy could be. Then Patsy pulled away the sheet that had been covering his lower torso. His left leg was horribly swollen and had surgical wounds and stitches on either side of the knee. The leg was made the more unnatural by discoloration from the iodine wash that had been applied in theatre. But it was not the scars and wounds to this leg that held C.J.'s horrified and transfixed gaze. It was the right leg, or at least the empty area on the mattress where the right leg should have been, that C.J. stared blankly at. He felt the blood draining from his face.

Patsy stroked the bandaged stump that stopped some nine inches below his groin and was all that remained of his right leg.

'What . . . what happened?' C.J. stammered.

'Apparently the bullet went through the artery – it happens sometimes. The surgeons did their best, they tell me I was in theatre for eight hours. But in the end there was nothing they could do to save it.'

C.J. motionless, continued to stare at the stump.

'You'd better watch out, C.J. It'll be worse for you. I'm one of their own. You're not.'

C.J. stood unmoving for a few moments more and then shakily made his way out of the ward. At the exit Nurse O'Connell smiled at C.J., but seeing his facial expression asked, 'Is everything all right, Mr McCormick?'

He didn't answer but simply hurried on out of the ward and out onto the street. He dived quickly into his car. He paused momentarily to light a cigarette, which he did with unaccustomed difficulty as his hands were trembling. Taking a few hurried but deep puffs, he turned the ignition key and pulled out into the oncoming traffic without any due care or attention and only just missing a transit van, which had to brake violently. He sped off down the road and back to the imagined safety of his home as quickly as he dared.

16

The story had first appeared in the newspapers, then it was taken up by the radio stations and finally it got aired on television. The outrage that the leaked memorandum had generated was also steadily mounting. The reports stated that the National Institute for Clinical Excellence had, as Dr Anderson predicted, allegedly turned down any possibility of expanding the use of beta interferon to other patient groups. But it was worse, much worse, than that. According to the reports in the media at least, the committee had deemed beta interferon to be perhaps too ineffective or perhaps too expensive, or more than likely a combination of the two; in any case, they had decided that its routine use within the NHS was in fact not justified at all. The leaked memorandum had gone as far as to state that no more new patients were to be treated with beta interferon in the UK. The committee's only concession appeared to be that those patients who were established on the drug should be allowed to continue to receive it. Virtually every day in the last week any tabloid that Harry read had carried individual and collective heartfelt stories of the very real suffering and misery from those afflicted with the disease. The charities and pressure groups involved in the field were quickly mobilising to try to have the NICE committee's decision reversed even before it had actually been officially announced.

Emma had rung just after the news had broken.

'Hi Harry, it's Emma here. Have you heard the news? It was on the television. Isn't it great?' She sounded overjoyed.

'Sorry, I'm not with you. I haven't had time to watch the TV, I've been a bit busy. What news are you talking about?'

'Beta interferon and MS, it's all over the news and in the papers.'

'What about it?' Harry asked somewhat mystified.

'The Government body, or think tank, or whatever it is, has just reported on beta interferon and its use in MS.'

'The NICE committee?' he added helpfully.

'Yes, yes, that's them. Well, a leaked report is all over the news,' she continued excitedly.

'You mean, they're going to allow us to prescribe it?'

'Oh, I don't know. I don't think so, I think they turned it down.'

'Well, why are you so excited, then?'

'Oh, Harry, you know it's only two weeks till our big day and the publicity machine was flagging a bit. Now with all this media hype we'll probably make the front page, if I can handle it right.'

'I'm sorry, Emma, I don't share your enthusiasm on this one.'

'Why not, Harry? What's wrong?' she said, and he detected the sudden change from her former ebullience.

'Well, for a start, if the NICE report is anti the use of beta interferon, then it's going to be harder for us to get Julie on the drug. Even if we come up with the money to pay for it, at least for a while, both she and I had hoped that the NHS would pick up the tab in the long run. If, as you say, the NICE committee's decision is a negative one then that makes that prospect even less likely.'

'I'm sorry, Harry. I wasn't thinking, I saw it all simply from a publicist's viewpoint. But you are quite right, it is a bad decision.'

'Still, I guess it can make us even more determined to succeed.'

Following Emma's phone call, Harry resolved to ring John Anderson. He eventually tracked him down in one of his country clinics. He confirmed that, although disappointed, he wasn't unduly surprised by the decision.

'How do you think it affects Julie McCormick?' Harry asked.

'I suppose that it doesn't really make any immediate difference,' he replied, 'in that, under the present guidelines, I wasn't going to be able to get her into our beta interferon treatment group anyway. And the NICE report won't stop you from being able to purchase the drug and for me to prescribe it to Julie on a private basis. However, in the longer term, there is no doubt it makes things much more difficult, particularly if you can only provide limited funding which may run out as time goes on.'

'I'm afraid that's very much what's likely to happen. We've set up this event as a one-off, so any money collected is likely to be finite.'

'Then, Harry,' he said, 'my best advice to you would be to release some of the funds as soon as possible and let us get Mrs McCormick started on the drug. Have you got any money in the bank yet?'

'C.J. and Emma have been taking care of that, but yes, I think we have a little. To be honest, I'm not sure how much.'

'Just release enough to get started. I think that's important, particularly if the nice people at NICE do recommend, as has been reported, that patients already on beta interferon should be allowed to continue on it. If Julie's on it when the report is officially published next month, albeit being prescribed privately, it does at least give us the option over time to reassess the situation and see if she has been benefiting from it. If we can show that she has, then that allows us to make a case for continued supplies through the normal channels when the private funding runs out. Do you think you can persuade your sponsors to come up with the cash a.s.a.p.?'

'I don't think there should be a problem, John,' Harry confidently asserted, but he was unsure of the actual position.

The next step was to call a strategy meeting. One was needed anyway as there were still a few loose ends to tie up and, with only two weeks to go, time was running out. Harry got hold of Emma and Julie fairly quickly and they agreed to meet anytime. Julie told him that C.J. was on his mobile.

C.J.'s voice came on the line after a couple of rings.

'Hi, C.J., it's Harry. How are you?'

'Oh, hi, Harry. Not too bad, How are you?'

'Listen, C.J., we need a meeting. There are a few things we need to discuss fairly urgently. Where are you anyway?'

'Here and there, ducking and diving, you know. Generally keeping a low profile.'

'Are you keeping busy then?'

'Well, I decided that with all the effort I've been putting into this ruddy event that I'd try to recoup something from it. I thought that I'd write a book about my experiences, once we've got it all finished. I've been making copious notes. I reckon it'll be a best seller – I'll make you famous, Harry.'

'Any resemblance between the characters in this book and any persons living or dead is purely coincidental. Isn't that what they say?'

'You'll be lucky!'

'Listen, we need a meeting, C.J. I've already contacted

Julie and Emma. Can you come tomorrow, at about seven p.m. Emma said to meet at her place – that way we'll not be disturbed.'

'I'll do my best, Harry.'

'Okay, see you then.'

Emma lived in a small cottage just outside the small County Down village of Killinchy, which lies just above the shores of Strangford Lough. An area recognised for its great natural beauty, Harry had known it from his childhood days, so he enjoyed the drive down to her house through the verdant countryside and then along the shore of the lough itself. The sea was a flat calm, that evening, as he drove slowly along, surveying the scenery as he passed. Over the lough, a group of seagulls swirled and circled, scanning the water below. Then, suddenly, one broke away from the rest and, folding up and then tucking its wings to its breast, plummeted straight downwards, crashing into the sea with a large but silent splash. A moment later the bird emerged beak first from the waves, a tiny silver line hanging from its tightly clenched bill. Up it rose, until it was joined by the other birds, which now swooped around the successful hunter, trying to dislodge its captured prey, so that they might have a share without the necessity of diving into the icy waters below. The successful seagull evaded the others' efforts and then made off into the distance to devour its meal in solitude. Harry could watch such scenes of nature for hours on end, such is their diversity, and leave the toils and tribulations of the city well behind. Emma was fortunate indeed, he thought, to live in such a wonderful area, and he was sure that she appreciated it.

Emma opened the door when Harry arrived. She had heard the crunching of his car's tyres as he turned into the gravel forecourt. Harry kissed her lightly on the cheek and she led him into the sitting room.

'First to arrive, as always, Harry. Do you fancy a beer?'

'I'll just have a coffee, thanks. I'm driving.'

'I'll get it. You sit down.'

Harry sat down in one of the comfortable and well-upholstered armchairs, and as he did so he heard another car pulling into the driveway. Rising and walking over to the window, he saw that it was C.J. and Julie. Harry called to Emma that he would let them in. Julie climbed slowly out of the car and stretched. She looked as if she had been driving for some hours though in reality the journey should have only taken twenty minutes. C.J. also appeared less than his usual self. His brow was furrowed, his expression worried. Harry guessed that the strain of Julie's illness and the bulk of the organisation, for which he was responsible, were starting to take their toll on his usual carefree attitude to life.

'Hello, C.J., Julie, long time no see. What have you guys been doing with yourselves?'

'Oh, just keeping too busy, that's all,' C.J. replied.

'How's the organisation gong down south?' Harry asked helpfully.

'I think it's all systems go, Harry. I've signed up golf clubs in all the counties that were missing and their levels of enthusiasm are high. I can't see a problem. The only county I don't know about for certain is Laois, but you told me that you would get that sorted, didn't you?'

'Umm, yes . . . I'll tell you about it inside.'

Emma reappeared and ushered them inside.

'I heard C.J. asking you about County Laois, Harry. You said that you were going down there over Easter to organise a golf club. Did you manage it okay? You never did let us know.'

'Well, umm, yes and no.'

C.J. looked over to Julie with an expression as if to say I told you so.

'What do you mean, yes and no?' he asked.

'Well, I have organised a venue, but it's not exactly a golf club . . . as such.'

'What do you mean, not a golf club *as such?*'

'I spent ages trying to source a golf club in Laois, but to be honest there really aren't many and those there were aren't suitable for our needs or just weren't interested.'

'So what have you organised then?'

'Have you heard of Portlaois golf club? Apparently it's one of the oldest clubs in Ireland.'

'That sounds all right.'

'Um, err . . . yes . . . but, well, it's like this . . . you see . . . ummm . . . I went to see them and there's no doubt that it is a nice course, but no matter what I said they wouldn't let us near it with a helicopter and a crowd of onlookers.'

'So what have we got then?'

'Well, while I was there, I got talking to a guy who knew somebody whose brother-in-law ran the driving range beside the club.'

'A driving range?'

'Well, yes. It was the closest I could get and they were really helpful and dead keen to get involved. All the staff there were up for it. The owner's promised to organise that one of the target holes becomes a proper par three. Of course Philip will still have to drive from one of the bays.'

'Oh my God,' moaned C.J.

Julie didn't say anything.

'Actually,' said Emma at last, 'it's probably not a bad idea.'

C.J. looked at her incredulously.

'No, look, Laois is probably going to be the second last

county, the one just before the Kildare County Club finish. Time at that stage is in all probability going to be very tight . . . The driving range has a car park, yes, Harry?'

'Of course.' But Harry remained confused.

'And the car park is where the chopper can land, and I bet the driving range is right beside the car park, yes?'

Harry nodded, and tried in vain to suppress the smile that was attempting to break out across his face. To be honest, before that moment he hadn't thought of any real advantages from his choice of venue.

'So no messing about getting out to some distant hole, farting about on a tee box, worrying about losing the ball in the rough – just land, drive off, putt, possibly putt again, back in the helicopter and away. Right back on schedule.'

'I can see the logic, now you point it out, Emma,' admitted C.J. 'Well done, Harry. So it looks like nothing can stop us now.'

'Well, actually . . .' added Julie sheepishly, 'just one thing . . .'

'What now?' Harry asked.

'Just before we set off Philip Watson phoned the house looking for C.J. Of course he was still at work, so I took the message. I told C.J. on the way here. He rang to say, that he's sprained his wrist.'

'Oh no,' Harry exclaimed. No wonder C.J. had looked so worried when he arrived, he thought.

'It's gonna be okay though isn't it,' butted in Emma. 'I mean, he can still play golf, can't he?'

'Nope. He can't. He's been told not to swing a golf club for at least a month.'

'Oh God.'

'It gets worse.'

'How can it?'

'Well, when Philip was told that he couldn't play, he tried

199

to recruit somebody else to take his place. But by this late stage all the other professionals have got commitments and none were willing or able to give them up for our event.'

'Shit.' The word was out before Harry could suppress it. 'Sorry.'

They sat in silence, engrossed in thought for several minutes. Then suddenly Emma cried, 'I've got it!'

They all looked towards her incredulously.

'Right, we're not beaten yet. If Philip Watson can't play golf and there's no other professional available, then there is only one other logical choice of who can go for the record.'

'Who?' they asked unanimously.

'C.J.,' she announced proudly.

C.J. stared at her, stunned, his mouth gaped fish-like. He couldn't speak.

'Of course,' said Harry, just glad it wasn't him. 'C.J., it has to be you. You, apart from Julie, are the closest person to this whole thing. You've got to do it.'

'But, but, how can I? I'm crap at golf, to start with.'

'You're not that bad,' lied Harry.

C.J. looked to Julie for support.

'Don't look at me, you got me into this in the first place. I agree with Emma and Harry, you should do it.'

'Look, C.J., I bet we can persuade Philip Watson to at least go round with you, carry your clubs, give you advice etc.'

'If he would, I think the proposition from a publicist's point of view would be even more attractive than if he was actually playing. I'm sure I can do something with it,' added Emma.

'Will you do it, C.J.?'

'It looks as if I've no choice in the matter.'

'No, you haven't,' the three returned in unison.

The period of self-congratulation continued for a few

moments. Emma brought in some coffee and sandwiches. And then it was Harry's turn to put a damper on proceedings.

'There's just one other thing we need to discuss . . .' he added, and went on to convey an overview of the NICE report and Dr Anderson's views regarding the supply of the beta interferon, particularly his view that if he were going to treat Julie then he would like to start sooner rather than later.

'So can we release some money as soon as possible.'

'I can't see that being a problem, Harry,' said Emma.

'How much have we raised already and how much can we expect after the attempt?'

'That's difficult to say, but . . .' Emma reached into her briefcase and produced a bulging pile of looseleaf papers. After studying these for several minutes and doing a number of calculations on her hand-held calculator, she announced, 'At the present moment we have taken in somewhere in the region of £10,000.'

'That's tremendous.'

'Yes, but don't forget we owe about £6,000 or £7,000 to pay for helicopter fuel, the venues, the catering, the bands etc., etc.'

'So we have about £3,000 profit at this moment in time?'

'Yes.'

'About four months' supply of beta interferon,' Harry musced.

'But there are plenty more pledges, in fact we could end up with as much as £70,000 profit. But only if . . . I hesitate to say, but a lot of the bigger firms with the bigger pledges have only agreed to sponsor a successful venture.'

'You mean to say, if we succeed then we get the money but if we fail we get nothing?'

'That's a reasonable summary, but not all the firms have sponsored us on this basis. If we were to fail then we still would probably make a reasonable profit . . . somewhere in the region of £10,000 to £12,000.'

'But if we succeed we get five to seven times that amount. It's one year's beta interferon against five to seven years'.'

'I'm sorry, Harry, but it was the only way to get some of the firms to come on board. It was easy to get them to buy a table at the dinner dance, and then we were able to persuade some of them to pledge more money on the success of the venture.'

'So from what you're saying, it puts more pressure on us to succeed.'

'I'm afraid it does, Harry. It really does.'

He looked over at C.J., who had visibly slumped in his seat.

17

It seemed to C.J. that he carried the weight of the world on his shoulders as he trudged his lonely way home through the gathering dusk. He had spent the morning at the driving range trying to ensure that his golf game was as good as it was going to get before the 'off' next week. Because of the few hours that he had spent doing this he had had to work later than he would have wished at the office. Now he just wanted to get home to Julie and the kids.

So caught up was he in his own concerns and worries that he didn't notice the car until it had pulled up right beside him. If he had have been more aware he would have seen it pull away from the opposite pavement as he had exited the office. He might even have spotted it crawling along, keeping pace with his own progress, but he wasn't aware of its presence until he had turned off the main street. Then the car had suddenly accelerated and just as suddenly pulled up beside him.

C.J. was jolted out of his daydreams by the car's unexpected appearance and by the loud screeching of its brakes. Startled, he stopped and jumped round to see what the reason was. Too late, he saw the two masked forms leap from the nearside seats. Too late, he tried to turn and run. He was only half around when he felt the strong grip on his shoulder and something hard pressing firmly into the small of his back.

'Get in the car – NOW.'

Dumbfounded, C.J. looked into the menacing eyes that gaped at him through the slits in the balaclava helmet. Then he looked downwards at the object pressing into his back. He could only see the short black muzzle, but knew the rest. C.J. did as he was told.

As he bent down to get into the back seat he felt a heavy push from behind and at the same time the one remaining occupant of the rear seat pushed his head downwards so that he was propelled onto the floor of the vehicle. Two pairs of feet and a revolver pressed hard against his temple pinned him there.

Silence. C.J. felt the car accelerate away and then speed through the city. From his position he could see only the occasional tall building or lamppost whizzing by. The car turned, accelerated, braked and manoeuvred at irregular intervals. The boots of his kidnappers pressed hard into his body and legs. One of his legs felt as if the circulation had been cut off. He tried to shift his position slightly to alleviate the problem, but received a sharp kick in the ribs for his efforts. C.J. lay still after that. At one point the car slowed, came to a halt and then edged slowly forward foot by foot. Some sort of traffic jam, he thought. His hopes started to rise. But as if to answer him the gun barrel pressed even harder into his temple, causing him to grimace with the pain. Then the car was on the move again, speeding quickly along its chosen route.

When the car finally stopped, C.J. was pulled roughly from it and manhandled into a building. He caught glimpses of countryside as he was pushed along, and the building itself appeared to be an old barn. Straw lay around the floor from a few discarded bales, one of which had been propped up to act as a stand for a small oil lamp that provided the only source of illumination in the gloomy interior.

That was as much as he could remember of the location because virtually immediately he was inside, a hood was forced over his head and his hands were bound securely behind his back. He was pushed further into the interior of the building. Then suddenly the grip loosened and he stood alone in the darkness.

Before he could gather his thoughts, he felt a sudden blinding pain in the stomach from a punch delivered with all the force and accuracy of one used to such work. C.J. dropped to his knees. The pain exploded inside him and a well of saliva and vomit surged into his mouth. Another blow; this time something hard struck him across the shoulders. C.J. was thrown forward, unable to break his fall; his face pitched hard into the concrete floor. More blows, and then followed a crescendo of kicks hard into his chest and abdomen. C.J. listened, seemingly now strangely detached, to the dull thud as each blow landed, he felt his body rise and fall with the impact but he seemed no longer able to feel any pain. Shortly after that even those sensations disappeared.

When he regained consciousness, C.J. opened his eyes and blinked. Everything around was dark. He tasted his own blood in his mouth and the pain surged up from his battered body. His breath was warm and clammy and hung about his face, then as his senses returned he realised that he still had the hood over his head. He was sitting, his arms were hooked over something behind him, the back of the chair, he guessed. He tried to move, but his arms were securely bound.

A sound to his left. Somebody was there. C.J. heard a movement. They must have been watching, waiting for him to regain consciousness. When he had tried to free his arms they had seen it. C.J. tightened himself against the beatings' return and cursed his own stupidity.

'So you're awake at last, McCormick?' came the voice in a heavy West Belfast accent.

C.J. didn't reply.

Another punch, this time just below the ribcage.

C.J. cried out and slumped forward in the chair but was prevented from falling by the bindings around his wrists. He struggled to get a breath, choked and coughed. Bloody saliva dribbled from his mouth and soaked into the cloth of the hood.

'Okay that's enough.' Another voice, this time from behind him.

C.J. felt his head being pulled upwards as he was forced back in his sitting position. He continued to gasp for breath.

'Right, McCormick.' It was the second voice again. 'Listen to me and listen good.'

'All right.' C.J. forced out the words. 'I'm listening.'

'You know why you're here?'

'No.'

'Don't mess with us.'

C.J. felt the pain in his neck as his head was forced further backwards.

'Okay, okay.'

'Brian Maguire was a mate of ours and now he's dead.' The pain continued even as the grip on C.J.'s head was relaxed. 'And some of us think that you're responsible.'

The hold released and C.J.'s head jerked forward.

'That's not—'

'Who asked you? Shut the fuck up.' There was no mistaking the aggression in the voice. 'When I want your opinion I'll ask for it. Okay? OKAY?'

'Okay.'

'Now, you just sit there and hear what we've got to say, okay?'

'Okay.' C.J. sobbed silently behind the hood.

'There's only a few of us real patriots left. Those boys that Special Branch murdered, they were part of our firm. You know what I mean? Now we can't let you get away with what you did, now can we? . . . CAN WE?' He screamed the last two words into C.J.'s ear.

'No.' C.J. continued to sob.

'Our army council has considered the matter, McCormick, and we're here to carry out the sentence. So, McCormick, say your prayers.'

C.J. felt the cold hard muzzle of gun being pressed against his temple. He closed his eyes. He thought of Julie, he thought of young Becky and of baby Tom. How could he have done this to them? Although an atheist all his life, he started to pray.

The pressure on his temple increased, then . . . CLICK.

C.J. slumped in the chair and shivered in panic and fear.

'No, McCormick, your time's not up, not just yet anyway.'

'You bastards. What do want from me?' C.J. couldn't stop his teeth chattering.

'We've got a proposition for you. We've been reading about you in the papers. This big money-making scheme of yours. We want to help.'

'Help?'

'Yeah, here's the deal. We let you live. You go ahead with it and then you give us £50,000.'

'£50,000? But . . . but we mightn't even raise that amount.'

'Well, you'd better make sure you do then. Hadn't you?'

C.J. felt the gun pressed hard against his temple once again.

'So, McCormick, we got a deal?'

It was his only way out and C.J. knew it. Right now he would have agreed to anything.

'All right, all right.'

'Okay, we'll take you back now and later we'll be in touch about the money. One word of warning, though. Don't you try anything smart like going to your friends the cops. We'll be watching. You go to them and it's not only you who's dead, it'll be that lovely wife or maybe one of those nice kids of yours ... Do you understand me?'

'Yes, I understand you.'

That was the last C.J. remembered. When he came to he was lying on his back in a pile of discarded rubbish. He blinked open his eyes and stared at the stars in the cloudless sky above. There seemed to be pain in every part of his body but the worst came from the lump at the back of his head. He reached back and rubbed the area. When he looked at his hand it was streaked in blood.

Shakily he got to his feet and looked around him. He was in some sort of park. He peered through the twilight ... something was familiar. Then he knew where he was. He was on the edge of Lagan towpath, no more than a few hundred yards from his own house – another warning, one that told him that they knew exactly where he lived and how to get to him or his family.

He sat on the bank of the river and thought about what had just happened and tried in desperation to figure out some way out of the mess he had got himself into.

C.J. looked at his watch as he entered the house. It was just after 2 a.m. All the lights were out. Julie had evidently gone to bed some hours earlier. C.J. was glad of that. He hadn't been able to decide much as he had sat on the riverbank but he had definitely decided not to tell Julie anything about what had just happened. He crept into the bathroom and closed the door quietly behind him before turning on the light. He pulled off his sweater and his shirt with unaccustomed difficulty and stood bare-chested in front of the mirror. His hair was matted with blood at the back where he had been struck, but it didn't seem to be actively bleeding and what remained would wash off easily. His face was largely unscathed, probably deliberately so, he thought

– nothing obvious to others. But there were welts across his chest and abdomen and dark bruises were already starting to form.

He soaked his head and prodded gingerly at the wounds on his chest and abdomen with a damp sponge. Then, satisfied that he had done all he could, he sneaked into the bedroom, located a pair of pyjamas, pulled them on and slipped silently into bed beside Julie.

Julie had let him lie in the next morning, so that by the time he eased himself painfully out of bed, she was busying herself downstairs and too occupied to see him struggling into his clothes.

'I'm off out,' he called as he pulled the front door behind him. By the time Julie had reached the kitchen door he was already gone.

C.J. looked up and down the street. There was nothing out of the ordinary. He walked to the end of the road, caught the next bus into town, walked around the city hall, then caught another bus to East Belfast. He got off outside the gates to Stormont, now once again the Province's parliament building. He walked up the long straight of the driveway and then sat down on one of the benches to eat the sandwiches that he had bought earlier. As he ate he casually glanced up and down the mile-long driveway. A black Labrador sensing food and making its escape nuzzled against his leg but was quickly summoned away by its owners. There did not appear to be many people about, just the couple with the dog and a solitary jogger ploughing his way painfully up the steep incline to Carson's statue.

Finishing his makeshift lunch, C.J. took another bus towards the city centre but got off after only one stop. Then he waited and caught the next bus going in the same direction and stayed on board for a further two stops. From there he walked down the Upper Newtownards road, turned left into the Knock road, then immediately right into the Kings road. C.J. walked slowly along the footpath for a further two hundred yards, then quickly spun around and made his way back along the same route to the Knock road junction once again. There he stopped and looked up and down the road. Finally, satisfied that he was not being followed, he turned right, walked briskly the final hundred yards and dived quickly through the gates into Police Headquarters.

'You've an inspector in Special Branch, tall, heavily built, rugged features, black moustache,' he barked at the startled PC behind the reception desk.

'Inspector Beattie?'

'If you say so. Tell him I want to see him. And I want to see him NOW.'

'Okay, buddy, just calm down. What's your name?'

'Tell Inspector Beattie, if that's his name, that it's C.J. McCormick. He'll see me.'

The constable retired to the rear of the small office and lifted the telephone, watching his unexpected visitor all the while out of the corner of his eye.

A few minutes passed and then the burly police inspector, whom C.J. instantly recognised, appeared through the security door at the side of the sealed reception area. He was accompanied by another, smaller and unfamiliar, officer. Without speaking, they ushered C.J. into a small interview room.

'All right, McCormick, what's your problem?'

C.J. didn't reply straight away. He just looked at the two men and then slowly and deliberately he pulled up his pullover and shirt, revealing the now confluent bruising that covered his chest and abdomen.

'Jezzzus. What happened to you?' asked the smaller of the two.

C.J. stared hard at the inspector. 'Friends of a friend.'

He went on to tell the two men about the events of the preceding evening. However, he deliberately left out any details about the pay-off. That remained his possible get-out clause and he didn't want to lose that, not just yet anyway.

'All right, McCormick, I hear what you're saying.' The smaller man was doing the talking, the inspector sat back thinking. 'What do you want us to do?'

'If it's not too much to ask, I'd like you to arrest these guys, lock them up and preferably throw away the key.'

'That might be difficult.'

'Why? You know what's going on out there, you must have some idea who could have been responsible.'

'We might have some ideas, yes. But proving it, that's another matter. For Christsakes, you didn't even see their faces, did you?'

'No, but . . .'

'But nothing. You can bet your life that anyone we pick up will have a cast-iron alibi for the time in question. Without proof, there's not a lot we can do.'

The burly inspector leaned forward over the table. 'I'm a bit confused here McCormick.'

C.J. shifted uncomfortably in his seat.

'I don't understand why, if they said they were going to kill you, they then let you go.'

'I don't know, I suppose they just wanted to frighten me first, just to let me know that they were out there . . . I don't know, do I?' pleaded C.J.

'Look, McCormick, the way I see it is, if they were going to kill you they'd have done it there and then. No, things have changed. Most of the terror groups have disbanded anyway, they're all into drugs, money-laundering, protection rackets, you name it they're into it. Whilst there's still a few punishment beatings around, nobody wants to break the cease-fire by actually shooting anybody. They know that would not only bring us after them, but people on their own side wouldn't stand for it either. No, all in all my guess is that you've probably just received all the punishment you're going to get from them. The threat to kill you is probably no more than the fact that they wanted to leave you in a state of perpetual fear and panic, that's all.'

'Then they'd be sure you wouldn't be bothering them again,' added the smaller policeman.

'I don't think it's that simple.'

'Look, McCormick, we can ask around if you want and we can offer you a period police surveillance. But to be honest, I think that it's all bluff on their part.'

'You weren't there, you can't know that.'

'Okay, here's what we'll do. I'll assign a couple of officers to keep a discreet eye on you round the clock for the next couple of weeks. How's that?'

'Big deal. Thanks a lot.'

'Look, it's the best we can do, okay?'

18

Harry felt terrible. It was Monday, June the twenty-sixth and this was the day. The months of what had felt to be interminable planning were about to be tested. Despite, or possibly because of, the restless night that he had just put in, Harry was finding it difficult to drag himself out of bed. Although he had not slept well and was awake when the alarm clock went off, it still startled him. The clock's bell roughly extinguished, all was quiet once again. Most normal people were still soundly asleep in their beds and would continue to be so for a number of hours yet to come. Harry felt tired and lethargic because of his lack of proper rest. He guessed that it had been the anticipation that had kept him awake, but equally it could have been the constant doubt that was intermingled with flashes of optimism and excitement.

Finally he sat up, climbed out of the covers and threw his legs over the side of the bed and reached for his wristwatch. Squinting at the small digits, for it was still dark in the room and the watch's light was dim, Harry confirmed that it was in fact 3 a.m. Just as, innumerable times throughout the night, he had confirmed it to be 1 a.m., 1.15 a.m., 1.30 a.m., etc., and just a few minutes previously registered it to be 2.55 a.m. He rose from the bed a little unsteadily and opened the curtains a little. Unsurprisingly, no light entered the room, for it was as dark outside as it was inside.

He dressed and quickly made himself a mug of strong, black coffee and then left to make his way to the golf club to rendezvous with the others.

As Harry drove along the dual carriageway on his way to the course, there were few if any other vehicles on the road. He felt the coffee starting to kick in and some degree of alertness returning to his senses.

As he rounded the wide, elongated corner known locally as 'the Devil's elbow', the sun started to appear over the horizon. The light it produced was broken into individual rays as it filtered through the leaves and branches of the horse chestnut trees that bordered the road at this point. The number of rays increased steadily and the horizon gradually brightened. The clouds became a blood-red colour as the sunlight penetrated them and then was dissipated. The rhyme;

> Red sky at night, shepherd's delight,
> Red sky in the morning, global warming . . . .

flashed into Harry's head. More worries: was the weather then to turn against them? Harry looked around, taking in the sky from different directions. No, there were very few clouds, it all looked generally clear and was brightening steadily. Emma had checked the weather outlook repeatedly over the last few days and all, she promised, bode well. Just forget those old wives' tales and get on with it, he told himself.

That cup of coffee had made him a few minutes late and he had to be there for the photographs and to see the first ball struck. He glanced down at his watch whilst simultaneously pressing the accelerator. The car's sudden rise in tempo made him look up and concentrate once again on the road along which he was travelling. At the lights Harry turned left onto the smaller road, which led towards the tree-lined avenue that greeted members and visitors of the King William golf club. As he neared the imposing Georgian building that was the clubhouse, Harry could see a group of people already milling around in the car park just outside the impressive colonnaded entrance. Amongst the group, which appeared to number about twenty or thirty, Harry spotted Emma chatting animatedly to the club captain. Others in the group carried cameras or notepads and were clearly journalists who had been dragged from their beds at this unaccustomed hour, far earlier than they would have chosen for themselves on any other day but today.

As Harry climbed out of his car, he could hear in the distance the unmistakable pulsating motorised noise that announced the approach of a helicopter. As one the crowd looked skywards, each person trying to be the first to spot its arrival. To be here so early, it must have left the international airport at the first hint of dawn. Suddenly, out of the early morning clouds, there it was swooping down towards the small gathering below. It hovered briefly overhead and then haltingly started its vertical descent until its runners alighted gently on the tarmac of the area of car park that had been roped off in readiness. Within moments the motor died and the blades ground slowly to a halt. The pilot remained in the cockpit in readiness for take-off, which was scheduled to happen in only a few short minutes. The passenger doors on either side of the craft opened and Philip Watson, who had been seated in the front beside the pilot, emerged first. Harry recognised him instantly from his appearances on television in golf tournaments around the world and from their own video link-up. Others also recognised the charismatic figure and cameras clicked furiously at his appearance. Flashes accompanied many of the photographs as the light was not yet sufficient to ensure a completely clear picture. Philip posed obligingly for the photographs and then attempted to answer many of the questions that bombarded him succeeding, but still overlapping with, the continuing photo-call.

From the rear doors emerged, almost unnoticed, the elderly sergeant major Harry and C.J. had first encountered at their interview at the club. He had clearly stuck to his guns about being the member to travel by helicopter the short hop from the international airport to the golf club. He leapt from the aircraft with great gusto, smiling from ear to ear. He had obviously enjoyed his trip and his opportunity to meet Philip Watson.

At that moment another car drove at speed into the car park behind the small crowd. Its tyres screeched as it came to a rapid halt. The club captain whirled around to glare at the driver. As the car door opened, Harry saw that it was C.J. Spotting Emma, he waved, but before he could come over, the club captain had cornered him against his car and was chastising him for arriving at King William golf club in such a reckless manner.

'I suppose you are one of these press chappies,' said the captain in the self-same condescending manner that C.J. and Harry had witnessed earlier in the year.

'Actually,' C.J. tried to explain, trying simultaneously to back round the car and away from the imposing figure of the captain, 'I'm here to play golf.'

Detecting C.J.'s difficulty Harry strode over to rescue him.

'Sorry, sir. Don't you remember C.J. McCormick from our meeting with yourselves earlier this year?'

Now that Harry was closer, he could see that C.J. was unshaven and was wearing a crumpled shirt that, if outward appearances were correct, might have been slept in. The shirt in parts hung out over a pair of trousers that also looked as if they had seen better days.

'Mr McCormick?' said the captain, looking disparagingly at C.J.

'Afraid so,' replied C.J.

'Well,' said the captain, turning to face Harry, 'will you kindly inform your colleague on the correct procedure and attire when visiting a golf club of the Royal and Ancient.' Then, with one last look of disdain directed towards C.J., he turned on his heel and marched off to rejoin his fellows.

'Who stuffed a bee up his arse?' whispered C.J., when he was sure that the captain was out of earshot.

'I think you just did. Anyway, weren't you supposed to be here nearly an hour ago for the photos etc?'

'Sorry, Harry, I didn't hear my alarm go off and I overslept.'

'Why didn't you hear your alarm go off, this morning of all mornings? Knowing you, you probably just didn't set it right.'

'No, you're wrong. I wound it, set it to go off at two-thirty a.m., as we had agreed, and left it ready to go on my beside table.'

'Well, why in God's name didn't it wake you then?'

'Because it was too far away.'

'Too far away? How far away can you get from your beside table, for Christ sakes?'

'I was in the living room.'

The conversation was becoming increasingly exasperating.

'After I set it, I then decided that it was unfair to wake Julie up at that time of the morning so I crept out and made myself a bed on the sofa downstairs. I just forgot to bring the clock down with me. The next thing I know, Julie's downstairs trying to wake me and I'm late. I guess I blew it, eh?'

'Don't worry, C.J., you're here now and there's a long day ahead and plenty of time to make amends.'

As C.J. strode over to greet Philip Watson a TV crew took in the scene, a background shot of the helicopter and clubhouse and the two intrepid adventurers on film and in full focus. Spotting the camera crew at work, the sergeant major moved into shot and waved furiously into the lens, clearly delighted with his moment of fame. C.J., at first, didn't notice the television crew, but looking around to see what the sergeant major was gesticulating so vigorously at, turned to be caught full-face by the lens. His face, as Harry was later to witness on television, was sallow and furrowed and betrayed his inner anxieties over the day's outcome. He attempted to force a smile for the camera, but Harry thought that the result was closer to a grimace than a look of pleasure.

The media scramble continued for a few minutes more, but then Emma tactfully stepped forward and announced that the light was now sufficient to allow the challenge to proceed, and then promptly ushered C.J. and Philip towards the tee behind the clubhouse. The par three had been chosen as much for its proximity as its particular appeal to members of the golfing fraternity. The drive was a blind one, over a moderate-sized copse and then on over a small undulating valley, to reach a well-appointed green. As C.J. stood on the tee box, Emma pulled a thin, nervous-looking individual from the crowd and announced that he had won the privilege from all the members of the club to play the hole with C.J. There was a round of polite applause, before C.J. carefully placed his ball, waggled the end of the club a couple of times and then struck a truly magnificent shot soaring high over the copse and out of sight. Cameras clicked furiously. Distant applause could be heard from that part of the crowd that had moved off earlier to reserve their places around the edge of the green; the ball had clearly flighted the valley and come to rest in a good position near the flag.

Now it was the turn of the thin, nervous individual. He bent down to push the tee into the ground. Even from

Harry's position a few yards away, he could see that his hand was shaking furiously. Once the tee was positioned, still bending over, he reached into his trouser pocket for the golf ball. In his anxiety to get the ball on the tee as quickly as possible, he fumbled it, dropped it from his grasp and watched as the ball rolled off the tee-box and into the crowd. The golfer looked suitably embarrassed as the ball was handed back to him by one of the photographers in the crowd. Harry turned to Emma and whispered that he didn't think that this guy looked like one of the club's best golfers. Emma replied that he wasn't, he had simply bought the winning £5 ballot ticket.

The golfer's second attempt at placement was a little more successful. Briefly admiring the ball sitting proudly on the tee, he stood back and took a couple of full practice swings, which, to be fair, were controlled and relaxed. Perhaps, Harry thought, he had misjudged him. The warm-up completed, the intrepid club golfer stepped forward and addressed the ball. After standing for what seemed an age staring intently at the small white sphere that was his target, he suddenly and almost unexpectedly jerked the club face backwards and then forwards again, striking the ball before falling backwards, off balanced by the force of the effort. The dissimilarity between the two magnificently executed practice swings and this attempt could not have been greater. That the mere presence of a small golf ball can make such a difference has never ceased to amaze, yet is something that can be witnessed in amateur golf competitions up and down the country, Saturday upon Saturday. The crowd on the tee box swung around to follow the path of the ball, which snaked along the ground before disappearing into the long grass at the base of the copse.

A frantic search ensued for the lost ball. The thin and nervous golfer became more and more anxious as the minutes ticked by. The club captain joined others pacing around and thrashing about with golf clubs or walking sticks in the long grass trying to locate the errant ball. Emma stood on the tee box, head in hands, waiting to usher Philip and C.J. back onto the helicopter. This she could not achieve until the hole was completed, and this required the detection of the lost ball.

The copse was now teeming with people searching frantically; two more would have made little difference.

'This challenge might take a bit longer than we had anticipated,' Harry observed.

'I think he was just a bit unlucky,' replied Emma, kindly.

At that moment a cry went up. The ball was found. The thin nervous golfer rushed up, took out a lofted club and swung aggressively at the ball, which had been lying in thick tuft of weed. The force of the shot lifted the ball from its resting place, but it rose only hesitatingly and uncertainly before plunging back into deep foliage still within the confines of the copse. The crowd in the vegetation surged forward after the ball to resume their search.

'Perhaps you do have a point,' said Emma as they continued to watch the comings and goings in the copse. 'Tell me Harry,' she continued, 'has Julie got started on her treatment yet?'

'The beta interferon?'

'Yes, did we manage to buy it for her?'

'Not yet,' Harry said, somewhat puzzled by the question. Harry had thought that Emma was aware of their agreement not to release any of the funds until the challenge was completed.

A cheer went up from the area of the green. C.J., under Philip Watson's guidance, had sunk his putt for a birdie two, just beating off the challenger, who was a close second with a well-deserved seven. Shaking hands, C.J. and Philip made their way quickly back towards the helicopter. The blades of the chopper were already turning. The pilot had been primed to start the engine as soon as the putts were sunk, in readiness for a rapid departure. More shaking of hands, this time with the club captain and other officials. Emma stood behind Philip, politely urging him forward. C.J. clambered into the back seat already occupied by the sergeant major, who alone was getting a second trip, but to be replaced by a member of the next club in the next county. C.J. had retrieved a suit-carrier and a small holdall and bundled them into the rear cabin between himself and the other passanger. Emma and Harry waited for Philip to break away from the crowd and climb aboard. Harry pushed C.J.'s golf clubs into the small hold, secured the door, ushered the crowd back from the helicopter and then waved at the pilot to ascend.

The engine noise increased, the runners at first shifted slightly on the ground and then lifted clear. The helicopter rose and hovered momentarily a few inches off the ground, before turning on its axis, lifting a few yards into the air, dipping its nose and then pushing forwards and upwards into the clearing sky. More cameras clicked and whirred. The club captain and other members of the crowd waved at the helicopter and those within, wishing them luck for the long day ahead. The outline of the aircraft slowly faded and became little more than a small black dot against the brightening sky.

The small crowd started to disperse and then Emma and Harry too headed for their car. Emma had arranged for them to take the second helicopter to the Kildare County Club, before it had to take over from its companion, to allow it to refuel.

Harry drove Emma to the international airport. Once there, they made our way through the terminal building and on to the business centre. Despite the early hour, the airport was already thriving with activity. Businessmen in sharp suits, smoking cigarettes and drinking strong black coffee, were waiting for the early morning shuttle flights, hoping to catch that important meeting in London. Interspersed around the terminal building were more casually dressed passengers, mostly in family groups, holidaymakers, Harry guessed, waiting patiently for some charter or other.

In the lounge Harry ordered coffee but couldn't contain his excitement, He was up and down off his seat, walking back and forth to the window every time a plane rolled by, or roared up the runway taking off for distant parts.

'Why don't you sit down and relax, Harry. You're starting to make me nervous.'

'Sorry,' he said, taking his seat once again. In an attempt to distract and settle himself, he asked: 'Why did you ask me at the golf club about Julie starting on the drug when you know we haven't got the money yet?'

'It's just that . . . No, it doesn't matter.'

'Emma, you're starting to worry me now. Is something wrong?'

'That's just it, I don't know. Well, okay, yesterday I went to withdraw some money from the account we set up to pay the hotel and caterers, as we'd agreed.'

'Yes, and . . .?'

'And somebody had closed the account.'

'What do you mean, closed the account?' yelled Harry. This particular attempt at relaxation was not going awfully well.

'Don't shout, Harry. It's probably just some sort of error, but they said yesterday that all the money had been withdrawn and the account was closed.'

'How much did we have in it?' he asked despairingly.

'About £10,000.'

'And it's all gone?'

'Look, it's probably just been shifted to another account or something. I'm sure it'll turn up.'

'Who had access to the account?' he asked.

'Just you, me and C.J. That's why I asked you if Julie had started on the drug because my first thought was that you'd gone ahead with the purchase to get her started.'

'No, no, I didn't.'

'So it wasn't you and it wasn't me, so it must've been C.J.'

'But why?'

'Maybe to go ahead and get the drug from John Anderson direct.'

'Possibly.' But in reality Harry didn't think that was the case. C.J. would have gone through him, and even if he hadn't, surely John Anderson would have let him know.

The conversation was interrupted when a dark-haired man wearing pilot's epaulettes approached.

'Ms Duncan?' he enquired.

Emma rose to her feet, confirmed her identity and shook the pilot firmly by the hand.

'We're all set to go. Are you and your friends ready?'

'We're just waiting for the other two.'

'Two?' Harry was puzzled. He had expected Julie but . . . The question was quickly answered by the arrival of Julie arm in arm with Olivia. He glared at Emma.

'Sorry, Harry, she insisted. She is, after all, co-ordinating all the video and audio equipment. I couldn't say no.'

Harry drained his coffee and feigned a smile in Olivia's direction as they set off down the stairs to the runway. The helicopter sat just a few yards away, and as they neared it the pilot informed them of the progress of the other group.

'The other chopper has just left Donegal and is coming back through Tyrone and then it's on to Fermanagh. So far so good,' he said in a refined English accent.

Harry looked down at his watch. It was nearly 6 a.m.

Donegal, that meant Down, Antrim and Londonderry, the northernmost counties, completed. He tried to do some mental arithmetic, 4 counties in 2 hours, then 32 counties in 16 hours, starting at 4 a.m. therefore finishing at 8 p.m. . . . fantastic, well on schedule. But a long way yet to go.

The pilot stowed the bags in the hold and they clambered on board the helicopter. Olivia sat in the front beside the pilot, Emma, Julie and Harry squeezed into the back seat. The pilot ran through some safety instructions and then handed around earphones and microphones so that they could talk when the aircraft was flying, he explained. The pilot started the engine and the blades above their heads started to turn.

'Ranger 125, can you wait till the aircraft ahead have cleared the airfield. Do you copy? Over.'

The headset boomed in Harry's ears. It was air traffic control.

'Roger,' The pilot replied.

It seemed odd to Harry to be privy to these private conversations between professionals. He looked around at the busy airfield, which was just beginning its day's work. On the slip road leading to the main runway three aircraft queued, waiting patiently to get onto the runway for take-off. Another, a British Airways Boeing 727, was positioned at the end of runway itself, awaiting instructions from the tower to start its take-off run. The three queueing behind were a British Midland Airbus, probably another commuter flight, Harry thought, a Logan Air Sky van and, looming up behind, was a TWA Jumbo Jet. The smallest of the planes, the Sky van, looked out of place, towered over as it was by the two larger aircraft. A small intercity hopper, with its twin propeller engines hanging from the overhead wings and its curious rectangular body, appeared alien to the modern jet liners which flanked it.

'Logan Air 237, Logan Air 237. This is TWA 4325, do you copy? Over.'

Harry could hear the slow Texan drawl through his earphones as he looked out of the window. It was the pilot of the Jumbo talking to the pilot of the Sky van as they waited patiently in the queue to take off.

'Hello TWA 4325, this is Logan air 237, over,' came the reply in a strong Glasgow accent.

'Logan Air 237, Logan Air 237. This is TWA 4325. Tell me what kinda plane is that you're flying there? Over.'

'Hello TWA 4325. It is Short's Sky van. Over,' came the reply. The Scottish pilot's voice speeded up, betraying his excitment at the enquiry from the larger relation.

'Logan Air 237, Logan Air 237. This is TWA 4325. Tell me son, didya build it yourself? Over.'

They sat and watched as the planes made their way forward one by one onto the runway and then accelerated, lifting off and disappearing into the sky beyond. Finally it was their turn to leave. The engine noise increased, the helicopter shuddered and lifted. It rose vertically above the buildings, then turned on its axis, dipped its nose slightly and accelerated forward and upwards, rising high above the fields. Harry could see cows and sheep grazing in neighbouring fields below, but they looked so small, like the little plastic farm animals that you bought as a child. A few Dinky sized cars raced along the roadways that crisscrossed the landscape. The helicopter swung south and continued its journey, never rising much above a few hundred feet, allowing for unparalleled views along the way. The chopper turned and followed the coastline. Emma pointed to an area below. Harry could see that it was Scrabo tower, a Victorian folly, on the top of a hill overlooking the end of Strangford Lough. Then on they went down the length of the lough itself, with all of its Drumlins. Emma was leaning sideways pressed hard against the window to take a photograph of her house from the air as they passed over Killinchy. A mountain range loomed ahead, the mountains of Mourne, which, as the song goes, sweep down to the sea. They skirted around the highest of the verdant green peaks, Slieve Donard. Along the rugged coastline, waves were crashing on the rocks far below, before they came to the long stretch of golden sands that borders the small seaside resort of Newcastle. Then they crossed the border. There below was the river Boyne, the site of the battle of 1690 which resulted in that oft-recalled Protestant victory, the one that the Orangeman of Ulster still celebrate to this day. They flew on over the green fields and the small towns and villages below towards their goal.

About halfway down Emma realised that Harry was starting to fidget in the seat beside her. He started to look about the cabin as if searching for something.

'What's wrong, Harry?' she asked.

'It's all that coffee I've drunk. I need to go to the toilet. I'm sorry, I didn't have time, what with all the rush before we left.'

Emma asked the pilot if a 'comfort' stop was possible, only to be informed that it was not, as any landing required to be entered on the original flight plan.

'Looks like you're just going to have to hold on,' she said.

It took about another half-hour to locate the Kildare County Club and by this time Harry was clearly suffering. He had both hands in his pockets and was rocking back and forth in an attempt to distract himself from the pain emanating from his distended bladder.

Olivia was first to spot the huge 'K' made up of flowers

in one of the large beds in front of the hotel. The helicopter swung around in a large arc and began its descent. The chopper hovered over the large lawn at the back of the hotel, before gracefully lowering itself down onto the grass.

'Can't you go down a bit faster?' asked Harry, now sweating profusely.

At last the helicopter settled firmly on the ground. Harry was about to leap out, when the pilot turned around to tell him that, as there was no ground crew, no one must leave the craft till the blades had stopped completely. Harry looked skywards in desperation, but reluctantly did as he was bid. The blades continued to whirl above their heads for several minutes despite being deprived of power. Immediately the blades finally did cease whirling above his head, Harry threw the small craft door open and leapt out. He turned and sprinted some ten yards across the neatly clipped lawn, to the nearest cover, a waist-high but immaculately trimmed hedge. Reaching it, without further ado he stopped and stood, the look of relief spreading across his face leaving no one in any doubt as to what was happening just below the level of the foliage cover. It was only then, as Harry looked up, that he realised the delay between landing and the final halting of the rotor blades had allowed a small crowd of onlookers to gather. The group consisted of the hotel manager, and a couple of porters, there to welcome those who must be guests of some importance to arrive by helicopter, followed by a posse of other inquisitive guests. Harry felt himself flush as he glanced around the sea of somewhat astonished faces staring blankly at him. From the corner of his eye he saw Olivia turn away in disgust. Behind her, Emma and Julie were giggling uncontrollably.

'Your rooms are not quite ready yet, Ms Duncan,' apologised the manager, who gave Harry a withering look as he approached, 'but you are welcome to take breakfast in the dining room.'

Breakfast, thought Harry. It felt as if it was the afternoon, so many hours had elapsed and so much had happened since he had left his bed. But, looking at his watch, he found that it was still only 7.30 a.m.

They gathered their bags from the helicopter's hold and made their way behind the manager towards the magnificent pale Georgian facade of the hotel. Porters discreetly removed the bags as they entered the spacious foyer and they passed on unburdened to the dining room beyond. A large landscape dominated one wall of the dining area but other equally impressive pictures were hung around the room. The manager offered seats beneath a portrait of a rather fierce-looking woman in a black Victorian dress. Harry recognised the expression as similar to that of the hotel manager on his arrival a few moments earlier.

Revived by a large Irish breakfast and lashings of black coffee, everything felt suddenly better. As they talked through plans for the day, Harry became aware of two portly gentlemen seated two tables to his left. Both were in their fifties, both spoke with loud American accents and both wore even louder golfing garb. One had round-rimmed spectacles and was only mildly in excess of normal proportions, the other was frankly obese. Hearing the discussion of Philip Watson and the challenge, the bespectacled one enquired: 'Hey 'scuse me, are you guys part of this challenge thing that's happening here tonight?'

Emma confirmed that they were. The Americans went on to explain that they were on an extended golfing trip to Ireland. They had picked up on the challenge only a few days previously when they had tried unsuccessfully to negotiate an extra night in the hotel.

'Where are you guys from anyway?' asked the large one, whose name was Jeff.

'We're from Belfast,' confirmed Harry. 'Where are you from?'

'We live in New York,' said Harvey, the bespectacled member of the pair, who continued, 'New York, so good they named it twice.'

'Frank Sinatra,' said Harry, confirming that he was aware of the line in the song.

'Absolutely,' replied Jeff. 'Hey you guys, we were thinking about going up north later in the week. Tell me, how long does it take to drive from Belfast to the Kildare County Club?'

Emma looked at Harry, Harry looked at Julie, and Julie looked back to Emma. Olivia looked down at her feet. Harry shook his head and raised his hands, palms upwards, as if to look puzzled and then replied, 'I'm sorry, but we have no idea.'

The Americans were somewhat bemused by this answer and looked quizzically at each other.

'So, how did you guys get here?' Emma asked them.

'We flew,' came the reply.

'Where did you fly into?' continued Julie.

'We flew into Dublin airport,' replied Harvey.

'Couldn't you have got any closer?'

For a moment the two Americans were lost by the question and then the penny dropped.

'Hey, was that *your* helicopter we saw landing earlier?'

Olivia fidgeted, while Harry, Emma and Julie nodded smugly and then dissolved into laughter. It was all going splendidly.

19

After breakfast Emma took her small band around the Kildare County Club to show them the preparations in hand. The hotel was to provide only the accommodation for guests staying overnight, though, in truth, only the more important guests could be housed within the hotel itself – many more were to be boarded in the many chalet-type buildings around the site. Some visitors, such had been the overwhelming demand, would even have to be farmed out to neighbouring hostelries. The hotel was also to host a drinks reception for a select and privileged group prior to the dinner. This was to be held in the Art room, so called because of the collection of paintings by famous Irish painters housed there. The main reception and dinner were to be held in the golf clubhouse, still part of the hotel complex but some five or six hundred yards distant. It had been deemed necessary to move the dinner dance from the hotel because of the numbers involved and the clubhouse's greater capacity. Emma led her group out of the hotel and down the wide sweeping driveway, Harry took Julie's arm as they walked slowly past the practice ground and on to the clubhouse itself.

The clubhouse was a large two-storey building with a balcony which ran round three sides of the upper tier. It stood in a slightly elevated position overlooking much of the golf course in general and the eighteenth hole in particular. The eighteenth was known worldwide as the 'signature' hole of the Kildare County Club course, the green being guarded by a large teardrop-shaped lake from which a fountain threw three streams of water high into the air. It was behind this magnificent finale that the clubhouse sat. On the ground floor there was a small bar and golf shop, but on entering the clubhouse through the main entrance one found oneself already on the second floor in a short foyer leading to the main bar and restaurant, such was the architectural design of the building.

Emma led the way into the restaurant and pointed out the layout for the night's dinner dance. Waiters in smart white jackets were already at work readying the tables. At the far end of the room another group of more casually dressed individuals were also busying themselves, in this case attempting to install a large video screen. Olivia explained that there was to be another similar screen downstairs in the bar area and that these were to enable a live link-up with the progress of the challenge over the last few holes. She expounded the virtues of such electronic wizardry, suggesting that it would enable guests at the dinner to really feel a part of the challenge and sense the tension rise as the event neared its climax. She explained that cameras would also be set up around the final tee box and green, again to allow revellers the chance to view the finale from the comfort of the clubhouse.

From the clubhouse they walked down to the course itself, and borrowing an electric golf buggy they skirted along the edge of the eighteenth, to reach the hole that had been chosen to close the challenge. It was the seventeenth, or it was usually the seventeenth, for the order of the course had been intermittently changed to accommodate a number of competitions – a par three, with a small river running down its right-hand side to catch unwary golfers with a slice, and trees behind the green for

231

those overestimating the distance from tee box to green. Harry could see a number of people frantically at work in the trees beyond the green and also to the left of the tee area. Cables were being laid and a huge generator was being pulled by a tractor, to be secreted, as far as was possible, behind a large foliated area at the side of the course. He presumed these preparations were for the television cameras and video link-up that Olivia had alluded to.

As they inspected the teeing area, Harry became aware of a rather dishevelled man in his early sixties with a pronounced weather-beaten appearance coming towards them. He sported a tatty tweed jacket over a creased checked shirt and a pair of dark blue corduroys. His face was deeply tanned from prolonged exposure to wind, sun and, in Ireland, rain. His deep facial wrinkles turned to furrows when he spied the party standing ahead of him.

'That's Joe Dolan, the greenkeeper,' whispered Emma as he neared. She waved gaily at him.

He ignored the wave; his facial expression did not change. A feat that Harry would have imagined difficult, when someone as attractive as Emma was offering a friendly greeting. Nevertheless he continued his steady course towards them.

'There's people playing golf here, you know. Why are you crew just walking about the course? This isn't a public park, you know,' barked the greenkeeper.

'We were just having a look at the arrangements for tonight, Mr Dolan,' replied Emma sweetly.

'Oh, it's you, miss. I didn't see you there, me eyes ain't what they used to be.'

Harry, spotting the glint in the greenkeeper's eye, strongly suspected that Joe Dolan's visual perception was not as bad as he had intimated.

'I don't mind telling you, miss, if weren't for the boss being so keen, I wouldn't have you here, I wouldn't, an' that's a fact. It ain't right, not so close to a major championship, you know. Damn silly the whole thing, if you ask me, tain't proper golf.'

'Well, you're right, of course. It's only the one hole but it is going to happen very late at night.'

'Tain't that. It's the thought of that chopper landing on me course an' the crowds tramping all over it. What with us trying our best to get it ready for the Open.'

Harry waited for the 'you know', but on this occasion it didn't come.

'But Joe . . .' Emma tried the more informal, friendly approach. 'It will be quite late at night and we expect most people will just watch the hole being played on video in the clubhouse.'

'That's as maybe but what about that?' He pointed at an area about a hundred yards distant where two men were busily bending over the grass with what appeared to be brushes in their hands.

'What are they doing?' Harry asked naively.

'They're painting the "H" for the helicopter landing site,' replied Emma, sheepishly.

'That's a fact,' returned Joe Dolan, 'and what am I supposed to do with that afterwards?'

'You could cut the grass, I suppose,' Emma offered.

'That's right down to the roots, that is, you know,'

'Wait a minute,' said Harry, as he strode over to the two painters and, after a brief word, picked up one of the paint tins and examined the label. Replacing it on the ground, he rejoined the group.

'I thought so,' he said triumphantly. 'It's that special dye they use at rugby matches and the like to advertise on the pitch. It means that it's not paint, it's a water-soluble dye.

The first heavy shower of rain and it's gone. Failing any rain, between now and the European Open, a decent hosing-down should do the trick, Mr Dolan.'

'Oh, well, that's all right then,' replied the unconvinced greenkeeper, who took his leave and wandered off to supervise the goings-on in the woods behind the green.

'I bet he knew that was dye all the time,' Harry whispered to Emma.

'He's been difficult to deal with all week,' she replied.

'I suspect he just likes to be difficult,' suggested Julie.

They returned to the clubhouse and sat round a table on the balcony. There they finalised their own personal duties for the forthcoming evening. Emma, as was her area of expertise, was to be master (or mistress) of ceremonies. Olivia would assist her and also supply regular updates on the progress of the challenge, with video link-ups where appropriate. Julie and Harry would simply do their best to be charming and welcome as many people as possible, thanking them, deeply and sincerely, for their support. Details completed, they relaxed and sat back to watch a few of the golfers making their way round the course.

Emma excused herself to make a few phone calls and Olivia went off to supervise her telecommunications network. Julie and Harry remained in the bar area.

'Harry, do you think C.J. is okay?' asked Julie.

'What do you mean?'

'Well, it's just that over this last week in particular, he's been so withdrawn and moody. He's had no time for me or the kids and that's just not the C.J. that I know.'

'I can't say that I haven't noticed anything, because I have, but I thought that he was just worrying about you and about having to take on the responsibility of the golf as well.'

'Well, I suppose it could be that . . .'

'It must all be a great worry to him at present,' Harry added helpfully.

'Would you have a word with him after this is all over, Harry? Try and snap him out of it. Becky, Tom and I need him back.'

'Of course I will, Julie. No problem.'

'Good news and bad news,' announced Emma on her return to the bar.

'Let's have the good news first,' said Julie.

'Twelve counties completed – they are just coming into Leitrim as we speak.'

'And the bad news?'

'Isn't it obvious?' Harry added, the concern apparent in his voice. 'Look at the time. It's eleven thirty. They've being going for seven and a half hours – they're behind schedule.'

Harry could see Julie furiously calculating the times and schedules in her head.

'But we can still do it, can't we?' she asked.

'I think it can still be done but it's going to be close,' suggested Emma.

'How close?' Harry asked.

'If it gets dark at about ten thirty p.m., then there is still eleven hours left. Twelve counties completed, twenty to go, it is still achievable.'

'But at their present rate of twelve counties in seven and a half hours, in another eleven hours, they will do . . . What's twelve divided by seven point five, multiplied by eleven?

'Seventeen point six,' said Emma.

Julie and Harry looked quizzically at her.

'We've set up a computer to monitor and predict the progress, along with the video system downstairs. I was just testing it out,' she added quickly.

'So seventeen point six plus the twelve we've already done. That's, to the nearest county, thirty. Two short. They'll need to speed up.'

'I'm sure they're aware of that, Harry. Olivia was talking to some of the communication people and apparently there were some problems at one of the holes in particular. It seems they got their times mixed up and they weren't expecting the helicopter so early. The golfer who was supposed to play with him hadn't arrived and they had to stand around for a while.'

'Typical.'

'Never mind, they're off and running again now. It all adds to the tension.'

'Tension like this I don't need, thanks.'

'The first video link-up should take place soon. The TV cameras are in Sligo. Olivia's hoping to get a slot in some of the news channels at lunchtime and it will also be beamed to us here.'

As it turned out, Olivia was better than her word. The challenge appeared on all of the local and many of the national news channels at lunchtime, all of which opened with views from the start at Belfast. C.J's fine strike off the first tee appeared on most channels, the thin nervous golfer's strike on none. There followed shots of the helicopter landing while a reporter explained the nature of the challenge and its aims. After that, a reluctant C.J. appeared, as a banner flashed onto the screen identifying him 'Charles McCormick, Event Organiser'.

'Charles?' Harry said, looking quizzically at the others.

'That's his name, Charles Jules McCormick,' explained Julie.

'I never knew that,' said Harry. 'I've known him for years and to me he's always just been C.J.'

'I only know because he had to admit it when we got married. He's never allowed anyone to call him anything but C.J. ever since I've known him.'

'It's no wonder he calls himself C.J. if his real name is Jules,' Harry laughed.

'I don't know, Jules McCormick . . . it has a certain ring to it,' said Emma.

'Apparently his mother named him after her two favourite authors, Charles Dickens and Jules Verne.'

'Actually it's all very appropriate. If C.J. does write a book about the challenge he can call it *Around Ireland in Eighty Golf Shots*, by Jules McCormick.'

They laughed in unison.

On the television, the scene had returned to the studio and an anchorman announced that the record attempt was due to finish at the Kildare County Club later in the evening. He then went on to report the current progress, and wished the project every success.

Julie, Emma and Harry couldn't help but smile with a degree of self-satisfaction. They laughed and joked and patted each other on the back. The reality that everything they had been planning for months was now actually taking place was finally starting to sink in.

20

Harry spent much of the rest of the day watching people arrive. The earliest generally tried to get in a game of golf, whilst their wives would disappear down to the main hotel for a few hours. Harry suspected that the manicurists, the hairdressers, the masseurs, the seaweed wrappers and all the other beauty salon practitioners were doing a roaring trade. The ladies, quite rightly, were taking advantage of the opportunity afforded to them by their husbands' own indulgences. From all corners of the island and beyond they came, their origins betrayed in the cacophony of accents that could be discerned, discussing this and that, as they busied themselves unloading cars, carting golf clubs or just sitting relaxing in one of the many bars around the complex.

They all agreed that they couldn't have chosen a better venue at which to finish. They were kept regularly informed about the progress of the challenge through frequent updates on radio and television. The outcome was still very much in the balance. No more time had been lost, but on the other hand they had not managed to speed up enough to catch up the time that had already been wasted. However, it appeared to Harry, one good thing was that, given the amount of publicity the event seemed now to be receiving, it had finally captured the imagination of the public, which in turn could only help their underlying ambitions of improving the provision of care to those who most deserved it.

'I suppose you brought your dinner jacket down folded up in the hold of the helicopter,' said Olivia. The evening's dinner dance was to be a formal occasion.

'I'm afraid so. It was probably at the bottom of my bag too.'

'Typical of you, Harry. I expect it's a crumpled mess by now.'

'If you want it ironed, I've got my travel iron with me. I brought it for my dress in any case,' Julie offered, and added for Olivia's benefit, 'You need a good woman to look after you, Harry.'

'It's nice of you to be so concerned about him.'

'Anybody would be.'

The afternoon passed quickly and it wasn't long before Harry was back in his room and preparing for dinner. He showered and slipped into his formal trousers and shirt and then spent a taxing few minutes trying to manipulate his cuff links. Having particular difficulty with the right one, he knocked on Emma's door seeking assistance. She was still in the bathroom but told him that she'd be with him in a minute and just to wait.

Sitting patiently on the edge of the bed, Harry picked up the television's remote control and channel-hopped, looking for something of interest. On channel four, he caught the end of a news broadcast and there they were again, the same initial scenes from Belfast but now a view of the helicopter landing in Cork and C.J. putting out. They didn't give the exact time but Harry reached for a map that Emma had discarded on the bedside table and plotted the planned route, counting off the counties as he went along. Not knowing the exact time of the film that he had just witnessed, he couldn't be sure, but it seemed as if maybe, just maybe, they had caught up a little time. Anything waspossible, he thought.

He conveyed the news to Emma as she got to grips with his cuff links.

'I'm sure everything will work out okay,' she reassured him. 'After all the work we've put in, we deserve to succeed. And if we fail this year we can always come back and do it all again next year.'

'I hadn't thought of that,' Harry said pensively. 'But I suppose you've got a point – and I would like to see a bit more of you in the future.'

'I was only joking, you know,' she smiled, revealing the perfect white teeth he had so admired on their first meeting. 'But which particular bit of me would you like to see a bit more of, then?'

Standing outside the Art room, with his cufflinks now perfectly fastened, his freshly ironed white dinner jacket, his black tie, and a red carnation in his buttonhole, Harry felt like James Bond, the James Bond played by Sean Connery – to Harry there really only was one James Bond. Emma was by his side chatting to some guests. Harry noted with some satisfaction that she looked absolutely stunning, resplendent in her black full-length evening gown.

'You're a shite,' he whispered to Emma as the guests moved off.

Emma looked at him gravely.

'You're a shite for shore eyes, Mish Moneypenny,' he continued in his best Edinburgh accent.

A waiter emerged and offered glasses of champagne from a silver tray. They toasted each other. Harry heard the elevator arrive in the foyer and its doors open. From it emerged Julie. It was, he remarked to himself, the Julie of old. There was a sparkle in her eyes and she flashed a radiant smile. She looked superb in her vivid blue evening dress. The only thing out of place as she turned towards them was that single health service issue crutch that she was using for support. It tugged at Harry's heart strings to see this one blemish on such an otherwise perfect portrait.

Spying Emma and Harry at the door, Julie gave such an enthusiastic wave that she nearly overbalanced. She clearly couldn't contain her excitement.

'Harry, this is wonderful, simply wonderful,' she enthused. 'Such a beautiful place and the people have been so nice to me. Did you know that they have put C.J. and me up in a suite?'

'I should hope so too – you are the guests of honour, you know,' he replied.

Julie blushed a little, and still unable to contain herself, continued, 'Never in a million years could C.J. and I afford to stay in a place like this, Harry. Thank you so much.'

'Don't thank me. Everybody's been very generous, and anyway you deserve it.'

'But you should see the room. It hasn't got a number it's got a name, "The Viscount Suite". I walked in and at first I couldn't understand why there was no bed, then I realised that this was a living room, with silk, real silk, curtains and sofa covers, a TV, drinks cabinet – the lot. Then the porter took me through a door to the bedroom. It's huge, Harry, nearly as big as our whole house, and it's got a four-poster bed. I couldn't believe my eyes. I suppose I started to babble. C.J. would have told me to calm down. He would try to act cool, like he stays in these sort of places all the time. Then the best bit, Harry. Through another door and into a huge marble bathroom, his and hers individual wash-hand basins. His and hers – I ask you, why? But then in the middle a massive sunken bath big enough for two. The whole thing feels like a dream. I can't wait for C.J. to get here and share it. In fact it's so good I wish the kids could be here as well.'

'No you don't, that's going too far. You guys deserve the

break. Take a few pictures to show them when you get home, make them jealous.'

'I'll do that, Harry. I can't thank you enough, you know. You've been so good to me.'

She leant forward and kissed him lightly on the cheek. Harry felt a tear well up in the corner of his eye, but he rubbed it away before she straightened up and saw it.

'It's all so wonderful, but the only thing that I've found difficult,' Julie continued, more seriously, 'is the fact that, because of all the publicity in the last few weeks, strangers, complete strangers, have been coming up to me in the street and wishing me good luck, or even starting a conversation, as if they know me. A child, he must have been about nine years of age, you won't believe it, asked me for an autograph the other day.' Julie laughed again.

'You're a celebrity now,' Emma quipped. 'They'll be asking you for a photograph next.'

'Don't mention photographs with Harry around,' said Julie, glancing in his direction.

Harry felt himself blush.

'What do you mean?' asked Emma inquisitively.

'You mean you haven't heard about Harry's collection of celebrity photographs?'

'I'm sure Emma doesn't want to be bored by stories of me off duty,' Harry quickly interrupted.

'Oh yes, I do,' replied Emma just as quickly.

'Well, sometimes when he and C.J. are out and about,' Julie continued, 'they bump into somebody famous – a celebrity, a television personality, a showbiz star, a well-known politician or somebody of similar ilk.'

'As you do.'

'Exactly. Well most of us would just take a confirmatory glance and then try to act as if they weren't there. But not Harry. He insists on approaching them and engaging them in conversation, and after a while, out comes the camera.

242

He has a little pocket camera that he carries around quite frequently, for just such occasions. Then holding the camera up, he says to the celebrity, "Look, I know this happens to you all the time, but would you mind a photograph?" The celebs invariably agree, smile sweetly and straighten their hair, waiting for their picture to be taken.'

'Seems okay, so far.'

'But then Harry hands the camera to the unwitting celebrity and stands back himself, hands firmly by his side, smiling broadly, and waits patiently for the celebrity to take his photograph.'

'I don't believe you,' laughed Emma, looking incredulously in Harry's direction.

Harry blushed even more deeply.

'He gets the celebrities to take *his* photograph? They're not even in it?'

'Honestly, it's true. He's got hundreds of them. They're all of him, all exactly the same and all taken *by* some celebrity or other.'

'How do the celebrities react?'

'Actually, most find it quite amusing,' Harry added, hopefully in his own defence.

'He calls it "the Irish celebrity photograph",' laughed Julie.

As they continued their conversation, Harry spotted Dr John Anderson passing through the hotel foyer. He waved and ambled over to join them. Emma and Julie greeted him warmly.

'Are you joining us for the champagne reception?' Harry asked.

'Actually, I was just going for a walk. I never feel particularly comfortable at these formal dos. And thanks to you, I've got to prepare my speech. I thought a little fresh air would help clear my head sufficiently.'

'We'll see you at dinner, then. Don't run off.'

243

'Of course not. See you later.' He gave a cursory wave and left for his stroll. Emma led the others in the opposite direction and into the reception itself.

The Art room was already crowded as they entered. A number of waiters and waitresses bearing trays of champagne eased their way carefully between the chatting groups. Some guests stood around admiring the collected artwork displayed on the walls, others gathered in larger groups talking animatedly. Harry spotted a number of well-known faces among the gathering, faces from television and politics, many of whom he guessed were regular invitees at such events. The captain of King William waved at them from a small group of men, all of whom looked as if they were golf club captains. Harry thought that he could over-hear discussions on golfing matters. He waved back a friendly wave of greeting but resolved to try to avoid that particular group at all costs. Over towards the window, two gentleman of middle years, each wearing a chain of office around his neck, shook hands and stood chatting amicably for several minutes. Harry turned to Emma.

'That's not something you see very often.'

'What's not?' she asked.

'Over there.' He indicated the two gentlemen at the window. 'That is the Unionist mayor of Belfast having a chat with the mayor of Dublin.'

Such a thing would never have happened before the recent peace process. It made him feel proud that it was happening now, and happening at an event with which he was so intimately associated.

Harry's moment of self-praise was almost immediately interrupted by a man in a town crier's hat, a loud red uniform and an even louder voice, who picked that moment to announce that dinner was about to be served. They were to make their way to the front door, where transport to the clubhouse was waiting.

Emma and Harry chose to walk. It was still warm and the cloudless sky and mild cooling breeze offered a few minutes' respite from the busy evening ahead.

'Did you ever think it would happen, Harry?' Emma asked, as they walked slowly along admiring the view on all sides.

'To be honest, when we sat talking about it all those months ago, I never imagined that we could pull it off.'

'We're not out of the woods yet,' returned Emma. 'It's still touch and go whether the challenge succeeds or not, but I know what you mean.'

They stopped and stood in the driveway and Harry gave her a hug, just a friendly, uncomplicated sort of a hug that conveyed the sheer joy that the day so far had afforded.

Above the doorway to the clubhouse a large banner proclaimed THE ROUND IRELAND CHALLENGE. Stepping below it and into the foyer, the first thing to hit Harry was the noise. When they had been down to the clubhouse earlier in the day, it had been quiet and serene, the way one had come to expect golf clubhouses to be. Now there was a general buzz of excitement and chatter. Crowds of smartly dressed men and women milled about, talking briefly with one group before passing on to the next. More waitresses squeezed through the melee, offering fresh drinks and removing spent glasses. A string quartet seated in the corner of the dining area struggled to be heard over the general level of background noise.

Many of the diners were already seated at tables in the main dining room, others were by now starting to make their way to their allotted positions. A large crowd milled around a board bearing the seating plan, trying to locate their predetermined table. Harry and Emma reunited themselves with Julie. She had been chatting with Olivia, who had spent most of the early evening in the clubhouse readying herself for the events to follow. They edged their way carefully to the top table, where Dr Anderson was already positioned. Harry noted the two lord mayors and lady mayoresses and the guest speaker, a television newsreader from RTE, who were attempting to make their way through the maze of tables to join them.

Formal introductions made, they were quickly seated. Almost immediately efficient white-shirted waitresses appeared at their shoulder, bearing plates of melon and Parma ham. Others, equally efficient, charged their glasses with chablis, and the dinner was under way. Harry glanced across at John Anderson, who was busily shuffling a series of small cards that he had pulled from his pocket. He guessed that he was going over his notes for his speech. He was suddenly disturbed from his revisions by a loud clapping and cheering reverberating around the room.

'What was that for?' Harry asked as the clapping died away.

Emma, who was seated a few places to his right, pointed to an area behind him with a large electronic map of Ireland. Harry had noticed it on the way in but had paid it no heed.

'Sorry, I know it's a bit tacky,' she said, 'but it does keep everybody informed of what's going on. The map charts the progress of the challenge. As each county is completed it lights up on the map. When it's all done, the whole country will be illuminated.'

Harry looked over his shoulder at the map. He hadn't appreciated it at his first cursory inspection, but she was right: the country was divided up by county boundaries, and by now, most of the counties were shining brightly. Down in the bottom right-hand corner, around the Dublin area, a small number of counties remained dark and unlit.

'So why the cheer?' he repeated.

'County Tipperary just lit up.'

'*It's a long way from Tipperary, it's a long, long way to go,*' sang the RTE television presenter who was seated beside Emma.

'Thanks for that encouragement,' Harry replied.

The meal passed pleasantly enough, with polite conversation from all sides. Two further cheers had gone up during dinner as counties Kilkenny and Wexford were illuminated on the map behind them. Coffee and liqueurs arrived and then it was time for the speeches. The gentleman in the red uniform appeared and placed a microphone in front of Emma. The usher banged loudly on the table with a gavel and asked for silence. Emma rose to her feet, with outward confidence. Knowing her now, Harry could detect that she was slightly nervous, but that just seemed to make her even more appealing.

'Ladies and gentlemen. To success,' she began.

There was a loud cheer and everybody raised their glasses.

'By the way, do you know what the secret of success is?'

Hushed silence. She had immediately and completely captured the attention of her audience, all heads were now turned towards her. Unsurprising, given her chosen subject matter in an audience made up of the rich and successful, to whom any added knowledge on how to accumulate even more money and power was always gratefully received. A few around the room whispered their particular secret to those seated next to them, but most listened on intently.

'Let me tell you the secret of success,' she continued,

deliberately surveying the faces around her. 'The secret of success is . . .' She paused, for dramatic effect. '. . . sincerity.'

She paused again. A few of the younger people present giggled quietly, but most of the older guests nodded wisely and glanced left and right to like-minded fellows, who nodded equally wisely back.

'Yes,' Emma continued, 'the secret of success is sincerity . . . Once you learn to fake that you can do anything.'

Raucous laughter broke out from all directions. Very clever. Well done, Emma, Harry thought, you've captured their attention and charmed them at once. As soon as the laughter had died back, Emma continued with the main body of her speech.

'Success, and I mean that sincerely – '

More sporadic laughter.

'That is what we are hoping for today, a successful outcome to a venture that has been many months in the planning. At the moment the success or failure of our record attempt remains very much in the balance. We have . . .' She looked around at the illuminated map. '. . . one, two, three, four more counties to get round. It is . . .' She glanced down at her watch. '. . . nine thirty. There are two and a half hours left of the day but, more importantly, only about one more hour of daylight. It's going to be very close. Olivia Newman has organised a live video link-up in the last two counties before here.' She nodded in Olivia's direction. 'And we hope that will happen soon. If the video comes on I'll shut up and sit down.'

Loud cheers.

'Though, to be honest, you know, the idea behind this whole event has not just been about the success or failure of a golf challenge. It has been about something much more important than that, it has been about highlighting the plight of people with multiple sclerosis and the inade-

248

quacies of treatment, both north and south of the border. In this I feel our efforts have already been successful.'

Emma looked over at Julie and, although she didn't say anything, the audience had picked up on the reference and followed her gaze. Applause rang out around the room. Julie looked embarrassed.

'To tell you a bit more about the reasons behind today's event, I would like to introduce Dr John Anderson.'

Emma gesticulated towards John Anderson, who was frantically searching his pockets for his notes and looking more than a little embarrassed at having been caught unawares.

'Dr Anderson is a leading consultant neurologist, at the world-famous Royal Victoria hospital in Belfast. Dr Anderson . . .'

The red uniform appeared from the shadows and carefully manoeuvred the microphone from in front of Emma to place it in front of John Anderson. The neurologist rose to his feet, pulled the now located notes from his pocket and then proceeded to give an astute and eloquent speech about the disease of MS, its manifestations, prognosis and consequences without once referring to the notes that he had so meticulously prepared.

Following Dr Anderson, the mayors of Belfast and Dublin each took turns at applauding the cross-border co-operation that was integral to such an event. Then it was over to the guest speaker from RTE.

He was well known for his television appearances and was greeted warmly by the audience. He stood up confidently and launched into a series of golfing anecdotes and jokes, most of which Harry, at least, had heard before. Still they had seemed to be well received, with the possible exception of the one about the priest, the nun and the hole in one, which Harry sensed some of the ladies present baulked at.

But when he sat down again some twenty minutes later, he received a generous round of applause.

Emma rose to her feet once more, but as she did so, the video screen to her left suddenly came to life. A ripple of laughter circulated the room. Emma, true to her word, immediately sat down again. A steward brought in another cordless microphone and handed it to Olivia. Harry's ex-wife stood up, moved over to beside the screen and announced that the first of the satellite link-ups was coming through. It was from Wexford, the thirtieth county to be played. A new face appeared on the large screen.

'Hello, the Kildare County Club, can you hear me?' said the unfamiliar broadcaster.

'Loud and clear, Damian, loud and clear. We can see you too,' returned Olivia into the microphone.

'That's great, Olivia. It's a glorious night here in County Wexford. I'm sure it's the same for you up at the Kildare County Club. Anyway, sorry to interrupt your festivities but the chopper has just come into view. It should be landing here any minute now.'

The view switched to a scene of green fields and then panned upwards to where the aircraft was now hovering a few yards up in the sky. Harry could see figures waving from the helicopter windows to those assembled below.

'There's a great crowd turned out here to see C.J. and Philip Watson play this hole,' said the now unseen announcer.

On screen, the helicopter could be seen to touch down and its passengers quickly alight. More shaking of hands and then on to the par three. C.J's playing partner on this occasion was somewhat more adept than the last one Harry had witnessed, and both players in a matter of a few moments had achieved their par threes. On the way back to the helicopter the intrepid reporter managed a snatched interview with C.J. himself.

'How's it going?' was apparently the only searching question he could think of.

'From my perspective, pretty good. You can tell Harry back there at the Kildare County Club that I'm actually only four over par for the round so far.'

A spontaneous burst of applause from the audience in the dining room.

'From a more general standpoint, though, not so good, we've still two counties to go and it's starting to get pretty dark. So, sorry guys, we can't hang around, gotta fly.' With that, C.J. broke away from the reporter and clambered back on board the helicopter, which within minutes was seen to lift off and disappear into the darkening sky.

Harry looked intently at his watch: 10.18. They had calculated nightfall at 10.30. Everything had been geared to finishing around that time. The receptions were to be followed by the dinner and speeches. It was then that the helicopter was supposed to fly in, C.J. would play the hole, sink the putt, the band would strike up and the party would start. Everything was running on time – except the main event. And now it looked, to Harry, at least, that because the light was fading so rapidly there wasn't even going to be a main event. He broke away up from his private and depressing analysis. He was aware that Emma was back on her feet.

'It looks as if C.J. and Philip won't be with us for a while yet, but we do have the magnificent Magic Moments show band here to entertain us into the wee small hours.'

More cheering and applause. Harry guessed that the wine waiters had carried out their task of refilling the empty glasses with more efficiency and enthusiasm than their employers had probably hoped for. The result was that the masses were becoming easier to amuse and entertain.

'But before the band comes on, I'd just ask you to join with me in thanking a few people here tonight. Firstly our speakers . . .'

Thunderous applause.

'I'd also like you to thank the caterers and our magnificent hosts, the Kildare County Club, who have treated us royally . . .'

More applause. Though personally Harry wasn't sure if 'royally' was the best choice of adverb in the Irish Republic.

'I'd also like to thank my fellow conspirators, Dr Harry Wallace, Mrs Julie McCormick and not forgetting Mr C.J. McCormick himself, who at present is riding around Ireland in the helicopter with the one and only Philip Watson, without all of whom today and tonight would not have happened . . .'

With that, Emma sat down to applause and whistles reverberating around the room.

At the other end of the room the band struck up. Plied with drink and already in good spirits, many of the guests were quickly up onto the dance floor and gyrating wildly to the music. By the time the band was halfway through their third number the dance floor was packed with bodies.

Then the music stopped, suddenly and unexpectedly. Some people on the dance floor booed, others looked around for an explanation. It was not difficult to spot. The video screen behind the top table was alive again and another fresh-faced reporter was trying to make himself heard.

'. . . the penultimate hole here in County Laois,' blared from the screen. 'It's pitch black here . . .'

Harry looked at his watch: 10.45.

'. . . but the helicopter was able to land by the lights of the car park and full marks to the organisers for choosing a driving range. The arc lights over the driving bays mean there should be no difficulty in seeing the ball to drive and putt.'

The camera panned around away from the reporter's

illuminated face, past the gloom and onto the brightly lit driving range with its newly constructed par three. A large vociferous crowd had gathered to witness the arrival of C.J. and Philip Watson in their small village.

The crowd watched C.J. and his new partner play the hole and as they made their way back towards the helicopter. In the background, Harry spotted Philip Watson strike a match and light one of his trade mark over-sized cigars. Clearly he was content with the progress so far. Harry watched with interest as they clambered back aboard the helicopter and the blades started to turn.

Harry turned to ask Emma whether she'd spotted Philip's cigar, when the sudden silence in the room and the sea of faces staring intently at the video screen told him something was wrong. He turned around. The helicopters blades were stopping again. The camera zoomed in on the cockpit. Harry could see some frantic discussions going on. For several moments there was no movement. Then the reporter's face came on screen again.

'There appears to be something wrong ... I'm going over to see if I can find out what's happening.'

The camera followed him as he made his way carefully over to the stricken aircraft. The passenger door was ajar and Philip Watson could be seen sitting impassively looking at the pilot, who in contrast struggled frantically with a number of buttons and knobs in front of him. He also appeared to be talking into his headset.

'What's the problem, Philip?' asked the reporter.

'It seems that a warning light has come on, something to do with the rotor blades. Apparently the pilot can't find anything wrong but he can't ignore the light.'

Behind Philip, the pilot shook his head and leant over towards Philip and the reporter.

'I'm sorry, we can't take off. I've requested the urgent

assistance of an aircraft engineer, but he's got to come from Dublin airport and then I don't know how long it will take to fix whatever's wrong.'

From the back seat C.J. leant forward into view. 'What about the other chopper? Can he come and get us?'

The pilot switched on his microphone and spoke into it for several minutes. Then he turned back to C.J.

'It's no go, I'm afraid. Control thought that the event was virtually over and ordered him back to base in Belfast. By the time they get hold of the pilot again, refuel the craft and fly it down here, it would be well past midnight. Sorry, chaps it—'

Before he had a chance to finish his sentence, there was a blur of activity as a crumpled golfer leapt from the aircraft and sped past the camera.

The crowd at the Kildare County Club stood or sat in silence looking up at the screen. Everything seemed to have stopped, suddenly everything was in limbo. Nobody knew what to say, what to do. Several minutes passed in silence. Then: 'Right, Philip out!' came a cry from off camera. Harry recognised the voice as C.J.'s.

The camera whirled around. C.J. stood in the middle of the car park, beside a middle-aged man in T-shirt and jeans whom Harry didn't recognise.

'Come on, I've got us a lift, we're going the rest of the way by car. Get my gear and let's get moving.'

A huge cheer went up all around. On the screen Harry could see Philip leap from the helicopter and, clubs and bags thrust under his arm, clamber into the back seat of a dilapidated Volvo estate, which then took off in a blur of red lights.

The band resumed the upbeat tempo and the dinner guests, festive spirits restored, returned to the dance floor or joined the throng at the bar. The background noise intensity escalated with anticipation. Harry sat on at the

254

table for a few moments longer but then rose, grabbed a bottle of Budweiser from the table top, and made his way slowly and forlornly across the room and out onto the balcony. Somehow he no longer felt inclined to partake in the premature celebrations.

The balcony was virtually deserted when Harry exited the function room through the panelled glass door, most guests preferring the noisy smoky atmosphere indoors to the cool breeze outside. Only one other couple stood on the balcony, by the rail, and they were too engrossed in each other's company to even register Harry's presence. He didn't feel inclined to talk in any case and made his lonely way to the far end of the balcony. There he sat down on one of the metal chairs, put his feet up on another, and sipped at the beer. There he remained in silence for a while, just sitting quietly, sipping, looking out over the lake that guarded the eighteenth green. The fountain of water even at this late hour still rose high in the air and then fell back, scattering and dappling the reflected lights from the clubhouse over the lake's surface. He stared out at the crazy patterns that resulted, which changed from minute to minute as the ripples moved out from their centre and overlapped. Harry looked past the lake as far as he could see, to where the seventeenth, their hole, their final hole, should have been. But there was nothing, just a black void. It was 11.15 and it was completely dark.

It was over.

Even if C.J. and Philip got here, and that wasn't certain – Portlaoise was at least twenty miles away, along Irish roads – and at night, C.J. couldn't play the hole, not in complete darkness. In his mind Harry started to conjure up crazy ways to solve the impasse. Perhaps they could persuade the guests to come out to the hole and to position themselves all around the green, in the rough, in the wood and then when C.J. hit the ball, they could listen for it landing near them. No, he thought, somebody would get hit by the ball and probably end up dying or suing them or something, and that would surely be a fine end to the day.

What if C.J. just hit the ball a few feet and they followed him with a torch? Then he hit it again a few feet, and again and again. That would be possible, but farcical. To finish a par three with a twenty or worse . . . no, C.J.'s pride wouldn't let him do that. No, there wasn't any doubt, it was finished, it was over. They had failed, and at the last hurdle too.

Harry drained the bottle and set it down on the floor beside him. He sat on, unwilling to rejoin the party, which continued inside unaware of, or oblivious to, the forthcoming disappointment. He continued to stare blankly into space, so engrossed in his own thoughts that he didn't hear Emma exit the party and step out onto the balcony behind him. She stood for a moment, but Harry remained unaware of her presence until she spoke:

'Penny for them, Harry.'

Harry jumped round, startled.

'What are you doing out here all on your own? Don't you know that there's a party going on inside?' she continued.

'Sorry, Emma, I didn't see you there. I just wanted a bit of time alone – you know what it's like.'

'Yes, it is a bit noisy in there.'

'No, it's not that. I just feel a bit down, that's all.'

'Down? What do you feel down about?'

'Well, we can't complete the event now, can we? It's pitch black. It's all very well having floodlights at a driving range but this is the middle of the countryside. You can't very well have lights out there, can you?' Harry pointed vaguely in the direction of the golf course now enveloped in a blanket of darkness.

'Oh ye of little faith,' replied Emma.

Harry stared blankly at her. Emma reached into her handbag, withdrew her mobile phone, dialled a few numbers and then, lifting the phone to the side of her head, she spoke a few quiet instructions into the mouthpiece.

Somewhere out in the distance, Harry heard an engine start and then continue to hum methodically. A moment later and the horizon ahead lit up. Huge floodlights blazed from trees around the seventeenth green, which now shone brightly and vividly in the near distance. Harry stood up, amazed. A cheer went up from inside the clubhouse; people had stopped to look out of the window when the lights went on.

'What did you think all that cabling was for this morning, Harry?'

'Emma, you are a star.' He hugged her tightly.

'What's going on here, then?' said Olivia as she walked across the balcony to find them in each other's arms.

'Er . . . nothing,' Harry coughed. 'Emma's just saved the day, that's all.'

Leaving the balcony, they gathered up Julie and then as a small group they made their way down to the front door to wait the arrival of the Volvo bearing C.J. and Philip. Outside, Harry paced about incessantly. Having faced up to defeat but then come to the realisation that success was still possible, he was more determined than ever not to sense failure again.

'Try to relax, Harry. You're making me nervous,' said Olivia. Then she and Emma disappeared down the path that ran alongside the clubhouse and led to the course itself. Julie watched as Harry continued his nervous pacing alone. A couple of minutes elapsed and then he heard an engine roar and the pair returned, each at the wheel of a golf buggy.

'These might prove useful,' said Emma as she disembarked.

*

Why is it that time, when you are waiting for something to happen, creeps by ever so slowly, thought Harry. And so it was as the four of them waited in the lonely car park. The party blasted out behind them, those inside apparently unaware or uncaring of the passing of the hour. Harry, his fidgeting abated, held Julie's hand. There they stood in that cold dark car park and waited, quietly and patiently, staring intently at the road that led from the front gate.

At 11.40, Harry thought that he saw a car's headlights in the distance, flickering between the trees. At 11.41, he was sure that they were headlights and at 11.42, he was convinced that they were moving rapidly in their direction. At 11.43, there was no doubt, a car was indeed snaking its way speedily down the drive towards them. The music faded from the clubhouse as the word spread and the windows behind them filled with spectators, many of whom now also spilled out of the doors to join the four in the car park.

The white Volvo skidded to a halt and C.J. and Philip Watson jumped out. Both looked exhausted by the day's efforts, something that hadn't come across on the video screen. Nevertheless, smiles abounded as they made their way through the sea of hands reaching towards them for celebratory handshakes. Time was short and the final hole a distance away. Harry ushered Philip and C.J. to one of the waiting buggies and then clung onto the back himself as it roared into life and back down the path towards the course. Emma drove the other buggy. Julie sat beside her and Olivia, like Harry, clung onto the back, like some bizarre stagecoach outrider clad in a flowing evening gown.

'Head for the lights!' Harry shouted at Philip, as they bumped over the kerb and onto the course itself.

Philip needed no further encouragement. Tired though he was, he pointed the buggy down the eighteenth fairway and it sped towards his goal.

As they arrived on the tee, Harry glanced once more at

his watch: 11.51. We can bloody do this, we can bloody do this, he thought to himself, but, keep calm, keep calm.

C.J's final playing partner was already on the tee box. He had been dispatched some time earlier so as to be ready and not delay proceedings. Joe Dolan, the greenkeeper, was also there, hovering about like the spectre at the feast.

C.J. stepped up onto the tee box and offered his partner the honour of striking first. Harry, having time to observe him properly since his arrival, thought that C.J. looked physically and emotional drained as he stood back to observe the other's strike. He looked back towards the clubhouse. A crowd of revellers were making their way along the fairway towards them. Others were hanging over the balcony, some clutching binoculars. More again, preferring the comfort and warmth of the interior, sat on in the clubhouse and watched events unfold on the large video screen.

The cameraman followed the flight of the ball from tee to the edge of the green, where it alighted softly and expertly. At least we had a proper golfer, when we needed one, Harry thought to himself.

Before C.J. could strike the ball, Joe Dolan grabbed Harry by the shoulder and growled in his ear: 'Can't you do anything about that lot?' He pointed at the stream of people coming from the clubhouse, the vanguard of whom were now surrounding the tee while others were filtering down towards the green. 'They're gonna destroy the course.'

Harry shrugged his shoulders, no longer caring. There was little, in truth, that he could do. Joe grunted and started to move off for the green as a burst of good-natured applause rang out from around the tee box. Thanks to the greenkeeper, Harry had missed C.J.'s shot. He squinted ahead, shielding his eyes against the brightness of the floodlights and trying to spot where the ball had finished. He could only see the first ball on the green, there was no sign of C.J.'s. Emma, seeing him searching for the ball, tapped him on the shoulder.

'He's in the bunker. There, just to the left of the green.'

Julie, who had remained seated in the buggy, shouted over to C.J. to get in, and they roared off down the fairway for his bunker shot.

In her enthusiasm, Julie slammed on the brakes as she approached the bunker. The locked wheels skidded along the damp grass, where the dew had already started to settle, leaving two long tracks in the turf behind the vehicle.

'JASUS!' Harry could hear Joe Dolan shout at the pair, as he made his way on foot towards the green.

C.J. pulled his sand wedge from the bag at the rear of the buggy and jumped down into the trap. A cursory swing. A cloud of sand. A thump as the ball landed on the green. A roar of cheers and applause from the crowd now ringing the green as the ball rolled slowly to within two feet of the hole.

Next it was C.J.'s partner's turn. A putt. The ball rolled up and came to rest a foot short of the hole. Polite applause. C.J. impatietly gesticulated to his partner to finish out. The other golfer stepped forward. One more putt . . . PLUNK, in the hole.

More applause.

Then silence around the green. All eyes were on C.J., who stepped forward nervously as he tried to mentally measure the distance and direction to the hole.

'BEJASUS, WILL YOU FOREVER GET ON WITH IT,' the greenkeeper bellowed, unable any longer to hide his own enthusiasm for the event to finish.

The crowd laughed heartily.

Philip Watson fixed Joe Dolan in a withering stare, and then strode forward himself onto the green to offer moral support.

C.J. stood beside the ball, surveying the green's contours.

He addressed the ball for the last time, drew back the club, then struck the ball. It rolled towards the hole.

The crowd held their breath and followed its path.

It ran straight towards the hole, then as it slowed, it wavered, an inch to the right. It reached the edge of the hole; momentarily it hovered over the edge, its path deflected by the cup . . . but then . . . it continued on – till it stopped, six inches past the hole.

A loud groan reverberated around the green. C.J. appeared disgusted with himself and was about to step forward to sink the return, when from somewhere behind Harry a huge firework rocket screeched skywards.

'What was that?' he said to Emma.

Emma stood motionless; she didn't reply.

The rocket exploded into a million red sparkles somewhere high above. The area of the green and the upturned faces of the surrounding crowd were illuminated by the sparkling display, such was its intensity. C.J. stood as if transfixed to the spot. He stared intently down at the golf ball, which still rested obstinately on the surface of the green, its glistening shell reflecting the skyward illuminations. As Harry watched he saw the colour gradually drain from C.J.'s face and then C.J. sank slowly to his knees. There he remained kneeling, still gripping the shaft of the golf club tightly between both hands. His head was bowed against its metal shaft.

Harry looked down at his watch: Fifteen seconds past midnight.

Philip Watson was the first to reach C.J. He tried to lift him to his feet, but C.J. continued to sag under his own weight. The enormity of the day and the heaviness of defeat continued to drag him down. Harry rushed over to help support him. As Harry held him up under his arms, his head continued to loll from side to side and Harry was aware of a wet tear running down his ashen cheek.

Julie was next to arrive. She hugged him tightly and tried to kiss some life back into his collapsed frame.

'It doesn't matter, C.J., it doesn't matter,' she wailed as she gripped onto him. 'You're my hero and that's all that counts.' Tears streamed down her face as she spoke.

As the small party stood unmoving on the green, those gathered about at first stood in silence and watched the sorry spectacle, but then tiring of the scene started to slowly disperse and wend their way silently back towards the comfort of the clubhouse.

As the crowds thinned, they lifted C.J. back on board his buggy. Philip Watson lit a cigarette and pushed it between C.J.'s tightly closed lips. Harry watched as he puffed slowly on it and the return of colour started to banish his previous ghostly pallor. As the buggies moved off and they made their weary way towards the clubhouse, Harry looked back towards the green. There, the only other figure now remaining was that of the green-keeper as he paced back and forth over his beloved turf, replacing and repairing it as he went along.

Nearing the clubhouse, it was quickly apparent that any semblance of the event's actual failure had not penetrated the party mood that had previously prevailed. The actual result seemed of little consequence to the crowds that hung out over the balcony rails and spilled out onto the course itself, cheering and frantically waving at the golfers' return. Pulling up outside the clubhouse door, C.J. and Philip Watson were instantly engulfed by a crowd of well-wishers pushing forward, smiling, laughing and trying to pat them on the back as they shouldered their way towards the clubhouse itself. Easing their way through the mass of outstretched arms and heaving bodies, Harry looked back at C.J., now independently mobile once more, as he shrugged off the applause with a look of dignified disappointment. As they entered the main ballroom, Philip Watson broke away and pushed his way forward to the band's microphone. There he made a short speech of thanks for all the support and help that he and C.J. had received during the day just past. Harry was grateful that he did so for the rest of the group, as no one else, at least at that moment, was in much of a speech-making frame of mind. The guests cheered loudly for the umpteenth time that night. So loudly that no one heard the errant helicopter, now repaired, landing outside the hotel.

The band struck up again and the dancing resumed with added enthusiasm. For a while Harry sat with C.J. and Julie at a table near the back of the room. Nobody spoke; the three just stared into the middle distance, giving the outward appearance, at least, that they were engrossed in the festivities.

From time to time, one wellwisher or another would stagger over and shake C.J. firmly by the hand or utter words of congratulation or perhaps of comfort. As time went by C.J.'s mood started to lighten as the shock and disappointment lessened. In the far corner of the room, Harry caught sight of Emma being buttonholed by the RTE presenter. Harry noted, by the leer on his face, that he was enjoying the experience. He could also see, from the look on her face, that Emma was not sharing in the enjoyment.

'I think you'd better go and rescue Emma,' Julie suggested.

Harry didn't need a second invitation. He left Julie to comfort C.J. and made his way across the room. As he approached, Emma gave him the widest of smiles. The RTE presenter's look was somewhat less welcoming.

'You've met Harry, haven't you? He's one of the organisers,' she said to the man from the television company.

'Oh, Harry. Yes. In fact, I've been hearing all about you.'

263

'All good, I hope,' Harry replied politely.

'Of course, of course, but I'm just a bit surprised, that's all.'

'Surprised?' Harry asked, a little bemused.

'Yes, surprised that you haven't asked me to take your photograph,' laughed the presenter.

Harry paused for a moment and then replied, 'Yes, sorry about that, but you see there's a problem.'

'A problem?' It was now the turn of the RTE presenter to appear bemused.

'Yes, you see, you are just not a big enough celebrity.'

The RTE presenter, his ego somewhat punctured, turned on his heel and left. Emma giggled quietly into her hand.

'Thanks, Harry. He was a terrible bore.'

'Not a problem, not a problem at all.'

Emma looked up into Harry's eyes and held her gaze there.

'Will you dance with me?' she whispered.

There was no need to reply, Harry simply slipped his arm gently around her waist and led her onto the dance floor.

21

C.J. sipped silently at his drink and watched the frivolity going on all around him. After recent events he felt no inclination to join in. Instead, he was simply content to sit and observe. Julie also seemed happy just to be there beside him. He held her hand tightly under the table.

'Cheer up, C.J. Everybody thinks you're a hero ... and that includes me.'

'That's a joke.'

'What's wrong, C.J.? You did your best and that's all anybody could ask. I'm very, very proud of you.'

A small tear ran down C.J.'s cheek. He reached forward with both arms and embraced Julie tightly. He kissed her passionately on the lips and then hugged her even more tightly.

'Look, my darling, I'm sorry but there's something I have to do. I'm going to the room for a while and I'll see you back here later.'

'I'm tired anyway, C.J. I'll come with you.'

'NO! Sorry, no don't. I just need to be on my own for a while. Look, stay here and I'll be back soon, I promise. If you go back to the room before I come back, I'll see you there, okay? I love you.'

'I know you do, and I love you too.'

He kissed her lightly on the forehead before disappearing into the scrummage of bodies that was the dance floor.

Back in the room, C.J. found the holdall that he and the helicopter had carried all around the thirty-two counties. He placed it on the bed, unlocked the small padlock that secured it and unzipped the bag. He removed the small bundle of clothes and then for several minutes he simply stood and stared dumbly at the remaining contents. For there laid out before him was £10,000 in used £20 notes. C.J. in all his working life had never seen that amount of money, not in cash anyway.

He glanced at his watch: 1.16 a.m. The phone call had told him to be there at 1.30. He had only a few minutes to make his mind up. He'd hoped that the event would have raised enough both to pay those murdering bastards off and to pay for Julie's treatment. But as he looked down at the money he realised that that was all there was and that was all there was going to be.

C.J. had watched Julie's condition worsen over the last few months. This new drug was her only realistic hope. And the money he stared at, it was hers, it was her future. Without beta interferon Julie's life was rapidly becoming a life not worth living. Yet Julie needed him, she needed him now more than at any time before – she needed his physical support and she needed his emotional strength and she was going to need it more and more as the years went by, as that terrible disease, that cursed condition, slowly gnawed away at her. He could never desert her, he wanted always to be there for her. But without this first pay-off, those bastards would surely kill him – he believed that. What would happen to Julie then? What about Becky and Tom? No, he could not countenance the thought of leaving them to cope on their own. And yet what would his life be worth if he gave away Julie's only hope of salvation? Julie would forgive him, he knew that, but could he ever forgive himself? C.J. stood unmoving, staring at the money – the money that represented a future for either himself or a future for Julie but not a future for both together. He debated for a few minutes more before finally making his mind up.

C.J. stood at the gateway and shivered, partially from the cold and partially in fear, as he looked up and down the road. He clutched the handle of the holdall tightly against his leg as he peered through the darkness. He cursed the fact that the road had no street lamps. From somewhere to his right he heard a car door open and then a second. He spun round; the holdall banged against his thigh. Two figures were looming up on him from the shadows.

'You're late,' barked the West Belfast accent.

'You got it, McCormick?' came the second voice before C.J. could answer the first. He instantly recognised both voices from the barn a week earlier and shook involuntarily.

'I failed.'

'What do ya mean, you failed?'

'I missed the putt.'

'So what?'

'So that's all there is.' He held forward the holdall. 'There's no more money, no sponsorship, you see. We only got the money if I completed the round and I didn't make it.'

The first figure to reach him grabbed the bag from C.J.'s grasp and tore it open.

C.J. could see their faces now that they were closer. They weren't as he had imagined; he had conjured up thoughts of hardened, scar-faced, crop-haired criminals. These faces were just . . . ordinary. Two ordinary, nondescript blokes, the sort of people that you might see in an ordinary street every ordinary day of the week.

'You bastard!'

'What is it?' the West Belfast accent asked.

'Golf balls! Fucking golf balls!' He swung the bag around and flung it angrily into the woods beyond.

The second man punched C.J. hard in the ribs. He sank to his knees, tensing his body as he did so, expecting more blows to follow.

None came.

As he spluttered for breath, he sensed that he was alone again. He clambered to his feet and peered in the direction of the car. It was too dark, too indistinct to see, but he heard clearly two doors being slammed shut.

They were bluffing, he thought. The cops were right. He turned to walk back to the hotel.

Behind him the car's engine fired and the tyres spun as it tried to move off.

C.J. turned to watch his tormentors leave, but was instantly blinded by the headlights accelerating towards him.

22

Harry was stirred from his deep and very restful sleep by a rapid pummelling on his right shoulder.

'Harry, Harry, wake up!' Emma's agitated tones broke into his dreams.

He raised himself up on one elbow and looked at the bedside clock. It was nearly four o'clock. He'd gone to bed only a couple of hours ago and after yesterday and last night this really was not the time that he had expected to wake up.

'What is it?' he groaned, rubbing the sleep from his eyes and turning wearily to find Emma lying in the bed next to him. Unconsciously he smiled as the recollections of the night before flooded back.

'Wake up, will you! Someone's knocking at the door.'

Harry sat up. Emma was right, somebody was knocking fiercely on the door of his hotel bedroom. He got up and in a single movement pulled on a bathrobe and stumbled across the room. He was taken aback to find the hotel manager standing outside, fist raised, ready to knock again. The door opening suddenly had taken him by surprise, so Harry was first to speak:

'What the hell do you want? Do you know what time it is?'

'I'm sorry, Dr Wallace,' he replied in an agitated voice. As the blurriness cleared from Harry's eyes he could see that the manager was breathless and sweating, as if he had been running. 'Please can you come with me? There's been an accident – a terrible accident.'

Harry dashed back into the bedroom without asking any more questions. His medical training had taught him to react first and ask questions later. He pulled on a jumper, a pair of trousers and an old pair of trainers, then turned to follow the manager.

'Harry, what's the matter?' asked Emma, sitting up in the bed.

'I don't know, there's been some kind of an accident. They need my help. You stay put.'

Harry followed the manager as he dashed down the stairs. Other guests, disturbed by the noise, were standing at their bedroom doors, trying to see what all the fuss was about. Harry continued to follow the manager at a pace through the foyer, then out of the front door and into the cold fresh morning air. Dawn was just breaking over the trees that lined the driveway. The manager continued at a jog, away from the hotel. Already a little out of breath, Harry caught up with him, which wasn't difficult as the manager was still wearing his heavy dark suit, a shirt and tie.

'Where are we going?' he asked.

'The gate,' he replied, breathing heavily.

As they reached the gateway to the hotel, Harry spotted a small group of men a hundred yards further up the roadway. They appeared to be huddled around something on the ground at the edge of the road. One of the group was kneeling down beside the object. Harry quickened his pace, leaving the hotel manager gasping for breath in his wake.

As he neared, he could see that the one who had been kneeling was John Anderson. Clearly he had been roused by a similar wake-up call but had been quicker to react. Hearing the heavy footsteps approaching, John looked up and, seeing that it was Harry, rose to his feet. He stopped

270

Harry a few feet short of where the group stood, and restrained him by putting his hand in the centre of his chest.

'Harry, hold it there for a second,' he said.

'What is it, John?' Harry gasped. 'Has somebody been injured?'

'Yes,' he replied, then hesitatingly, 'but I think it's your friend.'

Time stood still. Harry's blood froze in his veins. For several moments he couldn't speak.

'C.J?' he finally blurted out.

'Harry, he's very badly injured. It looks like he's been hit by a car and has been lying here for a while.'

'Is he alive?' Harry seemed to be struggling to breathe, but it was not because of the run.

'Barely, Harry,' replied Dr Anderson matter-of-factly. 'But we need to get him to hospital and quickly.'

'Let me have a look,' Harry said as he pushed past John Anderson.

'Are you sure, Harry?' The neurologist gripped Harry's arm.

'I'm a doctor, aren't I?' Harry said it with some irritation, but immediately apologised. 'Sorry, I just want to help.'

'Of course, Harry, I'm sorry.'

The group of onlookers parted to let them through. The first glimpse Harry got was of the torn sleeve of a woollen golf sweater lying on the mud and grass at the edge of the road. As the men stepped back he saw that it was C.J. He had terrible injuries. Even from where Harry stood he could see that both his legs were broken and that he had a bad head wound, from which blood oozed and congealed on the grass. He was unconscious, but Harry could just detect his shallow breaths. Harry knelt down beside him. Even with all his medical training Harry still struggled with quite what to do. This was different, this was personal. Harry

271

stroked the matted hair that lay across C.J.'s forehead. He was cold to the touch – hypothermic, thought Harry. John Anderson was right; he must have lain here for some time. The thought of C.J. lying there suffering while the rest of them had joked and laughed a few hundred yards away made him feel suddenly nauseous.

John Anderson knelt down beside him.

'Look, Harry,' he said, lifting C.J.'s eyelids. 'The right pupil is fixed and dilated.'

'What, . . . what does that mean?' Harry asked naively, his mind a blank. The thought of them enjoying themselves as C.J. lay injured just wouldn't go away.

'It means, Harry, that he must have raised intra-cranial pressure, probably from a subdural haematoma, given the head injury.'

'Of course, of course. I'm sorry, I just can't think straight.'

'Don't worry, it's just the shock. But he has to get to hospital immediately. He needs the pressure relieved or he won't survive. Can you help me?'

'Yes, yes, of course.' Harry tried to focus on the task in hand, to forget that it was C.J., just that it was somebody who needed his help urgently. He rose to his feet. At that moment, Emma pushed her way through the crowd. There she froze, then stepped back and stood motionless.

'Oh my God,' Harry heard her moan.

He stepped forward and put his arm around her. 'Emma, I need your help. It's C.J. and he needs to get to hospital straight away. Can you find out where the nearest hospital is and get an ambulance?'

'The nearest hospital is the General. It's only about ten miles away,' butted in the hotel manager, a sense of urgency in his voice.

'No, that won't do,' shouted John Anderson, who continued to kneel by C.J., supporting his head. 'He needs to

272

go to a neurosurgical unit. The nearest is probably at the Beaumont hospital.'

'But that's the other side of Dublin,' argued the manager. 'It'll take at least an hour to get an ambulance there through Dublin centre even at this time of the morning.'

'An hour we don't have, this chap needs neurosurgery and he needs it now.'

'The helicopter!' exclaimed Harry. 'It's sitting on the lawn in front of the hotel – it could get us there.'

'You're right; it's the only way. Emma, can you go and find the pilot and persuade him to fly us to the Beaumont?'

Emma turned and ran back up the road. As Harry watched her disappear in through the hotel gateway, he spotted another figure pacing up and down in the road. It was a local garda, he had stopped and was examining something on the ground. Then he spoke into his radio handset. Harry felt that he couldn't do much more to help C.J. or John Anderson till the helicopter arrived, so he walked over to find out what the policeman was doing.

'This is a terrible thing, Doctor,' he said as Harry approached.

'Can you tell how it happened?' Harry asked. He had guessed that the garda was examining the scene as he paced about and Harry needed some understanding to help him deal with it all.

'Was he hit by a car?' asked the policeman.

'It certainly looks that way from his injuries. Both his legs are broken, that's pretty typical. He's obviously been hit with some force, though. He's got a bad head injury and then he was thrown over there into the ditch.'

'There's some fragments of glass over here; they could be glass from a car's headlight, so that would fit. No, don't touch them, Doctor, we'll need to examine the scene in more detail later.'

'Why didn't the car stop? How could anyone just drive

off and leave him lying injured in the ditch? I just don't understand that sort of mentality at all.'

'There's something wrong about this,' mused the garda. 'Look at the road. What do you see?'

Harry looked up the road past the scene of the accident, but apart from the group huddled around C.J. he couldn't see anything out of the ordinary.

'Nothing,' he replied. 'I can't see anything unusual.'

'Exactly,' the garda replied. 'Nothing. That's what's wrong. Where are the skid marks?'

Harry looked back, up and down the road's surface, but the policeman was right, there were no marks.

'What does that mean?'

'It means that the driver didn't make any attempt to stop or swerve to try to avoid hitting your friend.'

'I don't understand, you mean he didn't see C.J., or what? Was the driver drunk? Or are you implying that C.J. deliberately jumped out in front of the car and didn't give the driver a chance? Just what are you getting at?'

'To be honest, Doctor, I don't know, but there is another possible explanation: that the driver didn't brake, because he wanted to hit your friend.'

'That's ridiculous. Why would somebody want to hurt C.J?'

'As I said, Doctor, I don't know. There'll be an investigation – perhaps we'll find out then.'

As the policeman finished speaking, the helicopter hovered into view over the trees that lined the road and set down on the roadway itself. He moved off to usher some of the onlookers away from the scene and to wave down any traffic that came along, in order to allow the helicopter to land in safety.

Carefully they manhandled C.J.'s broken body into the back seat of the helicopter. John Anderson clambered in beside him and Harry took up position in the front seat beside the pilot. This was his second trip by helicopter in as many days, but the pleasure he had felt on yesterday's flight was sadly lacking on this occasion. They soared high over the green fields that surrounded the Kildare County Club and on over the outskirts and then the centre of Dublin itself. Harry could see the city below just starting to come alive as they passed high over its commercial centre. He simply stared down, through the cockpit window, with unseeing eyes, unspeaking, unbelieving and totally numb.

The pilot had radioed ahead and a team of white-coated doctors and trouser-suited nurses were standing around a hospital stretcher trolley by the helipad as they circled overhead. As the aircraft settled onto the tarmac there was a flurry of activity. Venflons with intra-venous drips attached were pushed into C.J.'s veins, an oxygen mask was thrust over his mouth and nose and a rigid collar was placed carefully around his neck, his legs were bound together and then he was lifted out and clear of the helicopter. Before Harry could follow, C.J. was whisked off into the hospital through the A&E entrance.

C.J. was beyond his help now. He was with the professionals, they had all the necessary skills and equipment. Harry felt redundant. John Anderson had rushed into the hospital behind the crash team, to offer what help and advice he could. Harry was grateful that he had been there. He made his own way slowly into the hospital and took a seat in A&E reception. There he sat with his head buried deeply in his hands.

Harry continued to sit for the best part of an hour, unmoving, unhearing and unseeing, totally engrossed in his own morose reflections. The thought of C.J. lying injured and in pain, totally helpless, whilst he had enjoyed himself at the party hurt him deeply. I am a doctor, after all, he thought. Of everyone there, I at least could have helped. When C.J. needed me, the only time he ever really needed my help, I wasn't there for him. Even when I did get to him, I was useless. Despite all my medical knowledge, I felt totally helpless. Thank God that John Anderson was there. Then Harry came to the realisation that he was probably one of the last people to see C.J. before the accident. Why hadn't he stopped him? Why hadn't he taken better care of him? He should have seen him, not let him leave alone. He could easily have taken him by the arm and led him back into the bar, bought him a drink or gone with him back to the hotel. Just what had he been doing down at the gate anyway? The thoughts and recriminations just went around and around in Harry's brain, one upsetting image being quickly replaced by another.

His depression deepened. He started to think about what that policeman had said. Was it just a terrible accident? C.J. had been in bad form, things hadn't been going well lately for him and he had failed at the last hurdle of the challenge, but surely he wouldn't have tried to commit suicide by stepping out in front of a car. No, C.J. just wouldn't do that. He wouldn't do that, not to his friends, and he certainly wouldn't do that to Julie. Besides, Julie, Becky and Tom needed him, relied on him, loved him. No, C.J. had too much to live for; the thought that he might somehow, filled with remorse, have tried to kill himself was a non-starter. That wasn't C.J.'s way, not his way at all. The garda had seemed to suggest that somebody might have run him down deliberately, but that seemed just as implausible. The fact was that nothing seemed to make any sense, but that didn't stop the thoughts returning and revolving endlessly around in Harry's tortured mind.

Suddenly, he became aware that somebody was standing beside him. He looked up to find that it was John Anderson. Harry stood up quickly.

'Any news?' he asked, his voice betraying his anxieties.

'He has two broken legs, but we knew that anyway. He also has fractured ribs and a fractured skull. He may have some internal injuries also but they don't seem too severe. The major problem is the head injury. I went up with him for a CT scan.'

'Yes?' Harry asked, desperately hoping for some form of reassurance.

'As I suspected, he's got a large subdural haematoma. It's pressing on and distorting his brain.'

'Is he still unconscious?'

'I'm afraid so, Harry. Tom Byrne, the neurosurgeon, has been to see him and is going to take him to theatre for a burr hole decompression as soon as they can get a theatre ready.'

'This chap Tom Byrne, what's he like? Is he okay?'

'I know him well – C.J. couldn't be in better hands.'

'Thank you, John. Thank you so much, for all your help.'

'It's a dreadful thing that's happened, Harry.'

There then followed what seemed to Harry to be an eternity as he sat in a solitary and silent vigil. After what seemed to be hours of sitting and patiently waiting, Harry detected some movement and, glancing up to the far end of the A&E department, he spotted Emma, who was asking a nurse for directions. The nurse pointed in Harry's direction. Emma looked over and Harry waved. Then she disappeared for a moment, only to return, arm in arm with Julie. Both bore stern-faced and worried expressions. The nurse came over and guided the three of them into a relatives' room off the main A&E reception area.

In the small sitting area, Julie and Emma's faces were turned expectantly towards Harry; who told them everything that he knew and then went over it again and again, on request, until, finally convinced that there was nothing more to hear or to say, they lapsed into a patient silence.

Harry held tightly onto Julie's hand. There was knock at the door. He felt Julie's fingers involuntarily tighten around his at the sound. Emma leapt to her feet.

It was just a nurse offering them tea and biscuits.

There they remained, sitting in silence, consumed in their own private thoughts and personal grief. More tea came. More silence. Eventually, Harry couldn't stand it any longer. He disentangled his hand from Julie's, struggled to his feet and told them that he was going to find out what was happening.

Harry followed the signs, as the hospital was unfamiliar to him, to the theatre block. As he walked slowly along one particularly lonely corridor he was unceremoniously brushed aside by two doctors, white coats flapping behind them as they ran along pushing a red trolley packed with drugs and equipment. A breathless nurse followed closely behind. The crash team, Harry thought. Somebody's in trouble. He watched them burst through a set of doors ahead marked RECOVERY ROOM.

'No,' he thought, 'oh, no. Please, no.'

Harry eased one of the doors open slightly. Inside, a group of nurses and doctors, oblivious to his presence, were grouped tightly around one bed. The crash team doctors worked vigorously. One was pumping the patient's chest, the other monitoring a read-out from an ECG machine. The nurse was squeezing air from an Ambu bag into the stricken individual's lungs. Then at the rear of the group, Harry spotted John Anderson, who seemed to be directing operations. Harry slipped back out, letting the door slide slowly shut behind him. Then he stood propped up against the wall, helpless once more, in the empty corridor.

Minutes passed like hours, but finally John Anderson and another doctor wearing theatre garb emerged. They stopped, somewhat taken aback at finding Harry standing there. John Anderson put his arm around him.

'Harry, this is Tom Byrne, the neurosurgeon.'

Harry gawped blankly in his direction.

'Harry, the surgery went well, they got the blood clot out . . . but then there were some complications.'

'Complications?' Harry asked numbly.

'Yes, just after the surgery, your friend suffered a respiratory arrest. It seems that we were just in time. If we hadn't removed the clot when we did and if he hadn't been in the hospital when it happened, then I don't think he would have survived. In fact . . .'

'You mean C.J.'s alive?' Harry blurted out.

The two eminent doctors looked at each other with puzzled expressions.

'Yes, Harry, of course he is. I admit that it was touch and go for a while and he's not out of the woods just yet, but yes, C.J.'s alive and we think he's going to be okay.'

Harry grabbed the two men in all-consuming embrace and hugged them for several seconds, unable to contain himself and overcome with emotion.

Eventually John Anderson and the neurosurgeon managed to free themselves, and John Anderson asked: 'Do you want me to come with you to break the good news to your friends, Harry?'

'No, there's no need. I'm sure you could do with a rest. You've done so much, I can never thank you enough.' Harry hugged him again for several seconds, before turning back down the corridor and retracing his steps as he jogged towards the relatives' room.

'C.J.'s going to be okay, he's going to be all right,' he almost screamed as he burst through the door.

Julie and Emma were instantly on their feet, and then they were all embracing each other in a mixture of relief and joy. Two large tears welled up in the corners of Harry's eyes and then one of them trickled uncontrollably down his face.

C.J. lapsed in and out of consciousness over the next few days, but by the beginning of the following week when Emma and Harry visited the hospital, they found him sitting up in bed, apparently awake, alert and in good form, Julie by his side. His two legs were hung out before him by a collection of wires and pulleys and his head was swathed in bandages as if he was wearing some sort of bizarre turban. Most of the intravenous lines and life-support machinery that had remained cluttered around his bed for the last few days had now been removed in response to his improved condition.

'Hi, Harry, it's good to see you.' His speech was a little slow and slurred, but to Harry it was heart-warming just to hear him speak again after the events of the last week. 'Julie tells me that you and John Anderson saved my life.'

'Now C.J., why would I do that?'

'That's exactly what I told Julie, but hey, thanks anyway.'

'C.J., what were you doing out by the gate in the first place, and what happened to you?'

'Don't concern yourself with it, Harry, it's a long story. The police have been here and are on the case. I'll tell you all about it someday, but right now it's still a bit of a muddle.'

'Apparently the Irish police already have two men in custody,' added Julie quickly. 'They were picked up trying to dump a damaged Ford Escort somewhere near the border. They said something about a tip-off from Special Branch, though I didn't fully understand that. Did you, C.J?'

He reached for Julie's hand and pulled it across his chest and held it tightly there.

'Look, Harry,' said C.J., somewhat sheepishly, 'I took £10,000 out of our account – please don't ask me why . . . not right now, anyway. At the moment it's in Julie's suitcase back at the hotel. I want you to use that to get Julie started on that new treatment as soon as you and John Anderson can arrange it. Promise me you'll do that.'

He looked into Julie's eyes.

'I'm sorry, so, so sorry that I let you down. At least that £10,000 will get you a year's treatment, then Harry and I are going to have to think of some other scam to raise more money. I promise you that we'll get it, won't we, Harry?'

'Hey, not so fast,' replied Harry. 'Don't go involving me in any more of your hare-brained schemes.'

C.J. looked at him incredulously. 'You won't help?'

'I think he means he may not have to,' said Emma, smiling.

'What do you mean?'

'Well,' she continued, 'it seems the world loves a failure. With all the publicity we got following the event, and then your accident on top of that, the money's been pouring in from well-wishers everywhere.'

'And the sponsors have all agreed to pay up anyway,' added Harry.

'But how come? I missed the putt and you'd told me that most of the sponsors were only going to pay out if we succeeded.'

'The small print,' said Harry. 'Always read the small print. When we signed the sponsors up, I didn't appreciate at the time but they signed up to a successful completion of a hole of golf in all thirty-two counties in twenty-four hours.'

'So?'

'So, a day is always twenty-four hours but twenty-four hours isn't always a day.'

'I'm not with you.'

'Twenty-four hours, we started at four a.m., so according

to the contract they signed, although it was after midnight, you still had four hours to sink that putt.'

'Yeah, but I didn't actually sink it.'

'Actually, that doesn't seem to matter, Because Philip Watson's been on the case and he's told them that because that putt was only a few inches, it was officially a "Gimme". To be honest, though, C.J.,' Harry laughed, 'I've seen you miss putts that distance before and I certainly wouldn't have given it to you.'

'Oh ha, bloody ha.'

'Whatever,' continued Emma, glaring at Harry. 'The long and the short of it is, we think you would have had nearly four hours to sink a six-inch putt and, more importantly, given all the favourable publicity and public sympathy you've generated, none of the firms involved wants to get embroiled in any sort of public argument over the payment of the sponsorship money. So they've all come up with the goods.'

'I don't believe you.'

'You'd better believe it,' said Harry, smiling. 'At this precise moment we have something over £200,000 in the bank.'

'That's fantastic . . . I – I just don't know what to say.'

'Don't say anything. Just get better.'

'We're just glad to see you on the mend.' Emma smiled as she bent over and kissed him lightly on the cheek.

'Maybe I should do this more often,' quipped C.J.

The four sat and chatted and joked for the rest of the visiting period. Then an imposing nurse rang the bell indicating it was time to leave. As they got up to go, Harry turned and asked C.J. how long he thought he'd be stuck in hospital.

'Do you know what my surgeon said to me today when I asked him that very question?'

'No, what?'

'He said I was doing really well but I had had some bad injuries, so I might be here for another three or four weeks. So then I asked him if I'd ever be able to play golf again. Guess what he said?'

'What?'

'He told me that he'd seen my last putt at the Kildare County Club on television and it wasn't a neurosurgeon I needed it was a sports psychologist.'

'To be honest, C.J., I was thinking along the same lines myself. In fact, I was discussing that awful last putt of yours with Philip Watson and he agreed. He said he'd been observing your technique all the way round Ireland.'

'And . . .?'

'And he told me that he knew exactly what your game needed. He said the first thing you should do is take a complete break from the game. Put your clubs away, lock them in a cupboard or something, for the next few months at least. Don't touch them. In fact he said you shouldn't even go near them at all, give yourself a complete rest.'

'And after those few months are up, what should I do then?'

'Then, he said, you should sell the clubs and give the game up entirely.'